THE KINGSTONE RANSOM

A WILLIAM CHURCH NOVEL BY

JOSEPH W. MICHELS

iUniverse, Inc.

New York   Bloomington

THE KINGSTONE RANSOM

This is a work of fiction. All of the characters, names, incidents, organizations, and dialogue in this novel are either the products of the author's imagination or are used fictitiously.

Credit for cover art photo: © Stockphoto.com/Stacy Able

iUniverse books may be ordered through booksellers or by contacting:

iUniverse
1663 Liberty Drive
Bloomington, IN 47403
www.iuniverse.com
1-800-Authors (1-800-288-4677)

Because of the dynamic nature of the Internet, any Web addresses or links contained in this book may have changed since publication and may no longer be valid. The views expressed in this work are solely those of the author and do not necessarily reflect the views of the publisher, and the publisher hereby disclaims any responsibility for them.

ISBN: 978-1-4502-5034-4 (sc)
ISBN: 978-1-4502-5035-1 (ebk)

Printed in the United States of America

iUniverse rev. date: 8/10/2010

DAY 1

IT WAS ONE OF the larger mansions in Pacific Heights—a massive brick façade four stories high with carefully draped French windows and wrought iron fencing tall enough to discourage all but the most ambitious burglar. I pulled up to the curb and parked.

On-shore winds and the hot sun of mid-summer were struggling to break up last night's fog, but even at ten o'clock in the morning it seemed the marine layer might win out. I buttoned my woolen sports jacket as I walked over to the intercom next to the front gate.

"William Church to see Henry Kingstone," I shouted into the intercom after being prompted by some member of the house staff. The lock on the gate was remotely released, allowing me to push the gate open and walk through. The flagstone path leading to the front porch intersected a circular driveway. An expensive four-door sedan of German manufacture was parked directly in front of the steps leading up to the porch—almost as if someone had just arrived or was just about to leave. I went around the vehicle and climbed the steps. The front door opened as I came near and a soberly dressed middle-aged man stood to the side and motioned for me to come in.

"Mr. Kingstone is expecting you," he said, "please follow me."

He led me through the front hall and into a large, wood-paneled study facing the rear of the house. Large French windows, identical to the ones at the front of the house, offered a dramatic view of the San Francisco Bay. A man whom I took to be Henry Kingstone was standing behind a large antique desk, studying what appeared to be a map. He looked up as we entered.

"Mr. Church, sir," said the gentleman who accompanied me.

"Ah, Mr. Church, thank you for coming on such short notice," he said as he came from behind the desk to greet me.

"My assistant made it sound urgent," I said, shaking his hand.

"Won't you please sit down," he said, pointing to a matching set of leather couches facing one another across a long, highly burnished mahogany coffee table.

"Can I get you some coffee?" he asked as we sat down across from one another.

"That would be nice," I replied.

The gentleman staffer immediately left the room and the two of us took advantage of the interim before the coffee arrived to study one another.

Henry Kingstone was a large man in his early seventies. I could tell by the way he moved he was in reasonably good shape, but age had clearly take its toll—with face and scalp badly sun damaged and a tendency to treat carefully his lower back as he sat down. He had a friendly but enquiring expression on his face, clearly anxious to size me up—especially given the task he was about to engage me in. I sat patiently—letting him work through whatever assessment he'd finally arrive at.

"You must be William Church," said a beautifully groomed, gray-haired lady who entered the room briskly, followed by the gentleman staffer pushing a rolling cart holding a tray with coffee and a basket of assorted breakfast rolls. "I hope you don't mind if I sit in."

"This is my wife, Isabel Kingstone," said Mr. Kingstone as he rose from his seat," I've asked her to join us…this is a matter of great concern to both of us as you will easily understand once I've explained."

"Very pleased to meet you, Mrs. Kingstone," I said, standing up.

"Please sit down both of you," she said, coming over and taking a seat next to her husband. "I'll pour…thank you, Jackson," she added as the gentleman staffer transferred the coffee service tray to the table between the couches.

"Very well, ma'am," he said, then turned and left the room.

As Mrs. Kingstone poured each of us a cup of coffee she glanced at her husband who, catching her eye, got down to business.

"Mr. Church, the reason we asked you to come out here was to ask for your assistance."

"In what way?" I asked.

"You'll recall we commissioned you to review the travel itinerary of our daughter and her husband who were planning a tour of Latin America with their two children. We were anxious they avoid areas posing a risk due to high levels of crime or violence."

"Yes, I remember…it was just before I was scheduled to leave for Europe on another matter."

"Well, it seems—despite your instructions—our daughter and her husband chose to venture into areas you expressly warned them away from."

"And we've just learned our grandson's been kidnapped!" interrupted Mrs. Kingstone, her eyes tearing up.

"Perhaps you should start from the beginning…where precisely did this abduction take place?" I asked.

"Apparently, the family was on their way to a rural village some forty kilometers outside the capital…not far from a town called El Monte in one of those Central American countries they were visiting…I've been trying to locate it on the map," said Mr. Kingstone.

"I believe I know the town," I said, "and the country…not a good place to be without some sort of escort."

"They had a local guide with them who spoke English. I guess they felt safe enough," said Mrs. Kingstone.

"How'd you learn of this?" I asked.

"Our daughter called all hysterical," said Mrs. Kingstone, "They'd just gotten back to the capital."

"When did she place the call?"

"Yesterday…about eight o'clock in the evening our time," she replied.

"So your daughter and her family are still there?"

"Yes, they felt they should remain in the country until contact is made with the kidnappers," said Mrs. Kingstone.

"Has she contacted the police?"

"Yes, they're the ones who advised her to remain in the country...said it would simplify the payment of ransom."

"I take it they weren't too encouraging about their ability to rescue your grandson or capture the men who did it."

"My daughter didn't even mention such a possibility... presumably because the police didn't bring it up."

"That figures," I said. "Chances are, the abduction involved collusion with some members of whatever unit was in charge of policing the area in question."

"We're at our wit's end, Mr. Church, and that's why we call you in," interjected Mr. Kingstone.

"I take it you'd like for me to handle communications with the kidnappers."

"Certainly that, but also we'd like you to attempt a recovery of Matt. We've heard such horror stories of ransom being paid then ending up with a dead victim."

I didn't reply at first, my mind entertaining thoughts of what would be involved in such an attempt. Chances were, the gang involved in the abduction was large, well organized, ruthless and worst of all, well connected politically. Any overt effort at tracking them down would most likely be met with scarcely concealed interference by the authorities and end up making me the target well before I could manage the recovery. Something would be needed to balance the playing field. I had an idea.

"Mr. Kingstone, I think there might be a way to handle getting Matt back from the kidnappers but it would involve you taking a very large risk with a sizeable amount of money."

"What do you have in mind?" he asked.

"We need to take control of the negotiations—but in a way that doesn't antagonize them. I'm thinking we up the ante so to speak…cut your daughter and her husband out of the picture in exchange for you offering to foot the ransom bill."

"I don't understand," he said, "clearly I'm prepared to cover the cost. My daughter and her husband, although not poor, certainly couldn't afford to lose the kind of money I imagine the kidnappers will demand."

"Right now, the kidnappers are hurriedly trying to determine what your daughter and her husband can afford. That's why there's always some sort of delay before the initial contact: the kidnappers need to know how large a sum to demand. We need your daughter to inform the police her father will be handling the entire matter and that she and her husband and her little girl are leaving the country immediately."

"How will that help matters?" asked Mr. Kingstone.

"It'll put them off balance for starters, then force them to shift their attention to you and your wife. At first they'll be furious but once they discover how much wealthier you are they'll be excited…most importantly they'll not want to do anything stupid that might jeopardize a ransom beyond their wildest dreams."

"What do you mean by that last statement, Mr. Church? How much must I put up?"

"We won't know until they've made their initial ransom demand but whatever they demand you'll offer a bonus on top of that number to ensure good treatment of your grandson."

"But won't such a strategy result in delaying the release of Matt," said Mrs. Kingstone, worriedly.

"You're right, Mrs. Kingstone, it will delay his release, but more importantly it will encourage the kidnappers to value their hostage more than they might otherwise and to treat him with greater care. What we don't want is for them to terrorize Matt in hopes it will make his family more compliant. By offering a bonus on top of whatever demand the kidnappers make will reassure them you and your husband are already entirely cooperative—willing to do whatever they demand."

"But however well they treat him he'll be going through hell—you must admit that, Mr. Church!" she said, putting down her coffee cup noisily for emphasis.

"As I recall from my earlier work for you and your husband, Matt Richmond is about eleven years old—is that right?"

"Yes, he'll be eleven in two months," she replied, "but I don't see how that changes the picture."

"Mrs. Kingstone, an eleven year old boy is remarkably resilient. I don't know him personally but I imagine he's on the cusp of adolescence—both physically and mentally—and anxious to prove himself. I suspect he's secure in the thought his parents and grandparents won't abandon him and probably looks upon his present ordeal as something he'll be able to brag about for years to come. Unless they intentionally try to break him emotionally or physically I'd bet he'll be okay however long it takes to effect his recovery."

"Your plan seems a bit unorthodox, Mr. Church, but I'm inclined to go along," said Mr. Kingstone. "But tell me, how precisely do you fit into the picture may I ask?"

"A fair question. Assuming we come to terms regarding contractual details I'll be leaving for the area…probably as early as tomorrow. You won't know where I am since I'll be entering the country somewhat irregularly—not wanting to alert anyone to my presence—but I'll be always be reachable by satellite phone."

"How long before you'll be in position to begin the hunt for the kidnappers?" he asked.

"I should be ready to go to work just about the time you receive your first communication from them, but to ensure not too much time elapses have your daughter drop word before she leaves the country that the reason her father is handling the matter is because he's got enough money to satisfy whatever ransom demand they make. That should ease their minds and give them a fast take on your net worth."

"This all sounds very well, but shouldn't we also contact the FBI? After all, it's one of their specialties," said Mrs. Kingstone.

"Of course you should feel free to do so, Mrs. Kingstone, but keep in mind they would need to work through law enforcement agencies in the country where the crime took place. As I've pointed out, that might be counterproductive. However, if it should turn out their assistance might prove valuable I've got good connections with the agency—having once been an agent myself."

"Oh, I didn't know that," said Mr. Kingstone.

"Yes, not long after finishing college I was recruited by the agency. Spent three years as a Special Agent—mostly working on the recovery of stolen art as a member of the art theft staff at national headquarters."

"Why on earth did you leave the agency?" asked Mrs. Kingstone.

"Couldn't hack the bureaucratic mindset of the place," I said, "thought I could do the job just as well on the outside…freelance, without all the chain-of-command nonsense."

"Do they approve of your present career?" she asked.

"Well, I wouldn't say they approve but at least they value my work—enough to grant me a federal concealed weapons license and to ensure I receive cooperation with Interpol whenever I need to work outside the country."

"But you are a licensed detective are you not?" asked Kingstone.

"Yes, duly licensed in the State of California," I said, "but generally my work takes me out of state a good deal of the time."

"As in this case," said Kingstone.

"Yes, as in this case. But we're getting off the subject," I said, "we still need to work out the details of the plan so, Mrs. Kingstone, if you would provide us with some paper perhaps we can write down the proposed sequence of events so there's no confusion about what's expected of each of the actors, including your daughter and her husband."

* * *

It was close to noon by the time we'd worked out the details for both the game plan and my contract. Kingstone had written a generous check to cover my expenses and didn't flinch at the size of my fee. I begged off joining them for lunch, pleading a need to get on with the arrangements. Actually, I wanted to fly the plan past my sailing buddy, Jack, before getting too far down the road. I called him from the car.

"Hey Jack!" I shouted once I'd gotten past his secretary, "What say we meet up for lunch?"

"Suits me, Church. Where?"

"I'm already in Pacific Heights so how about you driving over to that place near the Presidio's Lombard Gate...you know, the place you like to call the 'joint'?"

"Yeah, I know. You hankering for an old fashioned Rueben?"

"That and a good martini."

"You're a lucky bastard, Church, those of us who work in law enforcement aren't permitted a drink in the middle of the day."

"As it happens I'm about to get involved in some action that's right down your alley...kind of hoping I can get your gut reaction to the case."

"My gut reaction or my access to FBI intelligence?"

"Well, if you put it that way I guess a little of both, partner."

"Thought so...okay, I'll see you there. Give me about twenty minutes."

"Will do...and thanks."

I broke the connection and started the car. Jack Barker and I jointly own a thirty-six foot sloop we keep at a marina in China Basin. We'd met during FBI boot camp some years ago. He stayed in and was now a highly ranked Special Agent in the San Francisco field office.

The sun had finally broken through the thick marine layer so I put down the top on my German sports car before driving off. I worked my way over to Presidio Drive and followed it through the eucalyptus groves of the Presidio all the way to the Lombard Gate where I began searching for a parking place. A space opened up to my left just as I hit the intersection. I made a quick turn and nailed the slot before anyone else could maneuver into position. Parking in the city was like that—you had to act fast. Available curbside parking spots lasted less than a minute before being occupied by one of the ceaseless horde of motorists cruising the streets in search of place to park.

Given the kind of neighborhood it was I didn't worry about leaving the top down as I turned off the ignition and climbed out of the car. The restaurant was less than a block away and I covered the distance quickly. A luncheon crowd had already gathered at the tables on the sidewalk out front. I headed inside.

"Hey, Church, how's it going?" asked Sam, the bartender, as I passed through the front area. "You want your regular?"

"Yeah, make sure it's well shaken and garnished with a lemon twist," I said, looking for Alice, my usual waitress. I spotted her coming from the kitchen and gave her a wave.

"You alone, Church?" she asked as she approached, carrying a couple of large plates intended for one of the tables outside.

"No, Jack will be joining me. Mind if I take that corner table?" I asked, pointing to a square table off to the right with banquette seating.

"No problem…you want me to put your order in or wait until Jack shows up?"

"I'll be having a Rueben and Sam's already got my drink order. Jack will be here in a couple of minutes so it won't matter if you want to put the order in right away."

"You think he'll be having the burger like he usually does?"

"Probably, but let's give him a chance to show he's capable of surprising us."

"What's this about 'surprising us'?" asked Jack as he slid on to the banquette across from me.

"What'll you have, Jack?" asked Alice as she continued to balance the two entrée dishes.

"By the time you get back from delivering those plates I'll have made up my mind," said Jack, picking up the menu.

"You really going to give some alternative to the bar burger a shot?" I asked incredulously.

"Hell no," said Jack, smiling. I just wanted to shake up poor Alice. So what's going on?"

I waited until Alice had taken Jack's order and I'd had a few sips of my martini before giving Jack a rundown of the case.

"So you don't think the FBI should be brought into this," said Jack once I'd described the kidnapping.

"At some point, perhaps," I said, "but given Kingstone's fear the boy will be harmed regardless of whether a ransom is paid or not a snatch of the boy while the ransom deal is still in the works would seem worth the gamble."

"And that's where you come in I take it," said Jack.

"It's what I do, Jack."

"Yeah, I know, but dammit, Church! You're going to need some sort of backup…this is probably a paramilitary gang you're going up against!"

"I've been thinking about that, Jack, and you're the one I'd most like to have covering my back but you're a government agent—it'd be a career breaker for you."

"It could be finessed, Church. We've got a Special Agent in residence at the embassy there. I could be seconded to her and assigned surveillance duty. That'd put me in the field."

About this time, Alice showed up with our plates. We cut off the discussion and concentrated on the food. As usual, the Rueben was excellent, as was the coleslaw. I ordered a cup of coffee. Jack was in no pain as he wolfed down the burger.

"Two problems with that plan come to mind right away," I said, taking a sip of my coffee.

"Yeah, like what?" asked Jack as he dipped a French fry into the mound of ketchup on his plate.

"First, if there's an official filing of a kidnapping case with your outfit someone in the Bureau is going to want to notify the counterpart agency in country and word will get back to the abductors. They'll monitor FBI and local investigative activity, making sure to keep a low profile and making my job just that much more difficult. Secondly, such a request on your part might jeopardize your position here in San Francisco. The Bureau might think you've got a yen to be assigned to an international post."

"Hell, Church, you've been out of the agency far too long… field ops can be given a 'need to know' status, making it possible to limit knowledge of the operation to about four people: my boss here, Elena Bolinas—the Special Agent at the embassy—and her boss."

"And the fourth?"

"The guy running the criminal branch—he's the guy both Bolinas and I ultimately report to."

"What about the ambassador?"

"Only if stuff hits the fan, and I'm thinking if that happens it'll be in connection with the end game—the actual snatch—and our victim will be back in official hands, making the ambassador a right proud dude for having the recovery take place during his watch."

"And my second concern?"

"Recovery of kidnap victims and the prosecution of those doing the deed is a top priority with the agency. My boss will be tickled pink to think the top guy in Washington values one of his men enough to seek his temporary posting in connection with a clandestine operation of this sort. I imagine it'll actually turn out to be a feather in my cap."

"Okay, let's say we do it your way, how're you going to explain my role?" I asked, grabbing a handful of his French fries.

"That's the tricky part," said Jack. "On the one hand, the agency will need to know it's providing backup for an independent operator but on the other hand it can't acknowledge your existence—especially since you plan on entering the country illegally."

"Perhaps if we get Mr. Kingstone to contact the chief honcho directly…let him know how important these arrangements are to the victim's family. A man of his wealth and West Coast connections would be difficult to brush off," I said.

"Yeah, that might work and I think I can get through to him by phone. Why don't we zip by the Kingstone residence after lunch and put the plan in motion," said Jack.

"Jesus, you're really hot to get a piece of the action!" I said mockingly.

"Go to hell!" said Jack as he pushed his plate away and stood up. "You finished yet?"

"Yeah," I said, taking a final sip of coffee. "Let's go."

We split the bill and stood waiting as Alice processed the credit cards. "God, you guys are really in a hurry today...something special going on?" she asked, looking at us speculatively.

"My friend here likes to hustle once he's got an idea," I said, patting Jack on the shoulder, "but never fear, he'll calm down come five o'clock—when he's off duty. Right, old buddy?"

"Don't listen to him, Alice, the fact is I'm trying to save him from doing something very ill advised, and since he tends to hit the ground running a little urgency is called for," said Jack.

"Well, I'm sure you boys will handle whatever it is," said Alice as she began to bus our table.

"Follow me," I said to Jack as we headed out the door of the restaurant and made for our cars.

* * *

Five minutes later we pulled up outside the Kingstone residence. Nothing much had changed except that the large sedan no longer blocked the view of the front entrance. Somebody must have left. I hoped it wasn't Kingstone himself. I climbed out of the car and walked over to the intercom and pressed the button. The butler,

Jackson, must have seen me because the gate opened without the need for an exchange of words. I signaled Jack to follow me in.

I figured Jackson must have been reassured by the business suit Jack was wearing and didn't regard him as any kind of threat to his employer despite his large muscular frame and athletic stance. I was a couple of inches taller than Jack and built pretty much the same but then again his employer had already vetted me and Jackson probably felt I could deal with anything unpleasant that might arise. In any case, we were greeted warmly by Jackson and ushered inside.

"Please make yourselves comfortable, gentlemen," said Jackson, "Mr. Kingstone will be down momentarily."

We'd been taken to Kingstone's study—a room I was already familiar with. I motioned for Jack to take a seat on one of the leather couches. I chose the one opposite and also sat down.

"Pretty nice digs," said Jack, looking around the room. "You sure know how to pick the clients."

"Actually, they picked me but I'll let that pass."

Just then, the door to the study opened and Kingstone came rushing in. He had on the same outfit he'd been wearing earlier—a pair of gray flannel slacks, a wine-colored cotton sports shirt open at the neck and a soft woolen sports jacket done in a muted plaid that captured the color of the shirt and combined it with a contrasting gray background.

"Have there been new developments already?" asked Kingstone breathlessly.

"Yes, one could say that," I replied as I stood up. "Mr. Kingstone, this is Special Agent Jack Barker of the FBI."

"Please to meet you Mr. Kingstone," said Jack as he stood and extended his hand.

"I don't understand," said Kingstone as he absently took Jack's hand, "I thought you advised us not to involve the FBI?"

"Agent Barker is a personal friend and after discussing the case with him he and I have come to believe there's a way the FBI can be helpful without in any way compromising the plan I set forth this morning."

"Please, won't you both sit down," said Kingstone, "my wife's gone out on some errands so she won't be joining us...please continue, Mr. Church."

"Agent Barker would like to join in the effort to recover your son, Mr.Kingstone, but it requires persuading one the FBI's senior executives that providing informal backup support for my efforts is in the agency's best interest. That's where you come in."

"What we would like you to do, Mr. Kingstone, is to talk with the guy—he oversees both the Office of International Operations and Jack's outfit here in San Francisco. You need to impress upon him the gravity of the situation and the importance you place in securing his cooperation."

"But I don't know the man."

"No, perhaps not, but you're a well-known figure here in California and there's every likelihood he's aware of who you are. We're counting on his not wanting to allow this kidnapping to become a public issue—especially one that might have political repercussions," said Jack.

"At least not until we've successfully recovered your grandson," I added.

Kingstone nodded thoughtfully and paced the room. "Perhaps you should fill me in on the details of how the FBI comes into this," he said. "I'd like to convince him I know what I'm talking about."

Jack and I took the time to brief Kingstone on the details of our strategy, stressing the need to give the FBI deniability should the recovery not succeed but allowing it to earn full credit should it succeed. When we were done, Kingstone was up for the call and urged Jack to proceed at once.

"It'll be about four-thirty Washington time," said Jack, "but I believe he'll still be in the office. Can I use your phone?"

"By all means," said Kingstone.

Jack had to go through three levels of assistants before he managed to connect directly with the guy. After identifying himself at some length and detailing the facts surrounding the kidnapping he put Kingstone on. Kingstone did a masterful job of conveying his grief as well as telegraphing the importance he placed on securing a positive outcome in my attempt at recovering his grandson. In that connection, he told the man, he was confident the FBI would wish to provide discreet support, especially considering I myself had once been a Special Agent.

"He wants to speak with you, Mr. Barker," said Kingstone, handing Jack the phone.

Jack was asked to lay out in detail the plan he and I had come up with. He did it with crisp professionalism, pointing out the deniability factor should it fail as well as the positive press the FBI would receive should it succeed. When he finished he turned the phone over to me. "He wants to talk to you," said Jack.

"This is some crazy stunt, Church," said the man once introductions were over.

"Perhaps a little irregular, sir, but given the cards we've been dealt I think it's the best way to proceed. The most important thing is to keep the operation quiet. As far as the kidnap gang is concerned I don't exist...same goes for officials in that country. Jack's role will be a supporting one, and then only if things turn ugly."

"You know the FBI doesn't countenance the paying of ransom, Church. There'll be one hell of mess if the Kingstone ransom actually gets paid, especially given the enormous sums most likely to be involved."

"I won't let that happen, sir."

"You sure as hell better not," he replied.

"So, can we count on your support?"

"Yeah, tell Jack he's got my approval for this caper. I'll make the necessary arrangements...on a need to know basis as he requested."

"Thank you, sir."

"And listen, there's no way the FBI is going to bail you out if you get snatched by the police over there."

"I understand, sir."

"Well anyway...good luck, son."

With that, he broke the connection. I turned to Jack and Kingstone and with a big smile gave them thumbs up.

* * *

Jack and I hurriedly left the Kingstone residence after having arranged for Kingstone to phone his daughter and instruct her to bring herself and her family back to California at once. We parted ways once outside the wrought iron gate—Jack to his office and yours truly to his one bedroom apartment high up in one of those glass-enclosed towers south of Market Street.

It was almost two-thirty in the afternoon by the time I pulled into the garage under the building. I hoped Chelsea was still on duty. Chelsea moonlights as my personal assistant. Her day job involves working the concierge desk at the high rise where I live, but her real passion is modern dance—something that gets her juices running but doesn't pay the bills, so for a few extra bucks she handles my travel bookings and other scheduling needs. It helps she's as sharp as a tack and unbelievably efficient.

I was in luck.

"Hey, Church," she called out as I emerged from the elevator, "where've you been all day?"

"Getting started on a new job. You able to break free for a few minutes and come upstairs?"

"Yeah, Peter will hold the fort, won't you, Peter?" she said to the skinny kid with an arm full of tattoos slotting some sort of circular into residents' mailboxes.

He just nodded and kept at it. Chelsea came from behind the concierge desk and walked with me to the bank of elevators.

"So what's the gig?" she asked once we were in the elevator and on our way up.

"The Kingstones…you know, the old couple living in Pacific Heights you had me contact this morning?"

"Yeah, what about them?"

"It seems their grandson was kidnapped yesterday."

"Jesus! Where?"

"Down in Central America…while the family was on that Latin American tour they asked me to vet."

"So that's why old man Kingstone sounded so agitated when he called this morning…Christ, what's he want you to do…handle the ransom?"

I waited until we'd reached my floor and stepped out into the hallway before answering.

"Actually, he wants me to go down there and get the child back…ransom or no ransom."

"Wow, sounds like a job for a special ops team not a freelance operative like you."

"Well actually this time I'll have some backup…Jack's coming along for the ride."

"How'd you work that?"

"I didn't, Jack worked it out himself…said he didn't want me going down there without some backup and volunteered for the job."

"I'll be damned, you guys are really tight."

"Comes from competing in all those beer can sailing races on the Bay," I said with a laugh.

I unlocked the door to my apartment and ushered Chelsea inside.

"Okay, we've got a few things to work out," I said, as I removed my sports jacket and draped it over one of the two kitchen counter stools that comprised the entirety of my dining furniture. Chelsea made a beeline for the leather couch facing the wall of glass that overlooked the Oakland-Bay Bridge and which, ostensibly, justified the steep mortgage I'd incurred when I bought the place. She kicked off her shoes and plopped her feet on the chrome and glass coffee table. I joined her.

"You need airplane tickets to this place?" she asked.

"It's a little more complicated than that," I replied. "Jack's transit will be handled by the agency since he'll be going in as a temporary posting to the embassy there, and it's not clear how long that'll take.

"And you?"

"I'm taking a somewhat irregular route…one that'll keep me below the country's official radar."

"You want to spell that out?" she asked, looking at me curiously.

"Book me first class on a flight to Santa Lucia…make it for tomorrow night."

"That the capital?" asked Chelsea as she thumbed the info into her smart phone.

"Actually, it's the capital of the adjacent country…as I said, I'll be entering the target country below the radar."

"You mean you're going to smuggle yourself in?" she asked.

"Precisely, so while you're getting me booked I'll be doing a little research on the web—checking out internet-based map and satellite imagery to see how best to pull it off."

"What else do you want me to do?" she asked as she searched the floor for her shoes.

"Book me into the city's Hotel Vallejo—it's reputed to be the capital's best.

"So much for going undercover...you think maybe you shouldn't announce your arrival in the region so ostentatiously?" questioned Chelsea.

"Probably not, Chelsea, but it'll be a while after that before I'll again enjoy the comforts of a first rate domicile so what the hell, I might as well do it."

"You're the boss," said Chelsea, slipping into her shoes and standing up. "Let me know if you need anything else."

"Will do...and keep in contact with the Kingstones. I need to know when their daughter and her family arrive."

"You think they'll arrive before you leave?"

"Hope so...give me a chance to get a handle on the type of men who pulled off the abduction."

"See you later, Church," said Chelsea as she left the apartment.

Once Chelsea had gone I put a call through to Boris, the owner and manager of a mixed martial arts gym on Folsom Street. Boris—a good friend of mine—was a middle-aged Russian Jew who'd immigrated to Israel after the collapse of the Soviet Union. He was quickly recruited by the Israeli Army and assigned to special ops. It seems they wanted to capitalize on the formidable skills in personal combat he'd learned during an earlier stint in the Soviet military. About a half-dozen years ago he showed up in San Francisco, set up this gym and began to pursue his real love: metal sculpture. I'd promised to hang one of his latest creations in my apartment—a mobile made of a long piece of copper belting purporting to depict three-dimensionally the mathematical concept of infinity—and thought I'd better honor the promise before I headed out of town.

"Boris here," said the gruff, heavily accented voice.

"Hey, Boris, it's me, Church."

"Where you been keeping yourself, old friend, you've been missed?"

"Sorry about that…it's been a little hectic since returning from that job in Europe. I'm calling to ask whether you've managed to finish that sculpture I expressed an interest in?"

"Yeah, it's all done and ready for hanging…you backing off from your offer?"

"Not at all. In fact, I was hoping you might be able to bring it around sometime this evening and help me mount it."

"So, you're a real art lover after all," said Boris affectionately. "Though I hate to part with this beauty it couldn't go to a better man…sure, I'll be over there just as soon as the night manager checks in. And, Church, I'll bring dinner."

"Sounds good, see you then."

I broke the connection then looked around my tiny one bedroom flat wondering where in hell I'd be able to hang the sculpture? As I recalled, it was a good three feet in height and about two feet in diameter. Fortunately, the ceilings in the building were high so chances were good I could suspend it in a way that would prevent me from continually bumping into it—that is, if I could find an out of the way place that wouldn't pose too much of an insult to Boris' artistic sensibilities.

Resigned to not having a clear idea of where to hang it I figured I leave it up to Boris to make the call.

* * *

Satellite images of the Central American region under consideration offered a few options. Clearly, highway connections between the two countries were off limits—they'd be closely monitored. A trek through tropical or subtropical forests was a possibility but any route would involve days of machete work clearing a path through otherwise impenetrable growth. The best option I could see was to take to one of the rivers that cut through the border. Unfortunately, the rivers ran downstream of the direction I had to traverse. This meant using a motorized vessel, that is if I didn't want to wear myself out trying to paddle upstream. Which of three river transects to choose posed the fundamental problem but here Boris could help out: he'd spent a year in country as a UN agricultural advisor back when he farmed avocados on a *moschav*, after military service.

Boris showed up a little after six o'clock that evening bearing a parcel full of his wife's cooking and a bottle of Chianti Classico Reserva.

"So, you ready to dine on a lasagna meant for kings?" he asked upon arrival, unwrapping the dish and shoving it into the microwave that constituted my only device intended—at least in my mind—for cooking. I could squeeze oranges and toast bread but beyond that I relied upon restaurants or frozen prepared dinners to sustain my soul.

"I'm at your disposal," I said, savoring the prospect of home cooked food.

While we waited for the entrée to heat up, Boris noticed the satellite image on my laptop and arched an eyebrow.

"I need to find a way to enter the country without attracting attention and figure it'll have to be by river. You know the area, what do you think?"

"Hold off, start from the beginning, what's the objective?" asked Boris.

I explained the need to extract the young boy from kidnappers using the ransom Kingstone was willing to put up as the bait to learn his location, but given my suspicion the abduction had at least the tacit support of some segment of officialdom I wanted to attempt the recovery off the radar of the authorities in country—hence the rather irregular entry into the country.

"So you imagine you can navigate one of the rivers bisecting the frontier undetected and gain uncompromised entry into the country?"

"That's my plan."

"You're a gringo, Church. The locals will have a field day broadcasting your presence to the local constabulary as well as to agents of the country you plan to penetrate. It's not going to work."

"You have a better idea?" I asked.

"Actually, no, but given a modest adjustment the plan might work."

"And that would be?"

"Take me along."

"How's that going to change the situation?" I asked skeptically.

"I know these people. Granted, it's been a few years since the wife and I spent a year down there but we made some mighty good friends…friends whom I think we could count on to persuade the local population in the rural areas you weren't just a gringo but an *hombre simpatico*."

"Come on, Boris, the wife would never let you go, and anyway you've been out of action for enough years to call into question your ability to handle the pressures of a clandestine operation."

"Don't put me out to pasture so quickly, my friend," said Boris, "Anyway, you've no choice—without me the plan won't work."

"Okay, suppose I acquiesce to your ultimatum, what river system would we select?"

"The Monte Rio, of course," said Boris without hesitation. "I've got good friends along that river, and anyway it's navigable with an outboard motor throughout the distance we'd need."

"And it would put us where?" I asked, looking at the satellite image.

"Here," he pointed, placing a finger on a section of the river that intersected with a dirt road inside the country we needed to enter.

"But it's miles away from any settlement, Boris," I complained.

"True, but then again I'm relying on your ability to pick up the operational baton once we've secured our entry into the country."

"Thanks a lot," I said sarcastically.

But actually, it made sense. If I could persuade Dora Perez, an archaeologist with the Archaeological Institute down there, to rendezvous with us at that spot we could make it to the next town and rent a car. Dora and I came to know one another at a post-graduate seminar in pre-Columbian archaeology some years back and had kept in touch. Whether she'd be willing to put herself at risk in this fashion was a big question. And whether it would be ethical for me to even ask her was an even bigger question.

"Okay, let me think about it. In the meantime, where the hell should I hang this masterpiece of yours?" I asked.

"Church, my good man, there's no contest, it belongs right here," he said, pointing to the corner of the main room farthest from the kitchen annex.

"Why there?" I asked.

"Two reasons. First, it won't be in the direct glare of the sunshine coming from the wall of glass you're so proud of, forcing you to illuminate it with artificial light which is much more manageable and therefore effective, and second it's not in the line of traffic so you won't have to hoist it above eye level just to avoid running into it whenever you move around this pathetically tiny apartment."

"Okay, let's do it," I said resignedly.

Boris pulled out the necessary hardware from his coat pocket and requisitioned a hammer and screwdriver from me, together with a stepstool. In no time at all the mobile was hoisted and Boris had maneuvered the ceiling lamps into position to cast a dramatic spotlight on what was now the aesthetic center of my apartment. I leaned against the back of the couch and contemplated the result.

"What d'you think?" asked Boris.

"You're the artist," I said, "but given my limited aptitude I'd be willing to wager you've chosen the best option."

"A good call, my friend, now let's get back to business. When do we leave?"

"Whoa, Boris, you've neglected to factor in your wife's opinion. What makes you think she'll go along?"

"She'll be okay once I persuade her it's the only way to insure you come through this operation alive. You know she's adopted you as a kind of surrogate son. No way she'll allow me to let you go off on this mission without old Boris looking after your welfare."

"So it's blackmail you propose?"

"Well, I like to think of it as making an emotional sales pitch for what otherwise might be construed as a self-indulgent escapade."

"God, you're good!" I said. "How in hell does your wife put up with it?"

"Don't worry, my friend, she knows what's going on...just pretends to be taken in by my spiel. So, let's not worry about her, let's worry about what kind of craft we'll need to make the journey."

We talked at length and settled on either an aluminum or fiberglass skiff powered by a four-stroke outboard motor—both of which we could secure once we were in country and had managed to make our way to the Monte Rio, a tedious journey by bus to a point some distance from the capital.

Having worked out the details, including alerting him to the fact we'd be flying out the following night, Boris said goodbye and assured me he would be in touch early the next day. I had no doubt he'd do what was necessary to get his wife to agree but felt a little guilty about the role I'd be playing in his alibi. I shut down the laptop, stood up and stretched. I wanted to head for the bedroom and sleep. It had been a long day and tomorrow was going to be no better, but I needed to contact Chelsea and let her know of the new development. She'd either be in the flat she shared with two other girls in a rundown building in the Mission District or at one of the spartan ad hoc theatres in her neighborhood where contemporary dance productions were performed. I pressed the button on my smart phone, triggering her cell number.

"Chelsea, it's Church, can you talk?"

"Yeah, what's up?"

"It seems Boris is going with me so you'll need to book him a seat and also a room at the hotel."

"Wow! How'd that happen?"

"You know Boris. He convinced me that without his help there'd be no way my plan to infiltrate the target country would succeed."

"And you bought it?"

"Let's say I wanted to be persuaded. Having Boris along is the equivalent of having that special ops team you argued would be needed in such an operation."

"Gee, Church, you actually listened to me."

"Yeah, how about that."

"I'm flattered all to hell, Church, and rest easy, I'll handle the bookings. Get some sleep, okay?"

"Will do, gorgeous…you dancing tonight?"

"Yeah, I'm on in about five minutes so you called at a good time. Wish me luck."

"Break a leg!" I said just before ending the connection.

I put down the cell phone and wearily walked over to the bar where I poured myself a snifter of cognac. I stood at the floor-to-ceiling window of glass and gazed out onto the lights of the city down below. I knew I should be thinking about what equipment to pack but all I could do was sip my drink and admire the restless stream of automobile lights passing into the city across the Oakland-Bay Bridge. Finally, I managed to pull myself away from the nighttime spectacle, give Boris' mobile sculpture a final approving glance then head for the bedroom.

DAY 2

THE SUN WAS WELL over the horizon, bathing the bedroom in bright morning light by the time I woke up—prompting me to get myself out of bed and into the shower. While I let the water stream over me I considered the pros and cons of calling Dora. It'd be late morning where she lived, which would most likely put her in the office or in one of the *bodegas* where artifacts were stored. I was hoping it was one or the other and not somewhere out in the field where cellular connectivity was non-existent. It was only after I'd stepped out of the shower and was toweling off that I made the decision to call her in any case, regardless of whether I'd ask for her assistance, just to say "hi" and to see how she was doing—at least that's what I told myself.

I planned to do a run this morning so I pulled on a pair of shorts, a cotton T-shirt and a pair of running shoes. After checking the headlines on my laptop I headed for the simple galley kitchen and began squeezing oranges. I continued to mull over the question of how to approach Dora as I drank the fresh juice.

No obvious solution seemed to present itself so I busied myself preparing a bowl of whole grain cereal, then sat down to eat.

With breakfast over with, I had no further excuses for delaying the inevitable. I made the call. Dora answered her cell phone on the third ring.

"Dora, it's me, William Church."

"William, how nice to hear from you. Are you all right?"

"I'm fine. Where are you…did I catch you at a bad time?"

"I'm in my office going over an excavation report so no, it's not a bad time."

"I'm calling to let you know there's a chance I'll be down your way rather soon."

"How wonderful! Will you be on business?"

"Yes, but that's the tricky part. I've been hired to serve as a kind of middleman in connection with a kidnapping of an American boy just outside El Monte."

"That's terrible! I haven't read of any such kidnapping. When did it occur?"

"Two days ago. The thing is, Dora, to do the job effectively I'll need to be in the country without the knowledge of the authorities."

"How can you work that? As soon as you step off the plane you'll be processed like anybody else."

"That's why I'm thinking of entering the country by land…in a remote spot."

"You mean sneak in?"

"That's what I was contemplating."

"But if they catch you, William, the authorities will be very angry. You would probably end up in prison."

"I'm fully aware of that, Dora, but I believe the risk is worthwhile if it means there's a chance I can rescue the boy."

She didn't say anything but I could hear her breathing. Finally, she spoke—but quietly: "What would you have me do?"

"Rendezvous with a companion and myself at a remote spot the location of which I can fax to you. It's an area that holds much archaeological promise. Perhaps you could arrange to undertake a quick reconnaissance of the area…in response to some fictitious report."

Again, she did not answer right away. I could hardly breathe as I waited for her reaction.

"You ask much of me, William," she said quietly. "I could also end up in jail were I to be discovered aiding and abetting an illegal entry into the country by *gringos*."

"I understand that, Dora, and you shouldn't hesitate to turn me down. Our cover story if discovered would be that we were fishing on the river and didn't realize we'd gone upstream so far. You happened to drive by just as we were standing next to the road examining our map, trying to figure out precisely where we were. It was you who informed us we had crossed the border and insisted we make our presence known to the authorities in the next town. It was for that reason we were in your vehicle making for Los Gatos."

"But why wouldn't the two of you simply get back in your boat and head downstream once I informed you about crossing the border?" she asked.

"We were scared the border patrol in the country we were returning to would take us for smugglers and shoot. Your suggestion that we announce our presence would allow the authorities in both countries to work out a transfer that would insure our safety. After all, we're just two *gringos* unfamiliar with the workings of international borders…hell, the only borders we're used to are those between states in the USA and they don't mean a hell of a lot!"

"That won't cut it, William, they'll know you—and probably also your companion—are seasoned world travelers engaged in quasi-police business once they catch a glimpse of your passports. They'll smell a rat if you try to put on the 'innocents abroad' act."

"Okay, we'll dump the pretended naiveté, but you get my point: there's always a way to give the operation an innocent spin."

"What if they dig deep and discover you and I know each other, and that you've been in the country before?"

"I'd agree, that'd be a hard one to finesse."

"What kind of distance are we talking about anyway?" asked Dora.

"From the point where we leave the canoe to the town of Los Gatos has got to be at least forty kilometers."

"Why not stash a couple of lightweight motorcycles in your canoe, concealed under wraps. That way you could avoid contact with anyone and also have a way to get around the country?"

"That's a great idea, Dora, why the hell didn't I think of it!"

"See, William, I can be useful even if I don't volunteer to be a part of your escapade."

"That you can! Okay, we'll do it your way."

"But, William, I insist you call on me once you've arrived. I would have no reason to question how you entered the country so there's no way our meeting could affect my standing with the authorities."

"Consider it a promise," I said.

"So when should I expect you?" she asked.

"In about three or four days I imagine."

"Take care of yourself, William."

"I will…and thanks for everything."

I broke the connection and paused to think about Dora's reaction to my plan. Her suggestion to use light motorcycles to get around in the country was a good one. The only snag I could think of was the possibility the police might wonder why two bikes with out-of-country plates were being driven in their jurisdiction. Two solutions presented themselves: brazenly assert we'd simply driven them across the frontier legally, or conceal the plates with mud—something no one would think surprising if the motorcycles were sports bikes, the kind of dirt bike that was road legal and engineered for long distance as well as off-road operation. I was pretty sure that type of bike would be available for purchase in the capital city, Santa Lucia.

With the phone call behind me I could focus on the rest of my day and that meant for starters getting over to Crissy Field for a run. I grabbed a sweatshirt and headed out the door. The elevator took me down to the parking garage below ground level. As I left the elevator I checked my watch. It was almost eight o'clock—much later than my usual morning run. The top was still down on my sports car and I left it that way as I started the engine and pulled out of the garage. The sun would feel good and who the hell cared whether my thick head of hair got blown around or not.

A stiff breeze was coming from the ocean, whipping up white caps and forcing sailors out on the Bay to reef their sails. I envied them and wished I had time to take out the thirty-six foot sloop Jack and I kept for just such days. But with a departure planned for later that evening I didn't feel I could afford the time. I put the thought out of my mind and focused on navigating the streets of the Marina District.

The parking lot of Crissy Field was packed. At this hour the recreation area was full of dog owners exercising their pets, young mothers jogging behind three-wheel baby strollers and retirees taking the air. Most of the serious runners were gone by now—back at their flats getting ready for the workday. I climbed out of the car, stripped off my sweatshirt and walked onto the wide pedestrian path that stretches some one and three quarter miles to Fort Point, at the base of Golden Gate Bridge. Taking care to dodge the erratic movements of dogs, kids, and ambling old men and women, I started my run. I began with a loping stride—not too fast, just enough to loosen up the leg muscles. Once I'd gone about a quarter of a mile I picked up the speed.

* * *

I was back at the car toweling off sweat from the three-and-a-half-mile run when my cell phone rang. It was Chelsea.

"Yeah, Chelsea, what's up?"

"Just got a call from Mr. Kingstone—wanted me to tell you the Richmond family's arrived, he thought you'd like to know. They're apparently staying at the Kingstone residence for the time being."

"Ring them up and tell them I'll be over there in about ten minutes…and thanks, Chelsea."

It made no sense to take the time to return to my apartment and change seeing I was already in the neighborhood. I removed the sodden T-shirt, finished toweling off then slipped on the sweatshirt that lay on the passenger seat—still fresh from having been only briefly worn. After passing a comb through my hair I climbed behind the wheel and started the motor. A cluster of pigeons drawn to a scattering of cracked corn at the center of the parking area fluttered out of the way as I drove towards the park exit. I worked my way along Marina Boulevard as far as Divisadero Street then turned right and headed up the steep rise leading to Pacific Heights.

I noticed the large black sedan was once again parked on the circular driveway in front of the entrance as I pulled to the curb and parked. Apparently, the whole family was home. It was almost ten o'clock in the morning and I imagined even with jet lag most everybody would be up by now. I got out of the car and walked over to the front gate, hesitated for a moment then pushed the buzzer on the intercom. Jackson came on and I identified myself. The gate opened and I headed for the front door. As usual, by the time I made it up the steps Jackson had the door open and was standing at the threshold waiting to welcome me in.

"The Richmonds are in the parlor," he said as he closed the door behind me. "Please follow me, Mr. Church."

A man and woman in their mid-forties rose from their seats as Jackson and I entered the room. He was slender and surprisingly pale—given he'd just returned from south of the border—with closely cropped hair and a somewhat tentative smile. She was almost his height and stepped forward without hesitation, hand extended.

"I'm Susan Richmond," she said as we shook hands, "and you must be William Church?"

"Yes, very glad to meet you, Mrs. Richmond, "and you, Mr. Richmond," I said.

Both were wearing comfortable but expensive country club attire, making me a little self-conscious. "I hope you'll excuse my appearance," I said, "When my assistant phoned to inform me of your arrival I was already in the neighborhood having just finished a run down at Crissy Field and thought it prudent to come right over."

"Of course, we understand," she said with a smile, "and it's a relief for us to know you've agreed to handle this awful matter, isn't it, Charles?"

Charles just nodded, letting his wife handle the conversation.

"Father has filled us in a bit but we'd like you to give us a rundown on how you plan to proceed," said Mrs. Richmond.

"Before we get to that perhaps you'd be willing to go over in detail the events surrounding the abduction?"

"Shall I bring coffee, ma'am?" asked Jackson, who'd been hovering near the door.

"Yes, please do, Jackson." Then, after a glance that took in the awkwardness of the three of us standing there, obviously discomfited by the formality of the moment, she smiled brightly and said: "Why don't we all sit down?"

"Let's begin with your guide, what was his name and how did you come to choose him?" I asked, having taken a seat on the couch.

"His name was Fernando something or other," said Mrs. Richmond, "but I can't really say how we obtained him...he simply showed up at our hotel the day of our arrival announcing his availability to serve as a guide should we wish to explore the countryside."

"You didn't check with the hotel whether he came recommended?" I asked.

"Well, he had all sorts of official looking documents and spoke excellent English. I suppose we were just relieved not to have to go to the trouble of looking for someone. Given what's happened, I suppose we were rather foolhardy in not going through a bonded tour agency."

"And was it his idea for you and your family to visit that particular rural village the day of the abduction, Mrs. Richmond?"

"Why, yes...yes it was, now that you mention it. We were originally planning to remain in the capital that day...visiting museums and the central market."

"Can you describe him?"

"A local man of average height...perhaps in his mid-thirties... well-groomed I would say, and quite formally attired."

40

"Did he appear at all menacing in his demeanor or in his behavior…perhaps not to you or your family but to those locals with whom he came in contact?"

"Well, there was a kind of officiousness in the way he dealt with his countrymen…always expressing himself in a curt, commanding tone whenever he had to speak with them."

"And how did the abductors treat him?"

"What do you mean?"

"Did they abuse him in any way…talk harshly to him or hit him?"

"I can't really say, the whole event happened so quickly and my husband and I were busy trying to protect the children."

"They ignored him," said Mr. Richmond.

"What do you mean?" I asked.

"Well, Fernando didn't even get out of the car. He was driving and came to a stop at the command of one of the men standing in the middle of the road. They pulled all of us out of the car but Fernando was left behind the wheel."

"They didn't have a gun on him?"

"Maybe they did…they all had guns…but my wife and I and the kids were forced to stand up against the side of the car and pull everything out of our pockets. Fernando just sat there…didn't make any effort to plead on our behalf."

"What did they take of yours?" I asked.

"Besides our son, you mean?"

"Yes."

"The stuff that's always taken, you know, money, jewelry, wristwatches, passports—that kind of thing."

At this point, Jackson returned, carrying a tray with the coffee Mrs. Richmond had ordered. "Mr. Kingstone instructed me to tell you he and his wife will be joining you shortly," said Jackson.

"Thank you, Jackson," said Mrs. Richmond. "You may go…I'll pour."

"As you wish, ma'am," he replied then silently left the room, closing the door behind him.

"Okay, let's focus on the men who pulled off the abduction," I said. "How many were they and what can you tell me about them?"

"At least five, I would say," said Mrs. Richmond, "wouldn't you agree, Charles?"

"Yeah, three guys out in the middle of the road and at least one on each side of the road. The guys on the side were the ones who opened the car doors and kept pointing their guns at us while the three other guys shouldered their weapons and reached in and pulled us out of the car…a bit roughly, I'd have to say."

"Were any of you harmed?" I asked, taking a sip of coffee.

"They sure seemed ready to hurt us," said Mr. Richmond, "but we were so scared and so worried about the children we offered no resistance…simply did what they told us."

"What did they look like?" I asked. "Were they wearing ordinary clothes, some sort of native costume, or perhaps pieces of a military uniform?"

"They were dressed like working-class men…but more like those who live or work in the city, not like the typical farm worker," said Mrs. Richmond.

"And they didn't act as if we were the first foreign tourists they'd had dealings with, I can say that!" said Mr. Richmond with emphasis.

"Did you get the impression they had a tight chain of command...you know, where one was clearly the leader and the others did what they were told, immediately and without question?" I asked.

"I guess so," said Mr. Richmond. "There wasn't much ordering about...the gang seemed to have worked out their moves beforehand, but I got the feeling one guy was in charge."

"How do you mean?" I asked.

"Well, it was the way the guy seemed to size us all up...took his time about it despite the risk some other vehicle could come along. He was the one who pointed to Matt, signaling to a couple of the others to grab him."

"So you had the impression this was a well-rehearsed team?"

"Yeah. They seemed to have known all about us beforehand... and I don't believe Matt's abduction was a spur of the moment decision. The only uncertainty, it seems to me, was which of us they were going to kidnap."

"Why do you think they chose Matt and not yourself, Mr. Richmond?"

"Hell if I know," replied Richmond.

At that moment, Mr. and Mrs. Kingstone entered the room.

"Sorry to disturb you all but my wife and I thought it best if we sit in...at least for a little of the conversation," said Kingstone.

"How's Anne?" asked Mrs. Richmond.

"She's doing fine, Susan," said Mrs. Kingstone, "I've been with her for the past hour…up in her bedroom reading one of those children's books you thoughtfully left behind when you went off to college."

"Have you learned any useful information, Mr. Church?" asked Mr. Kingstone as he joined me on the couch.

"Your daughter and Mr. Richmond have been quite helpful," I replied. "But I have a few more questions to put to them before I can let you people get back to whatever you were doing."

"Take your time, Mr. Church, we want you to have whatever information we can provide," said Mrs. Richmond.

"I appreciate that," I said, "especially since it's already given me a good mental picture of the event and those involved."

"Can you share your insights with us, Mr. Church?" asked Mr. Kingstone.

"Perhaps later, right now what I need to know is how Matt was treated once he was selected. Was he handled roughly while still in your presence or taken away quietly—without any threat of violence?"

"He didn't fight them if that's what you mean," said Mr. Richmond, "they just gripped him tightly and forced him to walk away from the car and into the tree line at the edge of the road."

"What happened next?" I asked.

"The team leader ordered the rest of us back into the car and instructed Fernando to drive on," said Mr. Richmond.

"Were they still standing there…in the road…as you drove off?"

"Yes, we could still see them even after we'd gone some distance. They didn't seem to make any effort to conceal themselves or to run away," said Mrs. Richmond.

"That meant they were expecting a car to pick them up," I said. "Did you see a car parked out of the way as you drove off?"

"No, I don't believe we did," said Mr. Richmond, "but, again, we were in such an agitated state—with Anne crying and all—we were in no position to make helpful observations."

"I understand, Mr. Richmond, but if you could, think carefully, what did Fernando do once you were away from the kidnappers?"

"He didn't say much, I remember that," said Mrs. Richmond, "just kept driving at high speed towards El Monte, saying we needed to report the abduction to the police."

"Did he seem to know who to contact once you arrived at the police station?"

"Yes, he asked to speak with a particular person…Captain Alvarez I believe it was," said Mrs. Richmond.

"Were the police dispatched immediately upon being informed of the abduction?" I asked.

"I'm not sure," she replied. "The captain seemed to want to record all the details of the encounter first…though I imagine he could've signaled to someone to mount a pursuit."

"But you didn't hear him give such an order?"

"No, I certainly didn't.

"Thank you…both of you…for being so helpful," I said, standing up. "I believe I've got all the information I need to move on to the next phase of the operation."

"I understand from my father you'll be going down there right away," said Mrs. Richmond.

"I leave tonight, Mrs. Richmond, and I'll be in touch with your father by satellite phone on a regular basis once I'm in the region. The next step will most likely be a ransom demand. It should come in a day or two and by then I'll be in position—ready to make use of all the information you've given me today."

"But what have we told you that could possibly lead to the kidnappers?" asked Mrs. Richmond.

"Let me worry about that," I replied. "I'll say goodbye then," I added, making my way to the doorway leading to the entry hall.

They all murmured their goodbyes and wished me good luck as I left. Jackson accompanied me to the front door and activated the release on the front gate so I could return to my car.

* * *

I checked the dashboard clock as I drove south out of the Pacific Heights area towards Bush Street where I could get a clear shot to downtown. It was approaching eleven. If I made good time getting back to the apartment and limited myself to a quick shower I could probably manage to make a noon lunch date with Jack. I pressed the speed dial option for Jack on my cell phone and let the Bluetooth link with the car's radio system take over.

"Hey, Jack, it's Church," I said once we were connected.

"Yeah, what's up?"

"Thought we'd best touch base before I take off this evening. You have time to meet for lunch?"

"I can manage it. What'd you have in mind?"

"How about meeting at that place on Sutter Street you keep raving about…say about noon?"

"Sounds good. By the way, orders have come down for my temporary assignment to the embassy. I fly out of here in a couple of days."

"Wow, that was fast! You think nobody put up a stink?"

"You forget, Church, this is a government bureaucracy we're talking about; if the top guy wants something done it gets done, period."

"Yeah, but what about your boss, no audible complaints?"

"Maybe a raised eyebrow or two but nothing further. The real reaction will surface once it's clear the operation was a bust… should that be the case."

"Gotcha. Let's hope it's not…see you at noon."

I pressed the telephone icon on the steering wheel disconnecting the call and returned my full attention to maneuvering through the buildup of traffic the other side of Van Ness Avenue.

I reached the high-rise apartment building minutes later, pulled into the belowground parking garage and hurried over to the bank of elevators. I pressed the button for my floor and caught a glimpse of myself in the mirror polish of the steel elevator door. I looked like a beach bum—a six-foot-four-inch, two-hundred-pound hulk in ratty shorts, soiled running shoes and a rumpled old sweatshirt; and my hair—a wind-blown thatch of sun-bleached sandy blond strands. Christ! The Richmonds must have entertained some uneasy second thoughts seeing me in such a getup. Good thing old man Kingstone was around to reassure them.

Once inside the tiny one-bedroom flat I call home I stripped off the workout clothing and jumped into the shower. While I was still in the bathroom toweling off I heard Chelsea come in.

"Hey, Church, you decent?"

"Be out in a second," I shouted, grabbing the terrycloth robe that hung from a hook on the door and putting it on.

"What's up?" I asked as I padded barefoot into the room.

"Brought your mail up and, noticing you made it back from your morning appointments," she said, eyeing the workout clothes scattered around the room, "I thought maybe there's something else you need me to do before your flight this evening."

"Actually there is, Chelsea, it'd be great if you could go online and see whether there's a motorcycle shop in Santa Lucia that carries sports bikes," I said, quickly gathering up the clothing.

"Sports bikes?"

"Yeah, they're light motorcycles designed for both off-road and highway operation. Lots of manufacturers market them… shouldn't be hard to find at least one or two brands being sold in the city."

"Any technical stuff I need to know?"

"Tell them I'm looking for two bikes weighing in at about three hundred pounds, with engines in the neighborhood of about 250 cubic centimeters. Oh, and also, they should be equipped with hefty storage racks."

Chelsea tapped the information into the notepad app of her smartphone. "Anything else?"

"One other thing, I'll need an outboard motor…probably one in the eight to ten horsepower range, again brand doesn't matter as long as it's got a four-stroke cycle."

"Got it," said Chelsea as she entered the details in her notepad. "I'll try to get back to you with whatever I've found out before you leave for the airport."

"You're an angel!"

"You off to lunch?"

"Yeah, I'm meeting Jack at that place down on Sutter."

"Have fun," said Chelsea as she left the apartment.

Once Chelsea was gone I padded back into the bedroom and began to dress. I put on a pair of blue jeans, a white shirt, a lightweight cotton blue blazer and a pair of black leather shoes. I checked my watch and figured I had enough time to walk the nine or ten blocks to the restaurant. A quick inspection in the mirror and then I headed out.

* * *

I took Market Street most of the way, enjoying the swirl of pedestrians let loose from their places of employment for the noon hour. When I reached the intersection of Sutter and Market I turned onto Sutter and walked briskly in the direction of Union Square. In no time at all, it seemed, I was within shouting distance of the restaurant. It was one of those quintessential San Francisco cafes—small, with a decent bar and an eclectic list of European-styled entrées. Jack was already sitting at a table out front—in the narrow strip of sidewalk set off with artificial hedges adjoining the restaurant. He waved me over.

"Hey, Church, you up for sharing a bottle of wine?"

"Sure, but come on, Jack, you're on duty…didn't think you'd ever wave the rule about drinking on the job," I said as I took the seat opposite him at the small table.

"Actually, I'm off duty…just hanging around until I'm put on a flight to the capital, San Rafael."

"You said it would be a couple of days."

"Yeah, but my boss doesn't think it's worth assigning me a fresh case given the limited time I'd be around, and my old cases are in the hands of my partner, Terry, who by the way has a temporary sidekick who'd just as soon not have me looking over his shoulder."

"So, what did you have in mind?"

"They've got a fine Italian *Barolo Riserva* at a reasonable price…goes well with one of their pasta dishes or any of the meat entrées."

"Let's do it," I said, looking over the menu.

I ordered a spinach salad and a plate of *fettucini carbonara*, Jack ordered a classic French steak with *pommes frites*. While we waited for the wine to be brought to the table Jack filled me in on developments at his end.

"I'm to report to Elena Bolinas, the embassy legat, who'll supervise."

"What do you mean, "she'll supervise?""

"She's to be the cutout between you and me. You'll touch base with her…give her your instructions and she'll pass them along to me."

"Why the hell for?"

"Headquarters wants thorough deniability in this caper... seems to think you'll screw it up and risk saddling the Agency with a truckload of bad publicity. By keeping our direct contact to an absolute minimum they believe they can stonewall any enquiries by pesky journalists or suspicious local authorities."

"Jack, this thing's going to heat up real fast once we're down there; how in hell am I supposed to keep you in the loop if I've got to ring up the embassy every time...and what for God's sake is a "legat"?

"Legal attaché...it's the standard FBI cover at most embassies. Listen, I'm not happy about it either but they tell me Elena has a plan that'll keep communication lines tight."

"What's the plan?"

"Damned if I know, she's to brief you on it once you've made contact with her."

"You got her phone number?"

"Yeah," he said, sliding a piece of paper over to me. "It lists her satellite phone number—the only one you're supposed to use, all her other lines are probably compromised."

We were interrupted by the arrival of the waiter with our bottle of wine. We held off further conversation while he uncorked the bottle and gave Jack a taste. Approval was evident as Jack lit up with a big smile. "You're going to love it!" he said, signaling for the waiter to fill both glasses. "Leave the bottle on the table", said Jack once the waiter had filled the glasses. The waiter nodded, did as instructed then headed off to attend to other diners.

"They going to let you bring you personal firearm into the country?" I asked.

"Yeah, no problem," said Jack, "and if I need something more powerful Elena can supply me from embassy stocks. How about you? You going to take along your thirty-eight semi-automatic?"

"Absolutely. I've still got my Interpol concealed weapons permit…don't imagine they'll give me any trouble at the airport in Santa Lucia."

A server approached with our food, once again cutting off further conversation. Once he was gone and we'd had a chance to taste the food all thought of resuming our talk disappeared as we concentrated on the meal at hand.

It was only after we'd finished eating and were enjoying our final glass of wine that I brought up the subject of Boris.

"You know, Boris spent a year down there doing agricultural pilot projects under the auspices of the United Nations."

"No, I didn't know that…always thought he spent his career in the military."

"Well, he did, but after marrying Gloria he retired from the Israeli Defense Force and the two of them settled on a *moshav* where they farmed avocados. I guess the work was pretty boring so he applied for a UN field assignment…caught a gig in Central America. It was shortly after that stint that they immigrated to the U.S."

"I'll be damned! That guy's no end of surprises."

"Well, there's one more," I said.

"What's that?" asked Jack.

"Old Boris is going to accompany me."

"You're kidding! What the hell for?"

"He figures he can be useful, knowing the country and the people as he does. Anyway, he says he needs to get some action... thinks riding shotgun for me should just fit the bill."

"And you're going to let him?"

"You ever try saying no to Boris? But seriously, he makes a good case. Situations will undoubtedly arise where I'll need someone covering my back—situations where you'd be too exposed if you were to play that role."

"I don't know, Church, seems to me having him along will just increase the likelihood you'll be discovered by the authorities down there—two *gringos* sticking their noses into a crime involving a bunch of locals with juice."

"It gets better, Jack. We'll be tooling around the country on flashy, high performance motorcycles."

"Jesus! You're out of your mind!"

"Let's just say it's a tad unconventional, but the way I figure it we're engaged in a fast-moving assault on a bunch of guys who expect us to approach timidly—afraid of incurring their wrath."

"You're saying you'll be going after some of the go-betweens as well as those involved in the abduction?"

"Hell yes!" I said. "The most direct path to Matt lies with the two guys I believe helped engineer the abduction: the family's in-country guide, Fernando, and the local *jefe* of the police detachment—a Captain Alvarez."

"You get that intel from the parents?"

"Yeah, during my debriefing earlier this morning."

"Okay, let's say having Boris along makes sense, how's he going to manage getting hold of some weaponry?"

"I asked him the same question…says not to worry, he'll improvise…maybe raid the armory of the police detachment in El Monte. Either way, any shooting we have to do will most likely leave a ballistics trail right back to our friend, Captain Alvarez."

"Christ! The guy's got a hell of a lot of *chutzpah!*"

"Well, he's an Israeli…and an ex-Russian at that!" I said with a smile.

* * *

It was close to two o'clock in the afternoon by the time I got back to the apartment. Chelsea had left a note on the kitchen counter outlining the arrangements she'd been able to make down in Santa Lucia.

> *Church—*
>
> *I've reserved two sports bikes, configured as you requested, at the Arena Cycle Shop in Santa Lucia— total price: $7,000.00 (they insist on cash, in American dollars). Had a devil of a time finding a place that sells outboard motors but finally located a marine supply store outside of town, on the way to the coast. They don't have what you're looking for in stock but can get it from their store in San Jose, a place popular with fishermen. It'll have a ten horsepower, four-stroke engine with a manual starter assembly and come equipped with two five-gallon auxiliary fuel tanks. I told them to go ahead but to be sure to have it ready for you by tomorrow afternoon. Hope this helps.*
>
> *Chelsea*

I folded the note and put it in my pocket. Fortunately, I'd stopped by the bank on my way back from lunch and withdrew an ample supply of dollars, enough to handle such transactions. What I needed to do now was pack.

There'd be no need for formal or business attire on this trip, I thought to myself as I pulled a couple of travel bags from out of the closet. Tactical clothing in the form of canvas shirts, blue jeans and a pair of cross-trainers should do the trick, together with a waterproof shell, cotton sweater and crushable special ops hat. As for the need of something a bit more presentable, I figured I'd just keep on the clothes I planned to wear at dinner this evening—they'd make do while traveling and at other times when circumstances warranted, such as during our stay at the Hotel Vallejo in Santa Lucia. With these thoughts in mind I headed for the bedroom, the travel bags slung over my shoulder.

* * *

Once I was all packed I figured I had a few hours of free time before I needed to get ready for my dinner date with Kate. I'd made the date well before all the events of the past two days had put a rush on my schedule and knew she'd have a fit if I tried to cancel. Anyway, I was looking forward to the evening—an evening now shortened to just dinner and drinks. We hadn't seen each other in weeks—not since I'd taken up the case of the stolen paintings that had me chasing through Europe. Kate, who taught fine arts at one of the city's universities, became an item in my life about a year ago when I sought her assistance in connection with some research I was doing on a couple of Andy Warhol silkscreens stolen from a home down near Palo Alto. We hit it off and made it a point to get together after the close of each of my cases.

I didn't feel like heading over to the gym for a workout but did hanker for some grunt work so I changed into a pair of old jeans, a sweatshirt and a pair of stained deck shoes and left the apartment.

The marina at China Basin was only minutes away by car from my so-called 'luxury' high rise south of Market and I figured I could get in a couple of hours of maintenance work on the thirty-six foot sloop Jack and I kept there. She was an elderly vessel requiring much tender loving care but rewarded all our labors by handling the strong bay breezes and late afternoon swells with grace and speed.

A scattering of cumulus clouds broke up the otherwise intensely blue expanse of the late afternoon sky making for a perfect day to be out and about on the Bay. And the musical chorus of breeze-driven standing rigging, halyards and sheets greeting me as I pulled into the parking area of the marina quickened my urge to climb aboard the teak deck of the *Eagle* and see to the maintenance of all the bright work that added so much charm to the nautical lady.

Eagle was tied up towards the outer reaches of E Dock and I couldn't help inspecting the condition of neighboring vessels as I made my way along the dock. Most were sloop-rigged sailing hulls in the same size range and battened down with canvas tarps to ward off sun, salt and seagull droppings. But enough of each vessel was visible to give a good idea of how well they were maintained. The ones taken out regularly seemed in the best condition; their owners giving immediate attention to wear and tear. It was the vessels seldom visited that showed real neglect. I couldn't help wondering why their owners didn't just put them up for sale, letting someone more highly motivated give them the attention they deserved.

When I finally reached the *Eagle* I grabbed the closest lifeline stanchion at the stern and climbed aboard, stepping carefully into the cockpit. It didn't take long to work the combination lock on the companionway door giving me access to the cabin below. I climbed down, savoring the smell of well-varnished tropical wood paneling and captive marine odors of saltwater and diesel fuel. After popping open the forward hatch together with several of the cabin windows fresh air began to stream in. I went through the routine of inspecting the bilge, engine compartment and head to ensure the boat was still seaworthy. Satisfied all was well, I switched on the electrical panel and powered up the CD player. Soon, the cabin was filled with the music of Schubert. I was tempted to remain in the cabin, lounging comfortably on the soft upholstery of the starboard couch, but pulled myself together and climbed back up into the cockpit.

My heavy-gauge canvas tool bag with all the items needed for maintaining the varnished teak was kept stowed in the aft cockpit compartment. I reached down and pulled it out. Jack and I had agreed our next job should be refinishing the toe rail that ran around the main deck. No way I could finish such a job in one afternoon but I could at least get a start on the sanding. I maneuvered myself into a comfortable position on deck and selected the proper grade of sandpaper for the initial removal of the teak's weathered surface. Focusing as much on the background music of Schubert as on the task at hand I whiled away the afternoon in a state of utter bliss.

* * *

I made it back to the flat in what seemed to me plenty of time to take a second shower, dress, and still get over to the tiny French restaurant on Russian Hill by seven o'clock—the time Kate and I had agreed to meet. Chelsea was just coming off duty at the concierge desk when I entered the lobby.

"So, Church, did you get my note?"

"Yeah, great work, Chelsea! It'll mean we won't have to spend a lot of time in Santa Lucia looking for all that gear."

"You need a ride to the airport?"

"No, I'll call a limo. Anyway, I've got to swing by and pick up Boris…probably spend a little time talking with Gloria who, as you've no doubt figured out, isn't real happy about his coming along."

"So what do you have on for this evening…going to slip out for a quick bite or what?"

"If you're angling for a dinner companion you're out of luck. I'm to meet Kate at seven this evening."

"No, Church, I wasn't angling for an invite…just thought you'd have trouble fitting in at one of the swankier places you favor dressed like that."

"Kind of thought I'd shower and change…that all right with you?"

"Probably be all right with Kate seeing as she's the one who'll be sitting right up close to you."

"Where you off to?" I asked, trying to steer the conversation away from my slovenly appearance.

"I've got a dance rehearsal over in the Mission...a bunch of us will probably go out for something to eat afterwards."

"That the piece about saving the whales?"

"No, Church, it's a serious piece of choreography depicting marine life around the Farallon Islands."

"But you play a whale, don't you?"

"I dance a complex set of movements evocative of a whale moving gracefully through the water—yes. Are you trying to make fun of me?"

"Only kidding, Chelsea. Thought I'd get back at you for trashing my present disreputable appearance."

"Well, go and fix it," she said, giving me a quick kiss on the cheek before heading out the front door.

* * *

Parking was a bitch on Russian Hill so I left my car in the garage and took a taxi. Kate and I were to meet at the restaurant at seven o'clock and I was pleased to see the cabbie knew all the shortcuts. I'd make it on time, I thought to myself as I touched the two pieces of flight luggage resting on the seat beside me.

A few sets of eyes turned my way as I entered the tiny French restaurant and headed for the table where Kate sat. Her eyes were on me as well.

"Why the luggage?" she asked as I bent over to give her a kiss on the cheek.

"Have a limo picking me up here at nine o'clock sharp…taking me to the airport," I added as I dropped the bags on the floor next to the wall and settled into a chair.

"You off on another job so soon?"

"Yeah, one of the downsides of working in a field that knows no scheduling boundaries…I must say you're looking very pretty this evening, new outfit?"

"Don't change the subject, William, come on, give me the low down on this new case."

"It's a kidnapping in Central America…a boy from a prominent San Francisco family. I've been assigned to go down there and get him out."

"Christ! That sounds dangerous!"

"It's what I do, Kate, you know that."

"Yeah, but I like it better when I hear about what you've been up to after the event…that way I know it all turned out all right."

"So why'd you ask me?"

"Just dumb curiosity I suppose…so let's not talk about what you're planning to do and get back to the subject of your recent escapades in Europe."

"Why don't we order first," I said, eyeing the waiter who'd been standing patiently off to the side.

"I already know what I want," said Kate, "spent the time awaiting your arrival to study the menu."

"And what would that be?" I asked.

"A small spinach salad followed by the *Fillet of Sole*."

"Sounds good…give me a minute to check the options," I said as I quickly glanced through the menu. "Okay, I think I'm ready," I added, signaling the waiter to come over.

"We'll start with an order of mussels in wine sauce to share," I said, "followed by the spinach salad."

"Make mine small," said Kate.

The waiter nodded, adding a footnote to his ordering pad.

"She'll have the *Fillet of Sole* and I'll have your *Beef Bourguignon*."

"And to drink, sir?" asked the waiter.

"Bring us a bottle of the *Saint-Emilion Bordeaux* you've got listed…the 2005 vintage."

"Very good, sir," said the waiter as he headed for the kitchen.

"But William, I'm having fish."

"I know, Kate, but trust me, the *Saint-Emilion* is a very elegant red, made of a blend of *Cabernet Franc* and *Merlot*, it won't overwhelm the sole and it'll be serviceable as a companion to the beef."

"If you say so…but I'll reserve the right to order a glass of *Chardonnay* if it turns out you're wrong."

"It's a deal," I said, taking her hand in mine.

"So tell my about this fine arts heist in Chicago," said Kate as she gently removed her hand from my grip and fixed me with an expectant stare.

I tried to limit the account to a barebones summary but she kept interrupting me with probing questions. The interrogation came to a halt only when the waiter brought over the bottle of wine and opened it. Once I'd assured him the wine was acceptable and he'd discreetly stepped away from the table to attend to other diners she quickly started in again. By the time the salad course had arrived she'd managed to get the full story out of me. We ate in silence as Kate reflected on the events I'd related.

"Okay, William," she said once a busboy had cleared the table and we sat back awaiting the arrival of our main dish, "Tell me about the paintings themselves...were they truly remarkable?"

I assured her they were and shared with her the professional appraisal given me by the art restorer in Chicago who'd had an opportunity to study them at length.

She nodded in quiet satisfaction, almost as if she was weighing the risks I'd been obliged to take in the quest for their recovery against the true aesthetic value of the paintings themselves.

"So what courses are you teaching this semester?" I asked, wishing to keep the conversation from reverting back to my activities.

"Oh, the typical intro course in art history...I have to say it gets harder every year; the kids are so into popular culture they don't know how to relate to a Michaelangelo or a Matisse."

"That your only class?"

"No, the other one is proving much more satisfying; it's a small class of more motivated students who seem serious about learning the history of American landscape painting."

"You going to take them to the De Young Museum in Golden Gate Park?"

"You mean on a field trip? Yes, towards the end of the course... when they're ready to really appreciate the paintings on display at the museum; it's such a fine collection—Bierstadt, Moran, Cole, Church, they're all represented."

"Wish I could come along…see how your male students handle that kind of proximity to their bombshell of a professor," I said with a laugh.

"Stop it, William, you're being outrageous! My male students always conduct themselves appropriately…as do the women students."

"Yeah, but what are they thinking as they try to ingratiate themselves to a teacher who's gotta be the hottest prof on campus."

Before she could lambast me for my politically incorrect comments the waiter intervened, placing our main dishes on the table and refilling our wine glasses.

Conversation turned to more mundane topics, like what the San Francisco Board of Supervisors was up to and whether our mayor would stick around for a second term.

Afterwards, we lingered over coffee until I saw the limo pull up in front of the restaurant. It was a large highly polished black sedan that stood out in a neighborhood of modest Victorian flats, old street-parked vehicles and scruffily dressed young men and women. I'd already taken care of the check so I helped Kate out of her chair, picked up my bags and waved goodbye to the proprietor—a thick-bellied Frenchman in a soiled white apron who surveyed his small culinary enclave from the vantage point of an open kitchen.

"I can walk, William, you go ahead," she said as we stood outside.

"Nonsense, Kate, let me drop you off...there's plenty of time."

"I only live four blocks away, for goodness sake...anyway I could use the exercise after sitting for the past two hours."

"You sure you'll be all right? It's nighttime you know."

"This is my neighborhood, William, and at this hour people still fill the streets. I'll be fine, believe me."

"Okay, but I tell you what, I'll walk alongside...gives us a little more time together."

"Oh William, that's silly...but in some ways rather nice," she said, stepping closer and giving me a lingering kiss on the lips.

"Just let me get rid of these bags," I said as I handed the flight bags to the limo driver, telling him to meet us in front of Kate's apartment building.

"Here's my address," said Kate, handing the limo driver her personal card with the address clearly printed out.

"Will do, Mr. Church," said the limo driver as he took Kate's card.

"Okay now, what's your real reason for volunteering to escort me home?" asked Kate as she took my arm and guided us in the right direction.

"Well, it can't be that I'm angling for a little lovemaking before setting off, given the fact I need to pick up Boris within the hour."

"Yes, there is that, but what then?"

"Frankly my dear," I said in my best Clark Gable voice, "It's because I just can't get enough of your inestimable charm and pulchritude."

"You're teasing me!"

"Perhaps, but you have to admit to being a gorgeous young woman—with striking blonde hair, and dressed in a pair of jeans and top that does full justice to an absolutely perfect figure."

"And the charm part?"

"Ah, fishing for more compliments are you?" I said, putting my arm around her waist and hugging her tight.

She gave me a punch.

We continued to walk without further conversation until we reached her street. Then she paused and looked up at me.

"Seriously, William, you will take care...this business with the kidnapping sounds terribly dangerous."

"Just the prospect of coming back to a city with you living in it is enough to insure I'll take every precaution," I said, taking her in my arms.

We kissed, oblivious to the aged Chinese couple approaching us, or of the unshaven young man sitting on the front stoop of the Victorian across the street who fiddled with his guitar.

We finally made it to her building. I waited until she'd worked the lock and had safely entered the lobby. She waved at me through the tiny panes of antique glass then started up the stairs. Her flat was on the second floor. I turned and approached the limo idling at the curb. The driver had the door open and I climbed in.

* * *

Boris and his wife, Gloria, lived in Hayes Valley, on the first floor of a nicely maintained Victorian with flowering bougainvillea climbing up the sides. The limo driver had cut over to Gough

Street to take advantage of the timed stoplights and we made the trip in less than fifteen minutes. I instructed the driver to wait while I collected my traveling companion, cautioning him it might take a while since his wife will probably insist on at least a brief conversation. He said he understood and would take the opportunity to grab a smoke.

I climbed out of the limo and, skirting the trash bins put out at the curb to await tomorrow morning's pickup, headed for the front stairs. One ring was all it took to get Boris to the door.

"So, my good friend, we are off," he growled in his deep Russian-tinged voice as he bade me enter.

"I've got a limo waiting outside, Boris, we'll need to be quick."

"He'll wait," countered Boris, "there's Gloria to attend to. Gloria, he's here!" he shouted.

We walked down the narrow hall of the railroad flat—a common floor plan in San Francisco, where all the rooms are lined up front to back and can be accessed from a single hallway running the entire length of the structure. Boris ushered me into the second room from the front that served as the living room and where Gloria was busy putting out small dishes of mixed olives, nuts, and crackers with cheese.

"What will you have to drink?" she asked as she came over and gave me a big hug.

"Gloria, this is lovely but we have to be off…we've a plane to catch," I said somewhat plaintively.

"Nonsense! Sit yourself down and tell me about this adventure you're taking my husband off to."

Resignedly, I took a seat on the large sofa and agreed to a shot of brandy.

"Well?" she asked as she placed the small glass of brandy in front of me.

"There's not much to tell," Gloria, "Boris and I plan to investigate a kidnapping involving an eleven-year-old boy, with an expectation that we can persuade those involved to honor the ransom payment I'm charged with delivering."

"When my husband uses the word 'persuade' he usually means threatening someone with violence, is that your meaning of the word as well?"

"I won't kid you, Gloria, these are bad men but I'm betting they're no match for someone as skilled and as experienced as your husband."

"He's an old man with fantasies of reliving his youth and you, you're helping him."

"Perhaps so, Gloria, but you and I both know Boris needs this. He's getting stir crazy and won't be fun to live with if thwarted, right Boris?"

"You're damned right!" said Boris, quite content to letting me take the heat from his wife.

"You promise me you'll make sure he doesn't do anything that's likely to get him killed?"

"It'll work both ways, Gloria, he'll watch my back while I watch his. And I can assure you I don't plan on giving anyone any opportunity to cause either of us harm."

"I don't know, William, it's been years since he's been involved in anything dangerous. I can't help but worry."

"I understand, Gloria," I said, getting up from the couch, "but your husband's in top physical condition with years of experience, he'll be all right."

"You'll look after him, you promise?" she said, with tears in her eyes.

"I promise," I said, taking her in my arms and giving her a hug.

"We've got to go," growled Boris.

"You two say your goodbyes, I'll wait outside in the limo," I said, giving Gloria a final hug then heading for the front door.

Boris came out a few minutes later carrying his flight bags. He handed the bags to the driver who put them in the trunk next to mine, then climbed into the limo and gave an audible sigh of relief. "Glad that's over," he said, settling back in the seat.

"Let's go," I said to the driver, "the airport…international departure terminal."

"Yes sir," said the driver who'd resumed his place behind the steering wheel. He quickly pulled away from the curb and headed down the street.

* * *

It was about half past ten in the evening when we arrived at SFO's International Terminal. Our flight was not scheduled to take off until after midnight so after checking in and clearing security we headed for the airline's first class lounge where we could sit comfortably and go over our plans for tomorrow's arrival in Santa Lucia.

DAY 3

WE HIT UPDRAFTS AS the plane began its approach, the descent buffeted by air currents rising up from the escarpment as we passed from the coastal piedmont to the mountainous highlands where the capital city was located. Cloud cover was slight allowing for a clear view of the intensely green foliage blanketing the hills. Small settlements connected by a network of narrow unpaved roads came into brief focus as we neared the ground. I signaled for the flight attendant to remove my breakfast tray and shook Boris who'd chosen to skip the meal.

"Wake up old man," I said, "we're almost there."

He roused himself and checked the view outside the cabin window. "I can see that," he said, "must be the Salinas highlands down below...city can't be more than a few miles further."

Breakfast trays were hurriedly cleared away and the craft secured for landing. It was half past seven in the morning local time and the city glistened as the early morning sun cast glancing rays down upon the buildings and streets still wet from the previous night's torrential downpour.

The airport was so close to the center of town I had the feeling we were landing on one of the city's wider boulevards rather than an airstrip, but we finally touched down and taxied over to the non-descript stuccoed building that served as the city's airport terminal.

We stepped off the mobile embarkation stairway onto airport macadam, pausing for a moment to let ourselves adjust to the warm humid air of the tropics.

"Christ, it's hot!" said Boris as he removed his linen sports jacket and slung it over his shoulder. "Let's go see what passport control has in store for us."

I nodded then followed him through the departure control gates and into the terminal. Boris was all but ignored as the control officers carefully examined my concealed weapons permit and the paperwork allowing me to transport the weapon in my personal hand luggage. Only when they were assured I had no intention of conducting police business during my stay in their country—just carrying the weapon in anticipation of needing it at my next destination—did they relax. Our passports were stamped and we were told we were free to go. We collected our luggage and headed out to the street in front of the terminal. The place was filled with people, honking cars, diesel-exhaust-spewing transit buses and garishly painted taxis. I signaled to one of them and motioned for Boris to follow me as I headed for it.

"The Hotel Vallejo *por favor*," I said, shifting to Spanish.

The driver acknowledged the request then began stowing our luggage in the trunk. Meanwhile, Boris slid in beside me on the rear seat. "Damn, it feels good being in the field again!" he said with evident feeling.

"Yeah, I know what you mean," I said

The hotel was set back from the street on a lot richly landscaped with bougainvillea, palm trees and lush lawns. The structure itself was a refurbished colonial mansion done up with Spanish tile, fountains, and heavy antique furniture. I left Boris to handle the luggage and strode through the front entrance and straight over to the registration desk. An attractive young woman with gorgeous eyes and lustrous black hair that fell sensuously around her shoulders greeted me with a warm smile. "You must be Mr. Church," she said as I reached for my passport.

"Yes, William Church, and despite the early hour I hope the two rooms I arranged for are available…it's been a long flight."

"Of course, Mr. Church. You'll find everything is in order. Your bags can be taken directly to the rooms."

"Appreciate that," I said with a smile.

"I'll also need the passport of the other party," she said as she took down the information from my passport.

"Here you are little lady," said Boris who had come up alongside me. "It's been a struggle to keep the bags out of the clutches of the bellhops," he said as an aside to me.

"It's okay, Boris, let them take the bags, our rooms are ready."

"Can I make any other arrangements for you two gentlemen?" said the young woman.

"Actually, you can," I replied. "We'll need a hotel limo…say in about an hour…to get us over to the Arena Cycle Shop here in the city."

"That'll be no problem, Mr. Church," she said, "a car and driver will be at your disposal whenever you need it."

"Pretty slick location, Church," said Boris as we walked out the open French doors leading to the rear courtyard. "Nothing like advertising our arrival—maybe we should shoot off come fireworks or maybe take out a full page ad in the local paper."

"Chill out, Boris, there's method in my madness. I want us to be seen as a couple of rich Americans out for some sporting adventure…you know, some off-road motorcycling, some fishing, maybe some hiking among the ancient ruins. We may need that cover if things turn out badly in the days ahead."

"I get it, but it's a little awkward for an old *Sabra* like me."

"You'll get used to it…anyway you're not a native-born Israeli and couldn't be taken for one what with a Russian accent as thick as yours."

"Go to hell," said Boris with a laugh.

Our rooms were on the ground floor and opened onto the courtyard. The bellhop had the doors to the two adjacent rooms open and stood outside waiting for us to arrive.

"Let's meet in about an hour," I said, "should give us time to get a shower and change into something more casual."

"Suits me," said Boris as he indicated to the bellhop which bags were his.

* * *

I stripped off the outfit I'd worn during the flight and jumped into the shower. It was a large glass enclosed stall—the kind often found in recently refurbished upscale hotels. I stood there for a long time, letting the hot water splash over me—feeling my tired muscles regain their strength and fatigue from the flight quickly slip away. The towels were large and soft and pleasant to the touch. I wrapped one around my waist and got on with the rest of the morning's ablutions.

The room itself was pleasantly cool, with shuttered French windows, a tiled floor and locally made wooden furniture that gave the room a rustic sort of character. I pulled on a pair of jeans, a pale, rock-washed canvas shirt and cross-trainers, letting the shirt hang out to conceal the thirty-eight semiautomatic holstered to my belt.

Before leaving the room, I bundled up the clothes I'd been wearing and placed them on the bed, then called down to room service and instructed the clerk to have someone take them for cleaning—making it clear I'd need them back before dinner time this evening.

Boris was already outside inspecting the central fountain that adorned the courtyard our rooms opened on to.

"Gloria would have liked to have stayed at a place like this during our stint working with the local farmers," he said with a sigh as I came up beside him, "but the stipend we received didn't allow for such luxuries, and anyway it would have gone over badly with the people in the villages if they found out."

"You going to tell her about the place?" I asked.

"Yeah, she won't be shocked, knowing that's the way my buddy Church always travels…right old friend?"

"Well, probably not for most of the time on this trip, sad to say. I figure we'll be roughing it once we leave Santa Lucia."

"Just as well, an old campaigner like myself doesn't like the idea of getting too comfortable."

We walked across the courtyard and through the doors leading to the hotel lobby. I caught the eye of the young woman who'd checked us in; she flashed a smile and gave us to understand through gestures that the hotel's car and driver were standing by outside. I gave her a thumb's up and steered Boris out the main entrance.

The Arena Cycle Shop was on the north side of town, some distance from where the hotel was located, but our driver was well-versed in the tactics of staying at optimal speed while navigating the congested streets and we made it to our destination in a surprisingly short time. I thanked the driver, gave him a generous tip and told him to return to the hotel—that we'd be returning on our own conveyances. He glanced at the shop skeptically but then shrugged and gave a wave as he put the car in gear and moved slowly back into traffic.

"I hope Chelsea was right and the bikes are actually here," said Boris, looking wistfully after the fading car.

"Let's go in and find out," I said, slapping him on the back.

The shop appeared to have been an auto repair garage in a previous incarnation with little evidence of any kind of refurbishment, but the grease-stained concrete floor was packed with motorcycles of all sorts—some used, some in various states of disrepair and a few that looked as if they'd just come out of shipping crates. A skinny guy in a tee shirt and jeans was working on one of the bikes and stood up as we walked in. He called out to someone in a back office and returned to his work.

"Bienvenido señor, cómo puedo ayudarle?" said the heavy-set man who emerged from the back office. He wore a rumpled dark suit, white shirt and tie, and figured to be in his mid-forties.

"I take it you are *Señor* Arena," I said in Spanish. "I'm William Church and this is my friend *Señor* Boris. We're here to pick up the two sports bikes my assistant ordered over the phone.

"Yes, *Señorita* Chelsea…I remember. She was very particular… wanted this and that…just so!"

"Are they ready?" I asked.

"But of course, come look," he said, pointing to two awkward looking motorcycles on kickstands up against the rear wall of the room. As we walked over he added, "I keep them back here so my customers don't see what clumsy looking machines I'm sometimes obliged to sell."

I could see what he meant. The rear seat assembly had been chopped off to allow for the installation of the storage racks I'd requested, giving the bike a boxy look that marred the otherwise sleek lines of the machine. I mounted the black leather saddle of the first one I came to, turned on the ignition and kicked the starter pedal. The engine started right up, giving a smooth, low decibel growl that climbed to a whine as I advanced the handlebar-mounted throttle. I dropped the engine speed back to idle and inspected the instrument panel and controls.

"Just as you requested they weigh just a little over three hundred pounds but have powerful engines. They will carry you far…and in much comfort," said the proprietor.

"What do you think, Boris?" I asked.

"I'd prefer something with four wheels but these will do I suppose," he said, putting all his weight on the horizontal storage rack mounted on the second bike to see whether it would carry a load as heavy as the outboard motor we planned to transport.

"We'll take them," I said. "I suppose you've filled the tanks?"

"Yes, of course, as you can see they are ready to be driven directly out of the showroom…that is, once the small matter of some paperwork and my receipt of payment have been taken care of."

"Chelsea mentioned you prefer cash…U.S. currency…that right?"

"Precisely," said *Señor* Arena as he ushered us back into his office.

* * *

By half past ten that morning we were cruising down the principal highway that led towards the outskirts of the city—in the direction of the coastal communities, including San Jose. The bikes were running smoothly and responded instantly to the throttle. I signaled to Boris to follow me as I swerved off the highway and onto a dirt path running alongside the road. It was still muddy after last evening's rain but the off-road tread on the tires held fast as we splashed through puddles and clayey soil at reckless speed. After about a hundred yards or so I swerved back onto the highway and brought the bike to a halt. Boris pulled up beside me.

"Handles well," I said, wiping the splashed mud from my face and hands.

"Yeah," said Boris, "but I've got to learn to keep further back if I'm to avoid getting plastered with mud whenever you get the idea in your head to plunge us into a godforsaken mud hole!"

"Well, at least we know the bikes will perform well regardless of the terrain…that's worth a bit of splashed mud…right?"

"Yeah, but warn me next time…okay, pardner?"

"I'll keep it in mind," I said with a smile, then cranked the throttle and kicked up dust as I accelerated down the road, Boris close on my heels.

The marine store Chelsea had contacted was about a half an hour's distance from the edge of the city, in a small town at the junction of the main road to the coast and a road that led to a lake reportedly large enough to accommodate water sports. We motored slowly through the town looking for the store but finally gave up and asked somebody. We were directed to an unpaved street off the main drag and instructed to go about a block. We'd see the store on the left. Sure enough, it was where we were told it would be. We pulled up in front and killed the engines.

"You go in and handle the business," said Boris as he climbed off his bike and set the kickstand, "I'm going to scout out a place where we can eat lunch."

I nodded and paused a moment to get the feel of the place. There wasn't much street activity, just a few women running errands and some kids scampering along—on their way to school or home, I couldn't tell. I watched as Boris strode down the street, heading for the busier commercial district we'd passed as we motored through town. The store itself was small—just enough of a storefront to accommodate one oversized display window and an entrance door. On display was a motley collection of kid's swimming inflatables, fishing gear and waterskiing equipment. I climbed off my bike and headed for the door.

A bell sounded as I entered and a young man in jeans and a cotton sport shirt poked his head out from behind a somewhat flimsy room divider at the rear of the shop. My guess was it was intended to separate the stockroom from the display area. He approached me—a welcoming smile on his face.

"May I help you," he said in Spanish, despite having sized me up as an American.

I reciprocated the compliment by answering him in English, "I'm William Church—here to pick up an outboard motor my assistant ordered by phone yesterday."

"Ah, yes…the order placed my Miss Chelsea of San Francisco," he replied in excellent English.

"That's the one…is it ready?"

"The motor and fuel tanks have not yet arrived from our store in San Jose but are expected by noon today…can you wait?"

"Don't have much of an alternative," I said. "By the way, my partner and I plan to do a little fishing…on the rivers the other side of the Salinas Highlands …any chance you can outfit us with the necessary gear?"

"No problem. Why don't I assemble two kits from the stock I have here in the store…have them ready by the time the outboard motor arrives?"

"Make sure the fishing rods are collapsible…got to carry them on the back of our motorcycles."

"I understand," he said, letting his glance fall on our two bikes parked outside—in full view through the shop's display window.

"Also, we'll be needing lunch. Any suggestion as to where we should eat?"

"The dining room of the town's only hotel, the Excelsior, probably offers the best food though the atmosphere is a bit boring. Perhaps you might try the *Cantina Rosa*, it serves local dishes and is popular with townspeople and travelers alike."

"Thanks for the tip," I said, turning and heading for the door.

"I'll keep an eye on the motorcycles for you," said the young man.

"That'd be a big help," I said, then opened the door and stepped outside.

I walked in the direction Boris had taken and spotted him once I turned onto the paved street we'd driven down when entering the town. He was coming towards me, a big grin on his face.

"Found a great place for lunch," he said once we'd come up to each other.

"Let me guess, it goes by the name *Cantina Rosa*."

"How the hell did you know!" he said, scowling.

"I'm not clairvoyant if that's what's worrying you, the proprietor at the shop recommended it."

"Makes sense," said Boris, "it's not even noon and the place is already packed."

"Think they'll have room for us?" I asked as we headed in the direction of the *Cantina*.

"Not to worry, old Boris worked his masculine charm on the proprietress; she's holding a table for us."

The place was only two short blocks away, barely giving me time to fill Boris in on my conversation with the proprietor of the marine shop before arriving in front of the place. As we walked in Rosa rushed over. She was a buxom lady in her late thirties dressed in a garish red dress and heels.

"*Señor* Boris, you are back! And who is this handsome young man who accompanies you?" she said in Spanish, eyeing me lasciviously.

"My friend, Church...but enough about him, where's that table you promised me?"

"You are such a grouch," she said with mock distaste, "come, I'll show you."

She led us to an unoccupied table near the bar "You sit here... that way I can keep an eye on you," she said to Boris as she gave him an exaggerated wink and a pat on the behind.

"Looks like you've made a real conquest," I said with a laugh.

"All in the line of duty my friend, so what will you have?"

"Whatever the Day's Special is...don't imagine she'd let us choose anything else."

Sure enough, there wasn't any opportunity to see a menu. A waiter began bringing out dishes moments after we sat down. Bottles of beer materialized just as fast.

"I ordered for you," said Rosa, who'd stopped by as we began to eat. "You are new in town and wouldn't know what is good—*es bueno, si?*"

"*Si, es buena, muchas gracias,*" said Boris, putting his arm around her waist.

Just then, a tall, heavy-set man sitting at a nearby table kicked back his chair and stood up. He was dressed in jeans, cowboy boots and a blue denim shirt and looked to be a local rancher.

"Hey *gringo,*" he shouted in Spanish, "keep your filthy hands off that woman!"

"You speaking to me, friend?" replied Boris, also in Spanish, not bothering to remove his arm from around Rosa's waist.

"Your goddamned right I'm speaking to you," he replied taking a threatening step towards our table.

"Whoa, *hombre,*" I cautioned, "you don't want to tangle with him," pointing to Boris.

"Keep out of it, *gringo*! That's my woman and I don't let anybody take such liberties."

"You're crazy, Ricardo!" said Rosa, pulling loose from Boris and turning to confront the rancher. "Go back to your seat and stop this nonsense!"

He shoved her aside and stood menacingly over Boris. "You going to get up or do I have to put my boot up against your head!"

Boris got up from his chair slowly, pushing the chair back out of his way then turned to face the rancher. "You'll want to sit down like the lady told you," he said quietly.

"You telling me what to do, *gringo*?"

"Yes, you overheated son of a bitch, I'm telling you what to do! Now get over there with your friends and let my companion and I eat in piece."

"Fuck you!" said the rancher and threw a punch directly at Boris' face.

Boris deflected the blow with a vicious upward swipe of his left hand that connected with the man's wrist, then threw a right-handed knockout punch to the man's jaw. The rancher crumpled, unconscious, to the floor.

"Hey!" shouted one of the rancher's table companions, scrambling to his feet, "who the hell you think you are?"

"Easy friend," I said, pulling up my shirt to reveal the thirty-eight holstered on my belt, "let's just all go back to our food and forget this little incident. I'm sure Rosa will tend to the guy on the floor."

Rosa was already on her knees, holding the rancher's head in her hands trying to revive him. "Everything's okay," she shouted, "Ricardo's not badly hurt...are you baby?"

Ricardo lifted his head, shook the dizziness from his mind and gingerly explored the damage to his wrist. He whispered something to Rosa.

"Nothing's broken...he's all right," she announced as she helped him stand up.

Boris nodded then slowly dragged his chair back to the table and sat down. The rancher, with Rosa's help, shuffled over to where he'd been sitting and spoke quietly to the two men who were at the table. Abruptly, they stood up, dropped some money on the table and grabbed the rancher, helping him make it to the front door of the *cantina* and then outside—to a pickup truck parked out front. Moments later, they drove off.

The rest of the customers in the *cantina* returned their attention to their food and resumed their conversations. Only Rosa seemed troubled by the incident. "He's a dangerous man, Boris, you should not have shamed him as you did."

"Couldn't be helped, Rosa, the only alternative was to let him hit me and that's something I just can't allow."

"People around here are afraid of Don Ricardo...we call him that because he is so rich."

"That why he thinks he owns you and feels he can do what he likes in your establishment?"

"It's best to humor him so I let him pretend I'm his girlfriend... it does no harm and keeps him from making trouble when he's here."

"Didn't seem to work all that well today," said Boris, "but we'll be out of your way just as soon as we finish this fine meal. You tell him you banned us from returning...in fact, you tell him you warned us we best get out of town. He'll like that...bullies always do."

Rosa didn't say anything, simply patted Boris on the shoulder and began attending to her other customers.

"Well, I guess we've added another dimension to our rich, sports loving *gringo* image," I said with a smile before taking a deep swig of my cold beer.

Boris just shrugged and kept his attention on his food.

* * *

The outboard motor and other gear were ready when we returned to the marine shop after lunch. The young proprietor had assembled two fishing kits as promised, both were packaged in separate canvas roll-up packs and rested on the two auxiliary fuel tanks next to the stand on which the outboard was clamped. I handed him the money he said I owed him.

"You going to get all this stuff on the back of those motorcycles?" he asked skeptically as we started taking the items outside.

"That and our luggage," I replied, hoisting the outboard onto the horizontal rack behind the seat of my bike. "You think you can locate some cargo straps, I think we're going to need them?"

"I've got a supply of nylon web straps…used to lash stuff to the roof of cars. That work for you?"

"Yeah, bring out a bunch, we'll see how many it'll take to get this equipment secured."

He brought out a cardboard box full of one-inch-wide straps, "S" hooks, and other tie-down hardware and Boris and I went to work. The fuel tanks were fairly easy to secure, they could be mounted on their side—their flat bottoms flush against the metal frame of the racks on either side of Boris' rear wheel—then lashed tightly with a web of straps. The motor was another thing entirely. It needed to be kept from rolling over when placed horizontally on the rack over my bike's wheel—the lower drive unit extending well out beyond the end of the rack. After a few unsuccessful strategies the guy from the shop brought out a U-shaped piece of stiff metal that he clamped to the rack with small U-clamps at a point about midway along the rack.

"Clamp the motor mount to the lip of the metal piece," he said.

I nodded then slipped the motor mount over the exposed lip of the piece and tightened the two mounting screws until the motor was rigidly secured. All that remained to do was to lash the motor with straps all along its length to ensure it wouldn't bounce around once we were on the road. Meanwhile, Boris had managed to slip the fishing kit rolls under the upper straps holding the fuel tanks.

"Thanks for the help," I said to the proprietor as I shook his hand.

"Hell, no problem, it's been a pleasure working with you guys…not often I get a chance to see a couple of crazy Americans in action."

"You mean the use of the bikes to tour the country with?"

"Yeah, that and the fight in Rosa's *cantina*."

"You know about that?"

"Hell, it's a small town…got a phone call about it while you two were out here struggling with the outboard."

Boris laughed then climbed on his bike and kicked the starter pedal. As the engine came to life he shouted, "Best we get a move on before the posse shows up."

I nodded, started up the engine on my bike and put the rig in a slow turn, checking to see how it would ride with the heavy outboard mounted behind me. Once assured the bike was in balance I gave the proprietor a wave and throttled up.

* * *

We cruised at a leisurely speed once we cleared the town, not in any hurry and anxious to get a better sense of the land we were passing through. Even though we hadn't actually left the plateau the landscape proved to be dramatic in its variety: cultivated fields, grazing pastures, dense groves of trees in steep draws and on hilly summits. And the road itself was an object of study, requiring a fair amount of attention due to frequent blind spots caused by the twisting and turning of the poorly maintained macadam as it sought to conform to the undulating character of the terrain.

It was at one of these blind spots about five miles north of the town that we ran into trouble. Don Ricardo and his two buddies had apparently monitored our approach from high ground adjacent to the curve, and seeing no other traffic approaching had pulled their pickup across the narrow highway, intending to block our way. Ricardo and one of his buddies stood behind the pickup, hunting rifles at the ready. The other guy was still on the summit of the hill, aiming down at us with a third rifle. We had no choice but to come to a halt.

"Things are a little different now, eh *gringo*?" said Ricardo as he stepped around the truck and poked Boris in the chest with his rifle.

Boris didn't hesitate—in a lightning move he ripped the gun out of Ricardo's hands with his right hand, tossing it laterally to where I was standing, while at the same time stepping up close and getting his left arm around Ricardo's throat. With Ricardo serving as a human shield and locked into a potentially fatal chokehold his buddies held off firing. But I didn't. I took Ricardo's rifle and shot the guy standing behind the truck, hitting him in the shoulder and causing him to drop his rifle. Before the guy on the hill could get a bead on me I dropped to the ground and rolled up against the side of the truck—out of his line of fire.

"Tell your buddy to drop his rifle and walk down with his hands up," ordered Boris, releasing his grip on Ricardo so his vocal chords would work. Ricardo complied and the guy did as ordered. As he was carefully making his way down the hill I scrambled around the truck and kicked the other guy's rifle away from where he lay.

"Now this is the way it's going to be," I said, once all three of them were assembled at the rear of the truck, "if you report this incident to the authorities or in any other way attempt to cause us trouble while we're in your country we'll inform the police that we observed Don Ricardo here shoot his friend just as we happened to pass by on our motorcycles. He's going to need professional medical help to remove the bullet and I'm going to confiscate Ricardo's rifle. I'll make it available to the police who'll be able to verify the bullet taken from this man's shoulder did indeed come from Ricardo's gun. With material evidence like that no amount of influence you might have with the authorities as a consequence of your wealth will persuade them your fanciful story about how two *norteaméricanos* got the drop on three guys with rifles could possibly be true."

"Nobody will believe you," sneered Ricardo. "Everybody knows I have no need to use a gun to discipline a subordinate. What would my motivation be?"

"Your motivation? I'll tell you why you shot the guy, it's because he shot out two of the tires on your truck after you threatened to fire him," I nodded to Boris who picked up the wounded guy's rifle and shot out the two tires on the right side of the truck.

"Jesus, you guys are crazy!" shouted Ricardo.

"And the reason you threatened to fire him was because he kept bringing up the embarrassing matter of you having been bested in the barroom fight at the *cantina*."

"But why would you be in the possession of my gun?" snarled Ricardo. "That in itself would be a criminal matter—foreigners are not permitted to have firearms without special permits."

"I've got such a permit," I said, showing them once again the handgun holstered to my belt, "and the means by which to have disarmed you. No, I think our story will hold up better than yours."

Ricardo slowly nodded his head, clearly convinced I'd made my case. "But everything changes if you return to my part of the country," he said defiantly.

"I give you my word we'll not be returning…at least not in the near future…so why don't you help your wounded companion back to town where he can get some medical attention while we continue on our way."

Ricardo, shaking his head in frustration, climbed into the cab of the truck and started the engine. As he maneuvered the pickup to the side of the road, Boris and I got back on our bikes, started them up and resumed our journey.

* * *

It was mid-afternoon by the time we arrived back at the hotel. We'd stopped at a nearby gas station to replenish the fuel in our tanks before motoring over—to ensure we'd have no difficulty getting an early start the following morning. Security at the hotel's parking lot was not up to the level required to guard the two bikes while all the gear was still strapped on, and the prospect of having to unload the bikes and then reload them just hours later held no attraction so we quietly pushed the bikes into the interior courtyard through a gate that led out to the parking area, then into our respective rooms.

We both felt the buildup of fatigue from the overnight flight, the roundtrip motorcycle ride and the tension stemming from the day's two hostile encounters; we agreed to get some shuteye before venturing out that evening.

But first I needed a hot shower. Maid service had already removed the wet towels from this morning's shower and had supplied me with fresh towels. I put my holstered thirty-eight on the night table, removed the jeans, canvas shirt and cross-trainers I'd been wearing and jumped into the shower. While I let the hot water wash off the road grit I began mapping out in more detail a plan for the coming days. The first order of business was to get close to where the kidnappers were holding young Matt. That would require either some bait—in the form of ransom—or by forcing them into the open by threatening their security. My plan was to work both angles simultaneously.

I toweled off, put on one of the hotel's courtesy robes and pulled the satphone from my luggage. It would be late morning in San Francisco—a good time to check in.

"Jackson, this is Church, put Mr. Kingstone on the line, will you? Thanks."

"Mr. Kingstone, Church here. Wanted to let you know I'm about to make my entry onto the field of operations…that's right, we should be in the capital city of San Rafael sometime tomorrow."

"I've heard from the kidnappers," blurted out Kingstone, clearly in something of an agitated state.

"What are their terms?" I asked.

"It amounts to two million dollars once the bonus is included. They want it in hundred-dollar bills and warn any delay would trigger painful retribution to the boy."

"How did they want it delivered?"

"They didn't say…just demanded I assemble the cash and await further instructions. They gave me forty-eight hours."

"That's a good sign…means they're professionals and know it takes time to round up large quantities of currency without tipping off the authorities. They insinuate you and your family are under surveillance?"

"How did you know?" asked Kingstone. "Yes, they said they'd be watching and not to try contacting the police."

"That's most likely a bluff," I said, "chances are they don't have the manpower to mount surveillance, and anyway they only learned of your involvement just a day or so ago—not enough time to get anything set up."

"I have to tell you, Church, I'm scared and so are the Richmonds. The man on the phone seemed angry and in deadly earnest."

"That's to be expected, Mr. Kingstone, they wouldn't be much of an outfit if they couldn't supply at least one spokesman who could scare the living daylights out of the guy with the deep pockets."

"I guess, but do be careful, I don't want anything to happen to Matt."

"We'll keep that in mind, Mr. Kingstone. Well, I'll sign off now…expect my next call early tomorrow evening—your time."

I broke contact and placed the sat-phone back in my shoulder bag.

Before climbing into bed I called down to the front desk and requested a wakeup call for seven o'clock that evening. "By the way," I asked the clerk, "what's the name of your colleague…that young attractive woman who checked us in this morning?"

"That would be Adriana…Adriana Rivas."

"She on duty this evening?"

"No, *señor.*"

"How can I get in touch with her?"

"I can have her call you…she's probably home…would that be all right, *señor?*"

"Yes, please do…and thank you."

While I waited for her call I slipped outside and knocked on Boris' door.

"What's up?" asked Boris once he opened his door—clearly surprised to see me standing there barefoot with just the hotel's courtesy robe on. He himself was shirtless but still in his trousers.

"Make your own arrangements for dinner, old friend, I've got plans to persuade a certain young lady to join me."

"You referring to that lovely lass who checked us in this morning?"

"The very same."

"Well, good luck…I guess I'll order something from room service and use the time to put through a phone call to Gloria. God knows, there's likely to be little chance for doing so in the days ahead."

"A wise choice, see you early tomorrow morning."

"Yeah," said Boris as he gave me a wave and shut the door.

As I reentered my hotel room the phone began to ring.

I walked over to the desk where the phone was located and lifted the receiver. "Church, here," I said.

"Mr. William Church?" said a delicate female voice I'd recognize anywhere.

"Yes, this is William Church."

"This is Adriana Rivas…you asked to speak with me?"

"That I did, Miss Rivas. I couldn't help admiring you during our brief encounter during check-in this morning and hoped there might be an opportunity to get to know you better. Your colleague mentioned you were off-duty this evening and I thought perhaps you might be willing to join me for dinner here at the hotel…say about eight o'clock?"

There was a lengthy pause before she spoke. "I…I don't know, Mr. Church…of course I'm flattered you took notice of me but honestly I don't…"

"I apologize for placing you in such an awkward position, Miss Rivas, but since I'm scheduled to leave in the morning and can't be sure when I'll be returning I hoped you'd forgive my presumptuousness."

"Well of course I don't wish to give the impression I'm offended by your invitation, Mr. Church, it's only that it comes out of the blue, so to speak."

"I quite understand, Miss Rivas. Let me suggest the following, why don't you agree to join me for cocktails at the hotel bar… say about seven-thirty. Then after a drink and some conversation perhaps you'll feel more comfortable accepting my invitation to dine, and if not we'll simply say 'good evening' and go our own ways…would that work for you?"

"Yes, I believe that would be all right…seven-thirty you say?"

"Yes, that's correct. I'll see you then."

"Yes, I'll be there," she replied, then hung up.

I put the phone down, walked over and closed the shutters on the windows then made my way over to the bed and lay down, stilled clothed in the courtesy robe. The prospect of an evening with the gorgeous Adriana Rivas was just the right thought to ease me into a deep slumber.

* * *

I woke to a soft knock on the door. "Who is it?" I shouted.

"It's the hotel's valet, Mr. Church, delivering your clothing," said a young man on the other side of the door.

"Give me a second," I said, sitting up and retying the robe's belt more securely around my waist.

I stood up and walked over to the door, opening it cautiously—conscious of the aggrieved parties Boris and I had cultivated earlier in the day.

A young man in a hotel uniform stood before me holding a plastic bag containing the items I'd arranged to have laundered and dry cleaned.

"Thanks," I said, taking the garment bag from his hand and slipping in a currency note.

I shut the door and tore off the plastic covering, laying the various items on the bed. I checked my wristwatch and saw it was close to the time I'd planned on getting up anyway so I called down to the front desk and instructed them to cancel the wake up call. Some minutes later—rested and all freshened up—I pulled on the gray light-weight slacks, white sports shirt and classic blue blazer I'd worn the previous evening and filled my pockets with the various items the evening required. And despite the seemingly harmless nature of tonight's agenda I thought it only prudent to slip the holstered semiautomatic onto my belt before going out the door.

The hotel bar was accessed directly from the lobby—a splendid little room with tiled floor, walls whose exposed structural beams stood out vividly against a background of white plaster, and furnishings that evoked the country's earlier colonial era. I was the first to arrive and chose a table off to the corner where I could monitor the comings and goings of other patrons but where we could expect to have our conversation remain private. I waved off an approaching waiter, signaling to him I was expecting a guest and would order once she arrived, which she did only minutes later.

"Thank you for coming," I said as I stood and took her hand in greeting.

"It was not an inconvenience, Mr. Church," she said as she settled into the chair I held for her, "I had no particular plans and my mother, with whom I live, was expecting an old friend to stop by, relieving me of any guilt for having left her unattended."

"Regardless, I'm indebted to you for making my one evening in Santa Lucia something memorable."

"I'm afraid you presume too much, Mr. Church, the evening may be quite brief; after all I've only agreed to meet you for a drink."

"But of course...still, should our evening's get together last no longer than a fraction of one hour and only consist of whatever conversation can be accomplished over a single drink I, for one, would still regard it as memorable."

"And why would that be, Mr. Church?" said Adriana as she leaned forward, a playfully inquisitive expression on her face.

Before I could frame a reply the waiter came over to the table and asked for our order.

"I'll have a glass of wine, Jorge," said Adriana.

"And you sir?" asked the waiter.

"Bring me whatever you're bringing Miss Rivas, Jorge."

"Very good sir."

As the waiter made his way back to the bar Adriana looked at me enquiringly, "But you don't have any idea what he'll bring."

"Perhaps you'll enlighten me," I said with a smile. "You see, I've put my evening's destiny entirely in your hands."

She shook her head dismissively, "I can see you're intent on making this difficult for me."

"Really I'm not, Adriana, I just want you to feel comfortable... to know I'm not about to dazzle you with worldly sophistication or any other ruse...we're playing on your turf with your rules."

"Very well," she said, settling back in her chair and letting a smile erase the otherwise stern expression on her face. "As for the wine, you'll be pleased to learn Jorge will be serving glasses of a California Sauvignon Blanc from a highly respected winery."

As surprise was clearly evident from my expression she continued, "Central American countries do not produce commercially marketable wines and as our tourist industry and our tastes have matured we've been importing more and more wine. California wines are favored, particularly the white wines made from the Sauvignon Blanc grape."

"And why is that?" I asked.

"Because, Mr. Church, chilled white wine is believed to go best with our native cuisine."

"And I have to believe there are several items of such cuisine on tonight's dinner menu...am I right?"

"Of course there will be," she replied, "the hotel prides itself on allowing guests to savor our national dishes."

"So perhaps it's not unreasonable to hope you'll feel inclined to guide me in the selection of an entrée in the hotel's dining room once we've finished our drinks," I said playfully.

"You're incorrigible!" she said, giving my hand a gentle slap.

At that moment, the waiter returned with our drinks. As Adriana had predicted, we were served a California Sauvignon Blanc—in beautifully shaped wine glasses of European manufacture.

"To a chance meeting…a very welcome chance meeting," I said as I touched my glass to hers.

"You still haven't really explained why you chose to invite me out for a drink," said Adriana with an air of pretended innocence.

"Actually, I have," I protested, "I confessed to having admired you as soon as I approached the reception desk…charmed not only by your beauty but also later, by the quiet competence you exhibited during the two times our paths met."

"Hmm," she murmured, idly fingering her glass of wine and gazing contemplatively in my direction—as if to ferret out what other motives might be concealed by my seeming candor.

"So tell me about yourself," I said, "did you grow up in Santa Lucia?"

"No, in a small town to the east of the capital, but when my father died my mother brought my two brothers and myself to the city where we could secure a better education."

"And I imagine that education continued up through university given the fluency with which you speak English."

"Yes, it did. I pursued a business curriculum and upon graduation was hired by the hotel's management."

"Your brothers, are they married?"

"One is…he's a banker here in Santa Lucia. My other brother is a sales representative for an agricultural supply company and travels a lot…probably why he's not yet married."

"So you live with your mother."

"Yes, just the two of us," she said, then paused, "you're wondering why I'm not married yet, aren't you?"

"The question did occur to me," I admitted.

"There's no easy answer, Mr. Church, I..."

"Please call me 'William', Adriana," I said, putting my hand on top of hers.

She left my hand where it was and looked up into my eyes, "If I'm to call you 'William' perhaps it would be fitting for me to know a little more about yourself."

"There's not much to tell, grew up in southern California, went to college back east...Princeton. Spent several years as a Special Agent in the FBI working the art theft detail—liked the challenge of detective work but couldn't hack the bureaucracy so I bailed out and went into business for myself."

"So you're a private detective?"

"Technically speaking, I am—with a California license and continuing links with the FBI, but I refer to myself as a recovery specialist."

"What's that mean, exactly?" she asked.

"It means people pay me to locate and retrieve something that's been taken from them."

"You mean like jewelry or works of art?"

"Yeah, but also anything that's been stolen—from valuable objects to kidnapped children."

"You enjoy that?"

"Sure, why not? It pays well and lets me do something I'm pretty good at."

"But it's got to be dangerous, I should think."

"Perhaps, but it's what I do."

"Is that why you're down here…trying to get something back for a client?"

"No, Adriana, this trip is just a chance for an old buddy of mine and myself to spend a little time together…do a little fishing, maybe check out some of the old ruins."

"Is that why you're leaving tomorrow?"

"Yeah, we're heading out early…heard the fishing is good on the Monte Rio."

"So when will you return to the capital?"

"Can't say for sure, Adriana, that's why I've been kind of pressing you to give me some time this evening."

She didn't say anything, just studied me with those gorgeous eyes of hers. I sipped my wine patiently.

"How old are you, William?" she asked, seemingly still not sure which way to proceed.

"Thought you'd have caught that this morning while handling my passport," I said with a smile.

"This morning you were simply a customer; I had no reason to occupy myself with biographical details."

"But now you do…is that what you're saying?"

"Just answer the question, William."

"Okay, I'm in my early thirties, I'm six foot, four inches tall and weigh two hundred and ten pounds; I've never been married and don't have a steady girlfriend—you satisfied?"

"Entirely, now let's go have some dinner."

* * *

Delightfully surprised, I rose from my seat and stepped around to pull the chair back for Adriana. The hotel's dining room was on the opposite side of the lobby and as we walked across the open space Adriana waved to the young man who was behind the reception desk.

"He a friend of yours?" I asked.

"That's Carlos, the young man who relayed your message. Thought he should know what the outcome was."

"Do we know the outcome?" I asked teasingly.

"I was referring to the fact we are dining together at the hotel... nothing more!"

"As you wish," I said, giving her my arm.

The Maître d' quickly escorted us to a table in the half-empty room and signaled for a waiter to attend to us. "Very pleased to see you this evening, Miss Rivas," he said as he helped her into her chair.

"Thank you, Ramon" she replied, giving him a smile.

"I expect you to order," I said as I placed the cloth napkin on my lap, "after all, it's my wish to have the benefit of your expertise—and your willingness to provide it—that seems to have brought us to this point in the evening."

"Is that so?" said Adriana, enquiringly, "Somehow I got the impression it had something to do with a certain young man's desire to be in the company of a young lady who caught his attention."

"That too," I said, "just as it seems likely the young lady's willingness to accompany the gentleman might in some measure be attributed to the favorable impression he's made."

She laughed then grew quiet, gently placing her hand on mine. "It's true, William, you are a very charming man…and a gentleman. I should like this evening to last a very long time."

I took her hand and gave it a gentle squeeze, "The length of the evening is entirely in your hands…but first things first, the waiter's going to require some instructions so why don't you take a look at the menu and order."

"Are you sure?" she asked.

"Absolutely, but keep in mind your country's culinary reputation is at stake."

* * *

It was close to nine o'clock before Adriana and I rose from the table and headed for the door leading from the dining room to the hotel lobby. I held her close, seeing she was a little tipsy from the wine we'd consumed over dinner.

"So did you like it?" she asked, looking up at me.

"It was wonderful," I replied, "and confirmed my opinion that the way you people prepare meat and fish is a compelling reason for us *Norteaméricanos* to make visiting the area a regular habit."

"So you'll be coming back…soon?"

I didn't answer—just continued walking. Once we reached the center of the lobby area I paused. Adriana sensed my indecision and looked first at the main entrance then at the opening opposite that led to the interior courtyard. "Let's go out to the fountain," she said, pulling me towards the interior courtyard.

"You sure you don't want me to walk you home?" I asked, turning my attention towards the front entrance.

"It's too far to walk, I'll catch a cab," she replied, "but first I'd like to sit for bit beside the fountain…you don't mind do you?"

"Of course not," I said, putting my arm around her waist and moving in the direction of the courtyard.

The courtyard, open to the dark evening sky, was lit by the soft yellowish light coming from handcrafted glass lanterns mounted above each guestroom door, producing a kind of halo effect that left the central fountain area clothed in darkness. The pool of water at the base of the fountain shimmered however as light emanating from bottom-mounted floodlights caught the delicate splash of water.

We stood next to the fountain, studying the graceful movement of water and enjoying the solitude of the darkened courtyard. She then turned towards me, her dark eyes intent on scrutinizing my face, "You didn't answer my question, William," she said in a whisper.

"It's because I don't have an answer, Adriana," I said softly. "In my line of work I can't predict where I'll need to go, or for how long. All I can promise is that my feelings for you are genuine…that whenever I return it will be as much to see you as anything else."

She didn't move, seemingly memorizing the subtle cues displayed upon my face, perhaps hoping to read in them the message she was after. I bent forward and met her lips. The kiss seemed to break the ice, emboldening me to take her in my arms and follow it up with a more lingering, more passionate kiss. I then broke our embrace and held her at arms length, gazing into her face as intently as she had mine, "How far do you want to go with this, Adriana?" I asked quietly.

She smiled ruefully and touched my cheek with her hand, "I'm a Catholic and this is a Catholic country, William, we're accustomed to painful sacrifices in pursuit of virtue and you've just framed my dilemma perfectly. How far do I want to go? Of course I would wish we could make love this evening…I wish you would simply pick me up and carry me to your room, but it cannot happen. You understand, I hope."

"Of course I understand," I said, drawing her close and kissing her once again.

"Perhaps you should walk me to the taxi stand out front before my determination weakens," said Adriana, playfully.

I nodded then took her arm in mine and headed for the lobby.

With other hotel employees hovering nearby we refrained from displaying any more affection. I slipped the cabbie money for the cab ride and made sure Adriana was comfortably seated. Then, after giving me one final caress she allowed me to stand clear of the vehicle. She waved goodbye as the taxi pulled out. I returned the wave, then once the cab past out of sight I walked back into the hotel and headed for my room.

DAY 4

THE SUN HAD NOT yet cleared the horizon when Boris and I wheeled our bikes out on to the street. The slight chill of early morning still hung in the air. Our luggage was now strapped to the bikes—mine to the two side racks, Boris' to the top rack of his cycle. I gave a sharp kick to the starter pedal and let the bike warm up. Although there was already some light from the gathering rays of the approaching sun we didn't hesitate to turn on our headlights—if for no other reason than to insure other drivers would see us as they barreled sleepily down the highway. I gave Boris the thumbs up, prompting him to move out smartly. He was to take the lead on this leg of our journey.

There wasn't much traffic in town this early in the morning but all the same we took our time navigating the streets. By the time we reached the edge of the capital the sun was well above the horizon. The principal highway at this edge of town was a two-lane affair, with a weed-infested, rubbish-strewn center divider that must originally have been intended for ornamental plants but had long since been neglected.

At first, the road was relatively flat but as we approached the surrounding hills it began to rise, taking us off the plateau and into the rugged landscape of the Salinas Highlands. Despite the early hour the road was thick with local foot traffic—farmers walking to their fields, groups of women heading for the market, their produce or handicrafts bundled neatly and strapped to their backs, and men pushing bicycles loaded with goods too heavy to carry on their backs. We found the motorcycles ideal for navigating the traffic and made better time than if we'd been encumbered by a car or truck.

The pavement came to an end once we turned off the main road that linked the country's principal highland communities and began our descent down the escarpment leading to the deep valleys off to our right. The dirt road was surprisingly well maintained but covered in loosely compacted soil, forcing us to ride side by side to avoid one of us having to eat the other's dust. We motored steadily for about three hours before finally reaching Los Padres—the tiny village on the banks of Monte Rio where Boris planned for us to begin the second leg of today's journey.

There couldn't have been more than two dozen families living in the village given the tiny cluster of homes we passed as we rode in. "Alejandro's house is the one on the right," said Boris, pointing towards a whitewashed concrete structure with a corrugated metal roof. He pulled up in front of it and killed the engine. I followed suit.

"*Alejandro, soy yo, Boris! Salid que Viejo!*" shouted Boris, hoping to rouse somebody inside the house.

"*Bienvenido, amigo. Ha sido un largo tiempo desde que hemos visto!*" said the old man who stepped out of the house in response to Boris's greeting.

The two men hugged each other briefly then Boris stood back and pointed towards me saying, "Alejandro, this is my companion, *Señor* William Church."

"*Con mucho gusto, Señor Church,*" said Alejandro, stepping forward and shaking my hand. "Please come in…you must be tired from your travels."

We followed Alejandro inside where several other persons were gathered. "This is my wife, Dolores, and these are my two sons, Benito and Pedro," he announced for my benefit. "And this is *Señor* Church," he added, pointing to me.

Dolores rushed forward to hug Boris who gave her a big kiss. "How is your wife?" she asked once their embrace was over. "Did she accompany you on this trip?"

"No, *señora*, our visit is very brief; she remains at home—but in excellent health I am glad to report."

"Please come sit," said Alejandro, "and tell us what is new with you and your wife."

Two full-length couches covered in old, cracked leather stood at right angles to one another and formed the anchoring point for a cluster of straight-backed, wooden chairs at the far end of the room. I walked over to the closest chair and sat down, thinking the family members probably preferred the couches. My instincts seemed to be good—the two young men sat down on one of the couches while Alejandro and his wife chose the other. Boris grabbed a chair and placed it directly in front of Alejandro and sat down.

Boris and Alejandro took time to catch up with the news of each other's family and to share favored memories of the year Boris and his wife spent working in the area. But finally Alejandro gently inquired what brought about this visit?

"Alejandro, I'll be honest with you, my companion and I are here to secure a boat large enough to freight the two motorcycles and ourselves upstream on the Monte Rio…as far as the road leading to Los Gatos."

Alejandro didn't say anything at first, just looked at Boris and nodded his head—as if trying to make sense of such a plan. Finally, he spoke up, "Boris, my friend, that would put you across the border. It is doable, of course, but there is much danger in such an undertaking: what if you are caught?"

"We understand the danger and wouldn't contemplate doing it unless the need to enter the country by stealth wasn't absolutely necessary. Will you help us?"

"What did you have in mind, exactly?" asked Alejandro.

"We need a boat that can handle a load of about six hundred *kilos*," I said. "We've brought with us a new outboard motor and fuel tanks so all we need is the craft."

"We'll pretend to be *gringo* fishermen who are unaware of the border—just a couple of guys out for a day's worth of excitement on the river…didn't know we'd gone too far upstream if anybody asks," said Boris.

Alejandro thought for a while, then brought up a difficulty we hadn't thought about, "if you abandon the boat and motor once you've reached the road to Los Gatos the authorities will learn of it and will initiate a search thinking whoever it was who left the boat must have been major drug smugglers; no one else would be so free with something as valuable as a new outboard motor and serviceable craft."

"Perhaps if we conceal it…or sink it?" I said.

"That might work," said Alejandro, "but if you will allow me perhaps I can suggest a somewhat better plan."

"By all means, my friend," said Boris.

"My son, Benito, owns a boat suitable for such an undertaking. Why not let him take you up the river? He knows the currents, the shoals and other hazards, and is less likely to raise suspicion should the authorities catch you on the wrong side of the border."

"But that would put your son in danger," said Boris, "we couldn't have that on our conscience."

"Not really," replied Alejandro, "you see, Benito could argue he's simply engaged in a fishing charter…one where the two crazy Americans who engaged his services insisted on trying their luck further upstream. Yes, he would confess to the authorities, he knew he'd passed the frontier but didn't know how to refuse his clients' wishes."

"But what about on the return leg of the journey…after we've left the craft and he's returning—still on the wrong side of the border?" I asked.

"You are right, that would pose a more serious difficulty," said Alejandro, "but it's not as if locals haven't always treated the frontier somewhat more casually than the authorities on both sides would like. Benito could say he was just taking his new outboard motor for a trial run and got a little carried away. They might exact a modest fine but nothing more."

"That's a point I'd like to make," I interjected, "if we agree to this plan of yours then Benito must accept the motor, fuel tanks and fishing kits as compensation for the risks he's prepared to take and for the service he'd be performing."

"You hear that, Benito?" said his father, "you ready to assist these men in exchange for a new outboard motor?"

Benito stood and walked over to Boris. He looked to be in his early twenties—short but stocky and well muscled. He extended his hand, "*Señor* Boris, it would be an honor for me to take you and your friend up the Monte Rio on my boat," he said in Spanish.

Boris rose from his chair and took the man's hand in his, "Benito, you do us a great service. I join my friend in insisting you place our new outboard on your boat and accept all the equipment…as a gift if you like."

"And keep in mind, Benito," I added, "if we were to do it the way we originally planned we would have to purchase a boat with the prospect of abandoning both it and the motor upon reaching our destination. Surely, you can see the merit of allowing your family to benefit rather than some stranger who happened upon the craft after we'd gone."

"I accept your generosity," said Benito soberly, but please understand my brother and I would offer our assistance even without such compensation…out of respect for our father's wishes."

"We understand, Benito," said Boris, pulling him nearer and giving him a big hug.

"When did you wish to leave?" asked the father.

"Unfortunately, there's some urgency involved," I said, "if it's at all possible we would like to be under way within the hour."

"I can manage that," said Benito, "come Pedro, let's get the boat ready."

Pedro appeared to be the younger of the two and responded quickly to Benito's urging. The two young men excused themselves and went outside.

"Please rest yourselves," said *Señora* Dolores, "I'll prepare some food for the three of you to take along. Goodness knows when you'll have a chance to secure a properly cooked meal."

* * *

It was a little after ten o'clock in the morning before we managed to free the lines and let the boat slip out into the current of the river. Benito and Pedro had successfully lashed the two motorcycles securely in the bow of the seventeen-foot-long fiberglass launch. They had replaced Benito's older outboard with the new one we'd brought with us.

"What about fuel?" I asked as Benito continued to play with the throttle, trying to get a feel for how the motor would perform.

"There's plenty," he shouted, "I filled both auxiliary tanks… and also the tanks on your bikes."

"From where? I didn't see any fueling docks or gas station while driving through."

"No," he laughed, "we don't have such things, I keep a fifty-gallon drum of fuel in the shed—with a pump. A tanker truck comes by every few weeks to replenish it."

Boris smiled to himself, amused by my apparent sense of surprise over the refueling. "These are very resourceful people, my friend," he said.

Satisfied with the throttle action of the new outboard Benito gave it full power and turned the boat directly into the current. I estimated the current to be around one knot, making our headway to be about four knots—at least on this section of the river. Alejandro and his wife, together with his son, Pedro, stood on the riverbank and waved; Boris and I waved back.

Dense, tropical vegetation lined the edges of the river, concealing us to a large extent from casual onlookers but unfortunately not from those locals who use it for bathing, fishing, as a source of drinking water or as an artery of transportation. Still, having Benito at the helm would allay most people's curiosity, or at least reassure them a full account of his actions and our presence could be secured by simply visiting Alejandro's family next time they were in Los Padres.

The sun had not yet reached a height that would allow the full effect of its rays to beat down on the river, nestled as it was in the bottom of the deep valley, but despite the shade I could feel my shirt getting soaked as the air—heavily laden with moisture—clung to my skin.

"I can see why you don't wear a shirt," I said to Benito whose sun-darkened skin seemed unaffected by the humidity. He just smiled and kept scanning the current in front of us, looking for submerged boulders that would need to be avoided.

"What's the depth here?" I asked him.

"A little over a meter," he replied, "but as we go further upstream the river will widen somewhat, causing shallows to appear."

"Can the boat handle it?"

"Oh yes, providing we don't get hung up on the rocks—at some places only narrow channels carry sufficient water for boat passage."

"Do we have to portage around any rapids?"

"No, the river rises gently, no rapids…at least not between here and our destination," said Benito.

I already knew that, having studied *topo* maps of the river before leaving San Francisco but it was reassuring having Benito confirm it. I sat back and focused my attention on the passing countryside, trying to gauge the likelihood we'd be challenged by a passing military patrol—either here or on the other side of the border.

* * *

Around half past noon, Benito suggested we eat something. We'd been on the river for about two and a half hours and the border between the two countries was less than a kilometer ahead—not visible from where we were, owing to the circuitous path the river was taking, but close enough to warrant caution. "Let's drop anchor and get lunch over with before pushing on ahead," I said.

Benito nodded, then steered the boat towards the left bank of the river where a quiet eddy in the current seemed deep enough to handle our draft. Boris hoisted the anchor—a gallon-sized cement-filled metal container attached to what looked like a thirty-foot section of stout rope. With a signal from Benito, Boris dropped the anchor overboard and secured the end of the anchor line to a cleat near where he was sitting. The boat drifted lazily away from the anchoring point, pulled by the nearby current, but once the anchor line grew taught the craft became stationary. Benito shut off the motor.

Boris took on the chore of serving the food Benito's mother had prepared. He removed the lid on a large, shallow metal pan filled with a mix of cooked rice, beans and chicken, placing it carefully on top of a wooden box Benito kept on board to store equipment in. Next, he unwrapped a tall stack of soft tortillas. I hungrily grabbed one and used it to scoop up some of the mix while Benito handed around bottles of beer—kept cold as we traveled by being submerged in the river in a net bag.

"Haven't seen many people so far," observed Boris between bites, "that going to continue you think?" he asked Benito.

"Mornings are mostly for farming and household chores," he replied, "people generally come down to the river towards the end of the day...when the fish are biting and when there's dirt to be washed off."

"And the border patrols?" I asked.

"If we're lucky we won't see any while we're on the river... they're mostly assigned to watch the roads," he replied.

We ate in silence after that, quietly reflecting on the uncertainties surrounding the impending border crossing. As the minutes passed, the cacophony of sounds emanating from the nearby forest became ever louder: bird calls, monkey screeches, and the droning repetition of insects seeking to attract others of their kind for mating. It seemed a bit too unsettling for Boris who after about a quarter of an hour impatiently wrapped up the uneaten tortillas and replaced the lid on the shallow pan then placed both items back in the basket in which they had come. "Need to leave something for Benito for the trip home," he explained, "and we might as well get this crossing over with," he added, motioning to Benito to start the motor and for me to pull up the anchor.

We approached the border region as unobtrusively as possible—hugging the river bank whenever possible, avoiding all loud conversation and instructing Benito to throttle back a bit so as to reduce engine noise. All three of us kept a keen eye out for any signs of government surveillance: Benito looking ahead, Boris to the left and myself to the right. Finally, Benito waved his outstretched hands up and down, silently signaling the fact we were at that moment crossing the frontier. There was no visible marker I could see: no sign, no barrier, no border post—and most importantly no military patrol.

Once past the frontier, however, we began to see more activity along the riverbank—clusters of women doing wash or bathing, children splashing, and the occasional man off by himself, smoking a cigarette and monitoring one or more fishing lines. They ignored us, at least in the sense of not waving or shouting a greeting, and we pretended to a comparable disinterest in their presence. But just to make sure we wouldn't unnecessarily arouse their curiosity Boris covered the motorcycles with a tarp he found stowed away in the equipment bin, and both of us broke out our fishing gear and pretended to be ardently engaged in fishing.

Two hours later, Benito turned the boat towards shore. "We're here," he said quietly as he suddenly increased power, the added surge intensifying the impact as the bow of the boat made contact with the riverbank, enabling it to ride up onto a low section covered with muddy grass.

"Christ! Give us some notice in the future!" muttered Boris as he picked himself up from where he'd fallen.

"This is where many boats put in," said Benito, "you can tell by the way the riverbank is worn down and the surrounding grass all muddy. I think we must be very close to the road you wish to take."

"Thanks, Benito," I said, stepping off the boat onto land. "Here, Boris, give me a hand, we need to beach the boat a little more securely. Grumbling, Boris climbed out and took a position one side of the bow while I gripped the opposite side. Together we dragged the boat further onto the shore—to a point where it couldn't slip back in even after its load had been considerably lightened. Benito was already busy untying the restraining ropes holding down the motorcycles. With Benito holding the bike upright Boris and I lifted the front end over the edge of the boat, allowing it to gently rest there, then while I kept the front end stable Boris and Benito lifted the rear end of the bike up and over the side of the boat.

After both bikes were once again on land, with our luggage still securely tied to the rear wheel storage racks, we shook hands with Benito and helped him shove the boat back into the water.

"*Buen viaje de vuelta,*" shouted Boris as Benito started up the outboard motor and slowly backed away from the shore.

"*Muchas gracias, señor…y cuidar!*" he shouted back.

We watched as Benito turned into the prevailing current and picked up speed.

"Without us on board and with no unusual cargo his boat should arose no suspicion," said Boris thoughtfully before turning to where his bike stood. "So my friend, lead the way."

"There's what appears to be a path from the landing area into the woods," I said, pointing to a spot where the undergrowth had been beaten down.

"Well, let's see where it leads," said Boris.

"Not so fast, old friend, first we need to cover the license plate and a good bit of the frame in mud so as to avoid anyone noticing we're riding bikes registered in another country."

"You're right…let's do it," said Boris who began wheeling his bike closer to the riverbank where a plentiful supply of viscous mud was to be had. I followed suit and before long both of us, as well as the motorcycles, were liberally spattered with mud. We stood back to admire our handiwork then removed our soiled clothing and without much hesitation jumped into the river—a bar of soap in hand—and began washing ourselves.

While we sat back on a dry patch of grass, waiting for the mud to dry on the motorcycles and for our bodies to dry after our brief dip in the river, we studied the maps we'd brought along—trying to get a clearer picture of where we were relative to the road that would take us to the town of Los Gatos.

"I make it to be no more than a half of a kilometer," said Boris.

"If the road's that close chances are that path I spotted probably leads directly to it," I said.

"Only one way to find out," laughed Boris as he stood up and stretched, "let's get dressed and head in that direction."

We put on fresh clothing, stowing the soiled garments in plastic bags that could be stuffed safely in our luggage then climbed onto our bikes, brought the engines to life and motored towards the path—with me riding point.

"Hold up for a second," I said as we entered the narrow trail, "I need to get rid of the rancher's hunting rifle."

"Christ, I forgot all about it!" said Boris.

I climbed off the bike, pulled the rifle out from under my large bag where it had been concealed, ejected the remaining ammo and disassembled the firing mechanism—tossing the parts deep into the surrounding woods.

"Okay, let's go," I said as I climbed back on the bike and throttled up.

* * *

"It's almost four o'clock," said Boris once we'd reached the unpaved road, "when do you figure we'll hit Los Gatos?"

"I'd estimate at least another hour given the road's poor condition," I replied. "Christ, it looks like it hasn't been newly graded in years!"

"Suggests nobody important ever uses this road," commented Boris, "might work to our advantage…no reason for patrols to be in the vicinity."

"Let's hope you're right," I said, releasing the brake and letting the bike pick up speed.

Boris followed suit and before long we were cruising in the proper direction at about forty kilometers per hour, dodging deep ruts and other impediments as we went. There'd been a lot of logging in these parts, at least that's what it looked like—not only the condition of the road but also the ragged strips of cleared timber that could be glimpsed every few hundred meters. Some of the clearings held cultivated fields but others were probably no more than grazing areas for livestock. We could see isolated farmsteads at the fringe of such clearings, probably squatters capitalizing on the bonanza of freshly timbered land to set themselves up with the means to scratch out a living. I kept watching all this, at least whenever my attention could stray away from the condition of the dirt track immediately in front of my bike, and failed to notice the military-styled vehicles parked alongside the road about five hundred meters straight ahead. Boris, who was a little ways behind me, pulled up alongside and shouted, "We've got trouble I think."

I snapped out of my reverie and concentrated on the two vehicles parked up ahead. Several uniformed men were climbing out of the jeep-styled vehicle on the right as we rode closer. "I think they intend to stop us," shouted Boris.

When we were perhaps a hundred meters out one of the men stepped out into the center of the road and raised his hand, signaling for us to halt. We did as instructed, bringing our bikes to idle and rolling quietly to a stop right in front of the man.

"*Sus papeies por favor!*" ordered the man. Meanwhile, several of his associates stood next to the two vehicles, guns carelessly held in their hands. Their uniforms were those of the national police but the unit must be on special assignment, I thought, given the remoteness of the region and the military nature of their assault weapons. I climbed off my bike and looked at him speculatively.

"You don't want to know who we are," I said softly in Spanish, "you don't want to even report having seen us on this road— you understand, *jefe?*"

"*Documentos, ahora!*" he shouted, putting his hand on the butt end of his sidearm.

I shook my head wearily then looked up at him and shouted, "You fool, you interfere with our mission and you're liable to be shot...you understand, shot!"

He stepped back involuntarily at the force of my indignation and his comrades quickly became alert, though not entirely clear on what was happening. But he quickly regained his composure and smiled mirthlessly, "So you wish to play games do you? Detain these two!" he shouted to his men.

"Halt!" I ordered while quickly grabbing the man by his jacket and pulling him close. "Any of you make one foolish move and your leader dies!" I added as I placed the muzzle of my gun against the side of his head. The men froze but kept their guns pointed at Boris and myself.

"Now listen and listen carefully you pompous son of a bitch, my companion and I are under the direct command of Colonel

119

Felipe Cruz of the army's counterintelligence unit. We're on a covert mission—a mission you don't want to interfere with if you value your rank, your pension…maybe even your life…you understand?"

He nodded and signaled his men to stand down. "Now I can tell you're somewhat puzzled," I continued softly, "but I've orders not to divulge our identity or the nature of our operation to anyone, including the police, so it'd be best for all concerned if you allowed us to pass through and forgot you ever saw us…you think you can do that?"

"But you are *gringos* are you not?" he asked. "How is it you are working for the army?"

"You are correct, *jefe,* my companion and I are Americans… been tasked to Colonel Cruz by order of the commanding general of the United States Army. Colonel Cruz seems to think he can make use of our special training…you want to argue with him?"

"No…not at all…come, men, we shall continue our patrol!" And with that he walked over to the lead vehicle and climbed in next to his driver. His other men returned to their seats and the two jeeps roared off.

"Boris just shook his head and smiled. "Who the hell is Colonel Cruz…did you make him up?"

"Nope, he's the real deal," I said as I holstered the semiautomatic and walked back to my motorcycle, "had a run in with him a couple of years ago…a mean-spirited bastard who scares the hell out of anyone who comes in contact with him. Seems our friend, the *jefe,* was familiar with his reputation and didn't want to press his luck challenging my story."

We restarted our motors and sped off, hoping to make it to Los Gatos before dinnertime.

* * *

Los Gatos was a typical small town in the middle of nowhere—a pretentiously elaborate cathedral-styled church at its center, yellowing plaster-covered single story buildings lining the main streets and rickety clapboard houses with *lamina* roofs scattered haphazardly around the town's perimeter. We rolled in just after five o'clock covered in dust and mud and hungry as all get out. Boris pointed at a *cantina* sign on one of the buildings on our right as we slowly made our way towards the center of town. I nodded and followed him over to the curb where we cut our engines and parked.

"No funny business this time, old friend," I said, slapping him on the back, "we need to keep a low profile from now on."

"Hey! I can't help it if there's a few gringo-baiting locals anxious to amuse themselves at my expense."

"No, but let's try not to give them any pretext."

We were in luck. It was too early in the evening for any serious drinking and the place was virtually empty. Boris and I took a table next to the front window where we could keep an eye on the bikes and waited for the barmaid to come around to take our order.

"*Bienvenido, señores. Qué puedo hacer por usted—un poco de comida, un poco de cerveza?*"

We ordered cold beers, grilled steak and the usual side dishes of rice, beans and a stack of tortillas.

121

"Is there a place where we can wash up?" I asked just as she was about to head for the kitchen to place our order.

"*Si, señor*, there's a washroom you can use through that door," she said, pointing to a doorway to the left of the bar."

I thanked her and got up from my chair and headed towards it.

"I'll wait until you get back," said Boris.

I nodded then pushed the door open and walked through.

It felt good to rinse the road dust off my face. As I stood there looking into the mirror I could see streaks of windburn were already showing up on my forehead and cheeks from hours of cycling without a helmet. It would get worse before this trip is over, I thought to myself. Then after pulling a comb through my hair I gave my reflection one last glance before stepping back into the room where Boris was waiting.

* * *

"So what do we have to look forward to on the final leg of today's journey?" asked Boris as he spread salt on a tortilla.

"Well, San Rafael's a good two hundred and fifty kilometers from Los Gatos so it's pretty certain we'll arrive well after dark," I said between bites of my steak.

"That's going to be one hell of a ride if the road looks anything like the one we've just come off," countered Boris.

"It won't," I replied, "the highway's paved and reported to be in good condition. Chances are we'll make good time...maybe even get up to a cruising speed that'll make us sorry we didn't think to bring helmets."

"Ah hell, Church, half the fun of riding these bikes is to feel the wind in your face."

"Yeah, but we're going to look like we've just slogged through a Saharan sandstorm by the time we get back to the states."

"Just think of it as part of our disguise," said Boris, stabbing the last piece of his steak with his fork.

"You keep that in mind, old friend, when Gloria gives you hell for acting like a dumb teenager."

Boris just shrugged and concentrated on his rice and beans.

Two beers and a solid meal under our belts, we paid our *cantina* bill and stepped outside. It was getting to be dusk and the streets were becoming livelier, with men heading into town now the workday was over and women hurrying between *bodegas* to secure food for the evening's meal. A police cruiser made its way slowly down the street but didn't seem to pay us much attention. But we took it as an omen and hurriedly started up our engines and made for the edge of town where the highway to the capital was to be found.

* * *

I knew San Rafael to be a more imposing city than Santa Lucia—not surprising given how highly regarded was its urban architecture but it was hard to appreciate since all we could see as we approached the outskirts were faint outlines of buildings and a random scatter of lights given the lateness of the hour.

Boris pulled up alongside me, "Where we headed?" he shouted over the rumble of the engines as we sped towards the capital.

"Western outskirts…I'm thinking we can put up at Dora's," I shouted back.

He nodded then dropped back behind me once again.

It took us another half hour before we reached the quiet residential neighborhood of Las Mesa with its modest—but gated—single story contemporary homes. We motored slowly, hoping to avoid any excessive noise that would bring attention to ourselves. It was now well after nine o'clock at night and although most homes still had their lights on there wasn't much traffic in the neighborhood. A few dogs barked as we passed and I could see the faint lights of patrolling night watchmen making their rounds behind the steep cinder block walls of some of the larger homes but generally we seemed to pass through the neighborhood without attracting much notice. I pointed to a gated driveway off to our right as we motored down her street and signaled for him to slow down even more. We came to a stop in front of the gates and shut off our engines.

"You think she's got a watchman?" whispered Boris.

"Probably…she's a woman living alone…can't blame her if she does," I replied as I walked over to the small metal intercom imbedded in the brick gatepost on the left. I pushed the button.

"*Hola, quién está allí?*" the voice of a woman called out from the intercom.

"It's William Church, Dora, may we come in?"

"William! You are here! *Bienvenido!*"

A metallic click sounded indicating the gates had been unlocked. I pushed them open and Boris and I walked our bikes into the tiny courtyard in front of the house. I noticed Dora's small European sedan was parked a little ways up the drive and motioned to Boris to follow my lead in parking the bikes just in front of it so they couldn't be easily seen from the street. I went on ahead where I could see Dora waiting expectantly at the front door, meanwhile Boris walked back to secure the gates.

"William, look at you!" she said, throwing her arms around me and kissing me on the cheek.

"Hi Dora…it's good to see you."

"Come in…come in; you must be exhausted."

"I expect we are…listen, that gentleman walking towards us is Boris—a good friend from San Francisco."

"Hello, Boris," said Dora, extending her hand for him to shake.

"*Es un gran placer conocerte, senorita.*"

"My, you speak Spanish very fluently, sir."

"Hardly, my dear woman, but I suppose the little skill I do possess comes from spending a year in the farming villages just beyond the Salinas Highlands."

"Well it's a pleasure to meet you," she added as she ushered us inside.

"Where will you be staying?" she asked as she settled them around the kitchen table and searched for a bottle of wine.

"We've no plans," I said. "Most likely we'll be off first thing in the morning…thought perhaps you wouldn't mind if we caught a little shut-eye here."

"Of course…you're welcome to stay as long as you wish, William."

125

"But won't your neighbors become suspicious…after all, you are a single woman; having two men overnight in your home would perhaps provoke a scandal," said Boris.

Dora laughed, "I'm an archaeologist, Boris, one who often needs to put up visiting foreign scholars—most of whom are graduate students without much money. My neighbors are accustomed to it…and the fact you both ride those ridiculous motorcycles further strengthens the case."

"I stand corrected, madam," said Boris.

"Enough talk, let me pour you some wine and we'll drink to the success of your mission," said Dora as she handed each of us a wine glass.

After a short while she showed us the guest room with its two single beds and urged us to retrieve our packs and settle in for the night. "The bathroom you'll be using is just down the hall," she said before heading to the kitchen.

"I think we'll have to dump the motorcycles, Boris," I said once we were alone, "I don't want Dora to be connected to what we're about."

"Yes, I was thinking the same thing," said Boris. "The question is should we get rid of the bikes tonight—before they're linked to Dora's residence—or tomorrow morning?"

"Let me ask Dora what she thinks." I went back to the kitchen where I found her washing out the wine glasses.

After I explained the reasons for our concern she shook her head, "William, there's no reason to abandon the motorcycles, just store them somewhere away from my home and let me chauffeur you and Boris back and forth."

126

"That'd solve the problem of the motorcycles, Dora, but it would just add a new problem—the fact somebody might recall having seen us in your company and connect it to whatever stories or bulletins might be distributed regarding our other business."

"I see your point, William, perhaps it would be best if you and your friend did leave before dawn tomorrow."

"That's what we'll do then," I said, giving her a hug. "I'll try to get back to see you at least once more before we leave the country but I can't promise."

"I understand," she said with a smile, "now go get some sleep."

"One last question, Dora, don't you have a night watchman?"

"No, William, I don't. Perhaps I should but I've always felt secure in this neighborhood…anyway my neighbors are quite protective of their 'little *senorita*, the professor'."

I went out to where the motorcycles were parked and retrieved our luggage. By the time I returned to the room Boris was fast asleep on one of the beds. I quietly took my small bag and returned to the kitchen. Dora had retired to her bedroom so I had the place to myself. I took the satellite phone from the bag and put a call through to Henry Kingstone.

"Mr. Kingstone, it's Church," I said once Jackson had given over the phone.

"Yes, thank you for calling…where are you?"

"I'm in San Rafael…have you heard from the kidnappers?"

"No, the forty-eight hour deadline won't be up until tomorrow morning but I have the ransom payment…what do you want me to do with it?"

"Give it to Jack Barker, the FBI agent I introduced you to. He should be leaving on a flight to San Rafael sometime tomorrow. I'll get hold of him and let him know."

"But what if they want me to hand over the ransom here…in the States?"

"They won't…the important thing is to convince them the money is on its way to San Rafael and will be in the possession of your agent—but don't give them my name."

"What should I tell them if they want to know how to get in touch with you?"

"Tell them I'll get in touch with them…have them give you a telephone number where they can be reached."

"All right…I'll do that…and you'll have Mr. Barker come by to pick up the ransom? Tell him it's in two five-inch deep aluminum attaché cases—a million in each?"

"Yes…and don't worry, Mr. Kingstone, Barker won't have any trouble bringing in the money…he'll be identified as a diplomatic courier and will be met at the airport by one of the embassy officials."

"Very well…goodbye then," he said softly just before disconnecting.

I immediately punched in Jack's number. There was a short delay then Jack picked up, "Barker here, who is this?"

"Your old sailing buddy, Church…what's your ETA for San Rafael?"

"Church, God Damn! How the hell are you …and where are you?"

"I'm in San Rafael…just arrived…along with Boris. Listen, I've got an assignment for you."

"What's that?"

"I need you to drop by the Kingstone residence and pick up the ransom money before you leave town."

"How the hell am I supposed to get it through customs?"

"Get the Department of State to make you an embassy courier…for this trip only. Shouldn't be a problem…only you'll have to get the boys back in Washington to move on it right away if you're going to make your flight…by the way when are you scheduled to leave?"

"Tomorrow morning…Jesus, Church, you're cutting this thing pretty fine."

"Can't be helped, Jack, I need that money down here ASAP and you're the guy in the right place at the right time…and listen, let Elena Bolinas know, she might be able to expedite the thing."

"Will do…Kingstone know I'm coming?"

"Yeah, he knows…just got off the phone with him."

"All right, I'll see you down there some time tomorrow I expect…you going to contact Elena?"

"Not until tomorrow…you might want to let her know to expect my call."

"Can do…and I'll warn her you start the day early…that maybe you'll wake her up well before she's ready to be woken."

"Go to hell!" I said then cut the line.

But Jack was right, I did plan to call Elena just as soon as Boris and I left Dora's place early next morning.

As I was repacking the satphone in my soft leather bag Dora returned to the kitchen. She had on a lightweight cotton nightgown beneath a terry cloth robe, and her long dark hair had a brushed-out look. She was a slender woman of average height who looked rather frail in her present getup—without the cosmetics and stylish clothes she'd customarily be seen in.

"I thought you'd be in bed by now," she said.

"Had to make a couple of phone calls...did I wake you?"

"No, William, I hadn't climbed into bed yet...everything all right?"

"Everything's okay," I replied as I gently took her in my arms and gave her a hug.

"You sure you don't mind leaving in the morning?" she asked as she rested her head on my shoulder.

"Not at all, Dora," I whispered as I continued to hold her.

She remained in my embrace for a few moments more then stepped back and smiled, "So off to bed with you my handsome young man and let me get some sleep."

"Yes ma'am," I said, feigning a military-style salute before picking up my bag and heading towards the guest room.

DAY 5

DORA MANNED THE GATE as Boris and I walked our bikes down the driveway and into the street. It was just before dawn and the neighborhood was still clothed in darkness.

"Take care of yourselves," she said as she swung the gates shut, "and William, give me a call once this whole thing is over and you're safely back in the States...okay?"

"Will do...and thanks for everything," I said as I started the engine and gingerly advanced the throttle, not wanting to make too much noise. Boris followed suit and we slowly moved out— giving her a final wave just before being enveloped in the early morning darkness.

"Where to?" asked Boris once we were some blocks from Dora's place.

"We need to make contact with Jack's counterpart in the embassy...a woman named Elena Bolinas. Let's pull into the first place that's open and serves coffee...I'll call her on the satphone."

"She going to be up and about this time of the morning?" asked Boris skeptically.

"She'll answer but I can't promise she'll be real happy about it."

We had to go another half-dozen blocks before locating a place where we could grab some coffee and something to eat. It was an oversized kiosk set in the middle of a large concrete parking area. A couple of trucks—their engines idling—were parked off to one side. Several men who I took to be the drivers and one assistant were walking towards the trucks carrying cups of coffee. Boris and I pulled right up to the kiosk and shut off the engines.

"Order me a coffee and something off the menu," I said to Boris, "I'll try my luck raising Agent Bolinas.

He nodded and approached the counter while I stepped some distance away where I could carry on a conversation without being overheard.

"Bolinas here," came the crisp greeting once the satphone was answered.

"It's William Church, Agent Bolinas, hope Jack gave you a head's up about my call."

"That he did...where are you?"

"At the corner of *Avenida* La Honda and *Boulevard* San Gregorio."

"That's about three kilometers from my apartment...wait there for me. I should make it in about ten minutes."

"Will do...see you then."

I broke the connection and headed for the cluster of tiny metal tables and chairs next to the kiosk where Boris had parked himself.

"You get through to her?" he asked as I settled into one of the chairs across from him.

"Yeah, she's on her way…so what did you find to eat?"

"Got us some coffee and ordered two plates of *huevos rancheros*… thought we'd need something more substantial than a stack of *tortillas* or a couple of fried plantains."

I nodded then picked up my coffee cup and took a drink.

"So what's our plan once she gets here?" asked Boris, putting down his coffee cup.

"Can't be sure until she fills us in on her plans…Jack mentioned she'd worked out a way to act as the go-between."

"Go-between…between you and who else?"

"Jack, of course. He'll be showing up later today…carrying the ransom money I might add."

Just then a teenage girl came out of the kiosk carrying two plates. We interrupted our conversation and watched as she put the plates down in front of us, then savored the aroma of the freshly prepared dish of refried beans spread thickly on *tortillas* and topped with two fried eggs and a generous amount of chopped ham and cheese. She smiled at our evident appreciation of the wonders such a tiny kitchen could produce then quickly returned to the kiosk.

* * *

We had just finished the *huevos rancheros* when a tan four-wheel-drive SUV turned into the parking area and sped over to where we were sitting. It came to an abrupt stop and out jumped a woman I'd guess was in her early thirties dressed in tailored blue jeans, a pair of black leather flats, a white T-shirt and a black cotton blazer. Her dark brown hair was worn long and pulled back into a ponytail. She hesitated for a moment then walked directly over to the table.

"Which of you is Church?" she asked.

"I am," I said, getting up and extending my hand, "and you must be Agent Bolinas."

"Please call me Elena," she said, shaking my hand. "I expect we'll be in one another's company a fair amount in the coming days and formal titles will just get in the way."

"How do you mean?" I asked.

"I'm to be your driver on this little adventure…it'll give me an up close vantage point on what transpires—letting me know in real time if and when to call in the troops."

"By troops I take it you mean Jack?"

"Yes."

"What do you propose we do with the motorcycles?" said Boris as he got up from the table and extended his hand. "I'm Boris, by the way."

"Hi Boris," she said as she shook his hand, "Jack says many complimentary things about you, though I had expected someone a little younger."

"Appearances, as I'm sure you're aware, can be deceiving," said Boris.

"And such deception can be capitalized upon I imagine you'd wish to add," said Elena with a smile.

"Yes, take you for instance, an attractive young woman fashionably dressed…who would expect a Special Agent for the FBI to be lurking behind such an innocent guise," said Boris with a grin.

"Well now that we're all properly introduced why don't you flesh out your plan so that Boris and I can weigh in with some of the operational practicalities," I said as I sat back down and picked up my coffee cup.

"Hey, no need to be patronizing, Church, there is no plan… just consider me another sidekick…like Boris or Jack…someone to back you up when things get a little frantic."

"I thought the FBI wanted to retain a healthy measure of deniability in this matter…you're active involvement would seem to contradict that. So what gives?"

"I'm ostensibly the legal attaché at the embassy. My involvement is to insure that once the boy is turned over by the kidnappers he's under proper embassy supervision and his repatriation back to his family in the States is handled expeditiously."

"And what about Jack?" I asked.

"Jack is here to deliver the ransom to you and to serve as escort for the boy as he flies back to the States."

"Okay, I can see how your cover stories keep you from being officially connected to the real action but if you're coming along with us you might witness events you'd have difficulty explaining."

"Let me worry about that, Church. Now, why don't you fill me in on what you're planning," said Elena as she pulled out a chair and sat down across from me.

The young girl from the kiosk came over to our table with a cup and a pot of fresh coffee. Elena thanked her in fluent Spanish for bringing the cup and instructed her to refresh the gentlemen's cups as well.

"Our first order of business, as Boris mentioned, is to decide what to do with the bikes," I said once the girl had returned to the kiosk.

"I take it you used them to travel from the frontier to the capital," said Elena, "so whoever is found riding on them might be connected to possible rumors about persons entering the country illegally."

"Actually, the only rumors we can expect are about two U.S. Military operatives over here on a secret assignment for Colonel Felipe Cruz of this country's army counterintelligence unit," I said, taking a sip of coffee.

"How the hell could that be?" she asked.

"It's how Church talked our way out of a hassle with a police check point on the road to Los Gatos," said Boris.

"That would mean there won't be any special police or military interest in you," said Elena, "the colonel is not someone the authorities would wish to antagonize."

"So you know about him too?" commented Boris.

"Yes, I've had some dealings with him…hard to avoid when your government insists on intelligence sharing."

"This might work to our advantage," I said, "any disruptive action we might engage in would be blamed on the colonel."

"And thereby deflect any suspicion by the kidnappers our actions are connected to an attempt to get at them," added Boris.

"I take it, then, you're going to continue using the motorcycles," said Elena.

"At least some of the time, surely," I said, "especially when the FBI needs to have convincing deniability regarding involvement."

"I see your point," said Elena, "but keep in mind I'll be close by whether you like it or not."

"Wouldn't have it any other way," I replied with a smile.

"Well, now that we've got that all cleared up what are we going to do about a place to operate out of…seeing that we've decided it's too risky for Dora Perez should we stay at her home?" asked Boris.

"Any suggestions?" I asked Elena.

"We've got a safe house at the edge of town that I can put at your disposal. It's got a six-foot perimeter wall and an enclosed garage…should make it possible to conceal the motorcycles when not in use, and to come and go without creating too much attention," said Elena.

"Sounds perfect," I said, "why don't we head over there right now, get set up then map out our first operation."

"Follow me," said Elena, getting up and walking over to her SUV.

Boris left some money on the table for the girl and the two of us got up and went over to our bikes.

* * *

The safe house was of cinderblock construction as was the surrounding wall. It looked more like a jail than a family residence—something of an indictment against the type of residents the neighborhood attracted. But it was well cared for and comfortably furnished. There were three bedrooms, a well-stocked kitchen, a common room with a large seating area, a bathroom and a serviceable dining area.

"Each of you can have your own bedroom, the third will be for Jack once he arrives," said Elena as we carried our luggage into the house.

"When will he be arriving?" I asked.

"I'm to meet him at the airport at five o'clock this evening," she said, "everything's been arranged, he'll have no trouble getting the money past customs."

"Listen, while the two of you begin working out the details of the rest of the day's schedule I'll roll the bikes into the garage and have a look around the neighborhood," said Boris as he came out of the bedroom where he'd stowed his bags.

"Sounds good," I said as I sank into one of the comfortable armchairs and motioned for Elena to join me.

"So where will you begin your search?" she asked once she managed to get seated on the couch, her feet carelessly perched on the coffee table.

"I thought we'd try and get a line on Fernando the guide… maybe hit the hotel where he hooked up with the Richmond family…talk to the staff."

"How do you want to travel?"

"We'll let you drive us…no sense linking the bikes to enquiries that might tie us to the kidnapping investigation."

"And after you've found him what then?"

"Well, we'll have a conversation…see how it goes."

"That's a little vague, Church."

"Thing is, Elena, we're improvising. I'm thinking either the guide or the police commander, or both, are connected to the kidnapping—so we'll have to lean on them a little and see what we can learn."

"I've no objection…just wanted you to be clear on what we might be getting into."

"How long have you been down here?" I asked, trying to change the subject.

"I'm on a three-year rotation…this is my last year."

"Like it?"

"It's okay…best part is not having any boss breathing down my neck. I report to a guy whose desk is at FBI headquarters in Washington."

"I can relate to that…it's one of the reasons I left the agency—too much bureaucratic oversight."

"Yes, Jack mentioned you'd spent some time there…the art theft unit I believe?"

"That's right, enjoyed working with Interpol and the art theft teams scattered around the country but the prospect of a career involving Bureau politics didn't entice me."

"So you've moved on…into freelance work of pretty much the same sort?"

"I guess you could say that, but being my own boss makes all the difference."

She nodded thoughtfully—almost as if she was evaluating the choice I'd made.

"Where do you think the Agency will send you next?" I asked.

"Probably another foreign assignment…at least that's what I'll put in for. If I'm lucky it'll be an embassy in Europe but with my fluency in Spanish it might just be another Latin American posting."

"You're not pushing for a *Special Agent in Charge* assignment?"

"That would probably require an in-country posting…worse, it would push me into management and away from the day to day action…so, no, it's not something I'm aiming for."

I laughed, "Sounds like you've got the same kind of itch I've got…a hankering for independence as well as lots of action."

"Could be, Church, but I like the legal trimmings a hell of a lot more than you seem to."

"You mean you don't want to have to worry whether what you do conforms with the law."

"Yes, that's right…from what I've heard you, on the other hand, don't seem to give that issue much thought."

"Perhaps, but as Boris has been known to say: appearances can be deceiving. I'll let you come to your own conclusion about that once you've had a chance to be in on the action."

"Speaking of that, isn't it time we head for the hotel?" asked Elena.

"Soon as Boris returns," I replied, "in the meantime why don't you share with me a little personal data…like whether you're married…have kids…that sort of thing."

"Why do you want to know…out of idle curiosity, or do you think it'll have some bearing on the operation?"

"Let's just say I've a healthy appetite for knowledge…especially when it involves someone with whom I'll be working."

"Hmm, so it would seem…well, to begin with, I'm not married…never have been, and no, I don't have any kids. Joined the FBI right after law school…been with the Bureau for six years now."

"Where'd you grow up?"

"Miami…my parents settled there after smuggling themselves out of Cuba. And, yes, I do have siblings—three of them, but I'm the only one who's chosen government work."

"They a little put off by your choice of career?"

"My brother is…he's had a run-in or two with local law enforcement down in Little Havana and doesn't have a high opinion of cops—federal included."

Just then, Boris returned. He dropped into one of the armchairs and gave us an inquiring look, "You kids playing nice?"

"Just shooting the bull," I said, "so, what'd you find out about the neighborhood?"

"Got the feeling it used to be a whole lot rougher than it is now…probably around the time this house was built. From what I could see it's full of young families—you know, the kind that have kids far too young to be gang-bangers or graffiti artists."

"Makes sense," said Elena, "the neighborhood probably got so run-down it lost real estate value, making it attractive for young families coming into the city from the surrounding countryside."

"How's that going to affect our stay?" I asked.

"Means the kids will be off the streets most of the time and parents will have their hands full making a living or caring for the children," said Elena. "That should minimize casual scrutiny of your comings and goings."

"So where we off to?" asked Boris.

"Elena, here, is going to drive us to the hotel where the Richmond family was approached by that tourist guide," I said.

"You think he'll still be around?" asked Boris.

"I think so. No need for him to pull a disappearing act since as far as he's concerned the payment of the ransom is already in play and there's no evidence of active police involvement."

"Well, let's get a move on then," said Elena as she got up from the couch and headed for the front door.

* * *

The hotel was 1970's vintage glass and aluminum modern with an oversized lobby sporting a registration counter that seemed to go on forever and plush seating arrangements scattered about like tiny islands. I approached one of the clerks at the counter.

"I'm not a guest here at the hotel but a friend in San Francisco recommended a country guide she met here...a man named Fernando. Any chance you could assist me in locating him...I'd like to engage his services if possible?"

"Yes, I know who you mean but I haven't seen him in some days now," said the clerk, "but he left some business cards with the hotel...let me see if I can locate them." The clerk, a slender, dark-haired man in his fifties, excused himself and went into the back office. He was gone for about five minutes and returned with an expectant look on his face.

"I couldn't locate his card but I was able to phone him. He says he'll be right over. It shouldn't be but a few minutes...he lives close by...why don't you take a seat and I'll point you out to him when he arrives."

"Thank you...I appreciate your help."

I walked over to one of the unoccupied seating areas and motioned for Elena to join me. Boris had taken a seat close to the front entrance.

"What'd you learn?" she asked as she sat down beside me.

"That the hotel staff is in on the take...at least when playing a role in drumming up business for the guide. The clerk phoned Fernando to let him know he's got a hot prospect and the old boy is heading over here as we speak."

"What's my role?"

"You're my girlfriend. We're here for just a couple of days and hope to squeeze in some tourist excursions."

"Do we have names?"

"Nope...we'll just deflect any such enquiries."

Elena picked up on her role effortlessly, settling back and displaying an air of bored impatience. I feigned an interest in the hotel's architecture—turning restlessly about as if intrigued by the wonders of modern construction techniques.

Ten minutes later, a man fitting Mrs. Richmond's description of the guide walked hurriedly into the lobby, hesitated for only a moment—just enough time to catch the eye of the clerk—then headed directly towards us.

"My apologies for making you wait sir...I am Fernando Alvarez, accredited cultural guide at your service," he said, bowing deeply and extending his hand.

I stood up and shook his hand. "Thank you for coming at such short notice, Mr. Alvarez. You come highly recommended."

"I am honored to learn of this," he said, "may I enquire who might the party be who referred you to me?"

"I forget her name, unfortunately...it was at one of those gala parties for the opera in San Francisco...but she insisted I write down your name and the name of this hotel after learning my girlfriend and I would be stopping off here on our way further south."

"It's not important...well, how may I help you?" he asked.

"We're only here for one night and hoped you might be available to show us some of the more important cultural sights here in the capital or in its immediate outskirts."

"Such a pity you cannot remain for a longer time...there is so much to see. But we must do what we can...it so happens I am free today and would be happy to serve as your guide. By the way, my fee is ninety dollars an hour with a three-hour minimum. Is that acceptable?"

"Perfectly."

"Do you have a car at your disposal or would you like me to secure one...it would be extra you know?"

"It won't be necessary, we have a suitable vehicle parked just out front."

"Well then, perhaps we should get started. I suggest we spend the morning visiting key architectural landmarks that are within the city such as the presidential palace, the cathedral, several of the more elaborate mansions…maybe also take a stroll through the city's open air market."

"That sounds fine, Mr. Alvarez, please lead on," I replied, placing a hand on his back and gently nudging him towards the front entrance. I hope you won't mind if my girlfriend drives… she's the one who rented the vehicle."

"Not at all, sir…though it might interfere somewhat in her ability to give due attention to any points of interest we might pass."

"Not to worry, Mr. Alvarez, she's not quite as keen as I on this whole cultural tourism thing…are you sweetheart?"

Elena just rolled her eyes but then turned to Alvarez and nodded affirmatively, keeping a big smile on her face.

We walked over to where the SUV was parked and I opened the door to the rear seat and motioned for him to climb in.

"But sir, it would be much better for me to sit up front where I can direct your attention to…"

I hit him hard at the base of the neck with the edge of my hand rendering him unconscious then carefully guided his slumped body onto the rear seat. Boris, who had quietly come up behind me, concealed the action from nearby pedestrians with his broad back.

"Jump in and prop him up," I said to Boris as I stepped aside and opened the door on the passenger side of the front seat.

Boris moved quickly to comply, shutting the rear door and letting Elena who had already slipped behind the wheel know it was okay to move out. By then I was securely in the front seat with the door closed. Without a single word, Elena put the SUV in gear and took off.

No one said a word for the first half-mile or so but then Elena broke the silence, "Well, Church, we've bagged your man. Now what do you want me to do?"

"Head for the safe house," I said.

She nodded and made a turn at the next intersection.

* * *

"I'm not sticking around, Church," said Elena once we'd removed the bound, blind-folded and gagged tour guide from the back seat of the SUV and dragged him into the garage.

"A need for deniability I suppose?"

"Let's just say whatever you plan to do with this guy probably falls outside FBI operational guidelines."

"I understand. You coming back later…after picking up Jack?"

"Yeah…you think you'll be done by then?"

"One way or another I suppose."

She nodded, then climbed back into the SUV and backed out of the driveway. Boris had been watching over our guest inside the garage and came out the side door to let me know Fernando was conscious and feverishly struggling to get loose from the bindings on his arms and legs.

"Good," I said as I followed him back into the garage.

Boris had shoved him up against the rear wall of the garage. I knelt down and untied the gag on his mouth. He was about to shout what I imagined would be a string of obscenities when I gripped his face tightly.

"Shut up and listen!" I said menacingly in Spanish. "We have things to talk about and you'll need to carefully consider your answers...not waste our time or yours with senseless displays of outrage!"

I removed my hand.

"What do you want? Who are you?" he asked with a sense of foreboding, his head turning from left to right as if somehow the movement would free him from the agony of not being able to see his tormentors.

"Where are they keeping the little boy?" I asked.

"What boy? What do I know about a little boy...what are you talking about?"

But his nervousness was evident and I let the question linger, not choosing to respond to his protestations.

"Can't you please tell me what this is all about?" he pleaded. "There must be some mistake...whatever it is...some terrible mix up...I don't know anything about a little boy."

"You don't remember having witnessed a kidnapping of the Richmond family's eleven year old boy named Matt?" I asked.

"Oh, that boy…yes, of course I do…but what has that to do with me? I reported that crime to the police…why do you insinuate I had something to do with it?"

I pivoted slightly and kicked out with my right leg, my foot connecting viciously with his left kidney. He attempted to scream but Boris covered his mouth with a gloved hand.

"Let's try once again," I said, "where are they keeping the boy?"

He shook his head defiantly once Boris released his grip.

"Stand him up," I said.

Boris grabbed him under the shoulders and pulled him into a standing position then stepped away.

I punched him just below the rib cage, letting the force of the blow drive all of the air out of his lungs. He collapsed, struggling to breathe.

I knelt down next to him and whispered in his ear, "Come Fernando, this is going to get ugly unless you cooperate. I know you set up the Richmond family…that run-in with the gang on the road to El Monte was no random event. What I don't know is where the boy is being held…and you're going to tell me even if I have to beat it out of you."

Fernando gasped for air as I stood up and stepped away. I gave him time to regain his breathing. Finally, he spoke, "Honestly, I don't know where the boy is…you must believe me…my uncle, he tells me I can make some money guiding rich *gringos* to a spot where men can rob them. I knew nothing about a kidnapping."

"Your uncle—are we talking about Captain Alvarez, *commandante* of the El Monte police force?"

"Yes, but he will kill me if he learns I told you."

"Kill his own nephew? That's hard to believe...especially since the two of you have probably been running this scam for some time now...and profitably too."

"Okay, he won't kill me but they will," said Fernando.

"Who?"

"The men who took the boy...the men who do the robbing."

"Who are they?"

"This I don't know...I never wanted to know...they are dangerous men."

"So, you haven't dealt with them directly?"

"No, only stop the car when they appear in the road...say nothing, then after the robbery take the *gringos* to the office of my uncle."

I stared at him for a moment, trying to sense whether he'd told me all he knew. "What do you think?" I asked Boris.

"I think he's given us about all he's got that's of any value to us. The real target is the uncle."

I nodded. "Okay, Fernando, we'll call a stop to this interrogation...for the time being. But you'll need to be held in our custody until we've dealt with your uncle...you understand?"

He shook his head, "You will never get to him...he's always accompanied by armed men. And when he learns I've talked he will be very angry with me...he might even tell the kidnappers who, I promise, will not hesitate to kill me."

"You're probably right, Fernando," I said, "so keep that in mind...the sooner we can neutralize these people the safer you'll be…might be a reason you'd be smart to give us any additional information you possess that will make our job easier."

"I don't know anything that will help you."

"Think about it…we'll be setting off for El Monte in the morning."

"Who are you?" asked Fernando in bewilderment.

"Not something you need to worry about…just try to make yourself comfortable…you've got a long time to wait before this thing is over." With that, Boris retied the gag and used Elena's handcuffs to cuff him to a metal pipe that ran along the base of the garage wall.

* * *

We returned to the house and settled into a couple of the chairs in the living room. It was almost ten o'clock in the morning and I was anxious to keep the momentum going.

"We've got most of the day left before Jack's arrival, any idea of how we can profitably utilize the time?" I asked.

"We'll need Jack here to keep an eye on Fernando before it'll be possible for us to head for El Monte," said Boris, "so I guess whatever we do will have to happen right here or at least well within the capital city itself."

Just then, my satphone rang. I looked enquiringly at Boris then answered it.

"Church, it's Elena, I've just come into the office…wanted to know how things were going with your guest."

"We've finished our conversation with him…at least for the moment, and can report he's been helpful. We were correct in thinking he was involved and learned the operation was a family affair…at least with respect to victim targeting and the subsequent police coverup. He claims he had no part in the kidnapping…said the take down was only supposed to involve robbery."

"Is he badly injured?"

"Aside from some abdominal soreness I suppose one could say he's as fit as a fiddle. Turns out he's not one of the hard types and saw the wisdom of cooperating. We'll keep him under wraps until this operation comes to a close."

"Thought I'd also give you a heads up," said Elena.

"Regarding what?" I asked.

"Seems your old nemesis, Colonel Felipe Cruz, got wind of your little escapade involving him and has made enquiries here at the embassy trying to nail down your identities, and whether you and Boris are on some sort of CIA mission."

"So what did the embassy do?"

"They routed the inquiry—and the complaint—to my desk, where it will sit and gather dust…unless you can think of a way to use it for your purposes."

"Thanks, Elena."

"My thinking is the colonel won't issue an arrest warrant for the two of you as long as he's not sure whether you aren't on some U.S. government mission but rest assured he'll be sending out his own agents to apprehend you as long as it can be done quietly. He'll want to know what's going on before he makes a public stink."

"In the meantime," I countered, "I'll bet law enforcement types will continue thinking we're on a covert mission under the good colonel's sponsorship and won't be easily persuaded to think otherwise."

"Can you make it work for you?" asked Elena.

"Perhaps...there's the outside possibility it may be the key to our getting access to Captain Alvarez."

"You're thinking Alvarez is the linchpin in the operation?"

"Yeah, one way or another he's got a more important role than just running interference for the kidnap gang."

"I think maybe it'd be a good idea to do a little background workup on the captain...see what his military record was...what units he was affiliated with."

"Can you get that information?" I asked.

"Ironically, I can get it courtesy of our colonel...you know, shared intelligence and all that."

"Why don't we meet for lunch and go over what you've learned... say about one o'clock? You think you might have something for me by then?" I asked.

"Possibly. In any case I'll swing by and pick you up...Boris be all right sticking around and watching the tour guide?"

"Yeah," I said as Boris nodded his head, "he's cool with that as long as we bring him some take out."

"No problem...and we'll be sure to bring enough for both him and Fernando."

"See you then...and thanks, Elena."

I shut off the satphone and looked at Boris. "Damn! She's turning out to be a real asset."

"What the hell did you think, she's FBI for God's sake!" said Boris.

* * *

Elena arrived promptly at one o'clock, still dressed as she was earlier that morning. I had changed into my traveling garb—tan slacks, white sports shirt and cotton blue blazer. She gave me a critical once-over as I climbed into the SUV.

"My, you clean up nicely," she said as she put the vehicle in gear and took off.

I acknowledged the compliment with a brief smile then asked where we were headed.

"Thought we'd go Spanish…you like Spanish cuisine…yes?"

"Love it, especially if they serve a good *paella*."

"That they do. The restaurant is relatively new but has already caught on. I've reserved us a table."

She drove with skill as she navigated the busy streets of the capital. I settled back in the passenger seat and relaxed, taking in the sights and letting the balmy midday air that rushed through the open side window of the SUV soothe the wind-burned skin on my face.

The restaurant was housed in an old Spanish-styled building just off the town's central square. Elena located a curbside parking space out front and deftly maneuvered the SUV into it.

"They've got a charming outdoor patio out back," she said as she took my arm and led me towards the front entrance.

The *maître d'* seemed to know her and without any instruction escorted us through the main dining room and out onto the rear patio where a handful of linen-covered tables had been placed under the shade of old Red Oak trees.

"We'll be having the *paella*, Antonio," she said as the *maître d'* helped her into her chair, "and have the waiter bring us a bottle of that lovely *rioja* you recently acquired."

"Yes, *señorita*...at once," he replied as he signaled to a waiter to attend to his new guests.

"I take it you come here often," I said.

"Perhaps once a week...for lunch generally. One gets tired of the region's traditional dishes and good American cooking is best enjoyed at the homes of my colleagues at the embassy."

"Is it awkward socially not having a husband to accompany you at these domestic gatherings?"

"Actually no. Nowadays there's a surprisingly high number of single careerists within the foreign-service community, and there's always a demand for someone like myself when dignitaries fly in for brief visits."

"I understand...still, it must be somewhat difficult for a young unattached woman—given the *machismo* culture of the region."

"Ordinarily, you would be correct but fortunately the kind of assertive training the FBI provides stands me in good stead in such situations."

I laughed and took her hand. "Well, I'll be careful not to incur your displeasure, knowing—what others may not—that you carry a nine millimeter semiautomatic in your purse. Still, I can certainly understand why any man would wish to impress a lady as lovely as you."

"My, Church, I get the feeling you're hitting on me."

"My apologies, Elena," I said, giving her hand a gentle pat before withdrawing mine, "I'll try harder to keep my attention on the matters before us."

"See that you do!" she said with mock severity.

Just then, our waiter brought over the wine, uncorked the bottle and filled our glasses.

"What do you think?" she asked as she watched me take a sip.

"It's wonderful," I exclaimed, taking a second sip. "Usually I prefer a *priorat* if I'm about to enjoy Spanish cuisine but this *rioja* is quite exceptional."

"It will be a some time before the *paella* is ready," said the waiter, "would you like a salad to start off with?"

"It won't be necessary," she said to the waiter, "we'll be fine… won't we Church?"

"Absolutely…anyway, it'll give us time to go over what you've learned about our mutual friend."

After the waiter had left us to attend to other guests Elena started in.

"The colonel was quite willing to arrange access to Alvarez' personnel records once I explained we'd received some disturbing information from an informant regarding the captain's alleged involvement in crimes against U.S. citizens. I assured the colonel it was most likely an innocent misunderstanding—Americans not being familiar with the way police procedure worked in his country—but nevertheless I was obliged to follow up."

"And what did you learn?"

"My suspicions were right on the mark, he did serve in the military...secured a commission shortly after he turned twenty-two, trained at the military facility in Santa Clara where he's reported to have achieved average ratings. Afterwards, he was assigned to an infantry battalion stationed east of the capital where he was placed in command of a rifle platoon."

"How does this help us?" I asked.

"I'm thinking perhaps this kidnap gang consists of a group of cashiered soldiers...maybe part of the platoon he commanded."

"Doesn't make much sense, Elena, wouldn't Alvarez, as platoon commander, be the guy who fingered them for dishonest conduct? And if so, wouldn't he be the last person they'd hook up with if what they were doing was outside the law?"

"You'd think so, but there's more to the story. Alvarez was later promoted to captain and placed in charge of the same company in which he'd previously been platoon leader. He served in that capacity until transferring to the national police."

"And?"

"And shortly before his transfer the leader of Alpha Squad and four of the men in his squad were dishonorably discharged...this happened about a year ago."

"I still don't get the connection."

"Assume for the moment the complaint against the rogue squad had to do with extortion...threatening local merchants and farmers residing in the military zone to which the company was assigned. And assume Alvarez, as company commander, got a cut."

"He'd go down with the squad if the authorities found out about it," I said.

"Maybe, maybe not. If Alvarez persuaded the squad to take the rap but not incriminate him in exchange for his providing police cover once they were all out of the military."

"So the gang hides low until Alvarez gets a posting to El Monte then runs their highway gambit in his jurisdiction, using his nephew as the facilitator."

"That's how I see it," said Elena.

"So, what do we know about the squad leader?"

"Nothing yet, and I'm reluctant to press the colonel for information on these guys...it'd convince him I might know more than I'm willing to share."

"Well, I'm thinking if your hypothesis is true then this kidnapping stunt suggests the squad leader, who ever he is, is no longer under the finger of Alvarez...maybe we can use that as leverage."

"How do you mean?"

"Get Alvarez to believe his life is in danger...warn him we'll put the word out that he's fingered the gang and is willing to testify against them in court."

"Not bad, Church, but we're getting way ahead of ourselves... we still don't know whether any of this is real and we still haven't worked out how we'll get to him in the first place."

Just then, the food arrived—a classic *Paella Valenciana*—in steaming iron skillets. The waiter refilled our wine glasses and bid us *buen apetito*. Conversation diminished as we concentrated on the flavorful mix of seafood, chicken and rice.

Once we'd finished the meal and were enjoying our coffee Elena brought up the question I'd been about to.

"Church, I hope you don't get the impression I'm trying to run this operation."

"Well, let's just say your input has been greatly appreciated… though I've come to wonder just how much distance you're really looking for…in pursuit of deniability."

"It's complicated. I'm anxious to be of help and I want to do what I can to insure you're successful in this venture, but at the same time I'm worried I'll blow my cover and get myself shipped back to the States before this thing is over and done with."

"It's a risk you don't have to take, Elena," I said softly, once again taking her hand in mine. Boris and I will run the operation, Jack can ride herd on the tour guide, and you can remain at a distance…but not too far I hope since I've already come to rely on your analytical skills."

"Is that code for something else? She asked with a smile.

"Perhaps. You know what they say, " There's nothing more irresistible in a woman than a fine mind…especially when it's combined with a beautiful smile and a gorgeous body."

"And I always thought men liked their women dumb."

"Only dumb men, I'd wager. But seriously, we make a good team and I'm looking forward to the next several days when I've the privilege of working with you."

"You're very sweet, William…may I call you William?"

"Absolutely," I replied as I got up from my chair and came around to help Elena out of hers. "Now, why don't you give me a lift back to the safe house and arrange whatever you need to arrange to get Jack through customs."

She smiled and took my arm. After passing through the main dining room where she said a brief goodbye to the *maître d'*, who handed her the parcel of takeout food we had ordered, we left the restaurant and headed for the parked SUV.

* * *

It was close to three o'clock by the time Elena dropped me off and headed back to the office. Boris was just coming in from the garage when I walked through the door.

"How's are guest?" I asked.

"Probably as hungry as me," he said, eyeing the takeout package I was holding.

"Brought you both some *paella* and a bottle of *rioja* wine to share…that do the trick?"

"That it will! Let's bring it into the kitchen and heat it up."

"It's still hot, just scoop it out onto a couple of plates," I said as I handed the package to Boris.

While Boris prepared servings for himself and Fernando I changed out of my good clothes and put on a pair of jeans and a rock-washed blue canvas sports shirt, then returned barefoot to the living room and lay down on the couch. I wasn't really tired but I needed to sort through the information Elena had given me, and maybe also get a handle on the new twist in our relationship.

"So what did Elena have to say?" asked Boris when he returned to the living room after giving Fernando his meal and a generous glass of wine.

"She came up with a fairly plausible scenario that connects Captain Alvarez with a squad of cashiered soldiers who, according to her theory, might be the guys that pulled off the kidnapping."

"You buy into it?" he asked between bites.

"Enough to want to run with it once we get our hands on Alvarez."

"Jesus, this stuff is good!" said Boris as he sampled some more of the *paella*.

"Yeah, that was my reaction…and wait till you try the wine."

"So, what's are next move?" asked Boris, just before taking his first sip of the wine.

"We can't do much until Jack arrives…or, for that matter, until I've had a chance to touch base with Kingstone—he should've received contact information from the kidnappers by now."

"You might want to have a little talk with the tour guide," said Boris, "he's been thinking about what you said regarding how much safer he'll be once his uncle and the others are neutralized. I think he's got something more to tell us."

"Will do…so, what do you think of the wine?"

Boris took another sip, turned towards me and smiled broadly, "It's gotta be straight from heaven! You choose it?"

"No, Elena. That woman's got talents wherever you look."

"You kinda like her, don't you?"

"She's definitely a winner…I'll give you that, and it's getting harder and harder to think of her as just another FBI agent."

"Well, don't fight it, Church…nothing in the freelance world rules out fraternization with a colleague, especially one with looks that'd make a cover girl green with envy."

I shook my head in mock dismay, got up from the couch and headed for the garage. "Why don't I let you eat your meal in peace," I said, "and in the meantime I'll have a chat with our boy Fernando."

* * *

Fernando was sitting on the garage floor, chained to the metal rod running along the back wall, totally engrossed in putting away the lunch I'd brought from the restaurant. He looked up as I approached.

"I take it the food meets with your approval," I said as I squatted down next to him.

"It's good all right!" he said, taking another sip of the wine.

"You doing okay?" I asked.

"Yeah, the old man's taking good care of me...lets me go to the bathroom, brings me water, lets me stretch...things like that."

"Shouldn't be much longer, Fernando, maybe another day or two. It'd be quicker if you could help us get to your uncle."

"I've been thinking about that...hell, haven't thought about anything else since you left."

"And?"

"Okay, I've been thinking the best way to get to him is to catch him at his house."

"You want to spell that out?"

"At the police station he's always surrounded by armed guards... other policemen...you know."

"But at his house?"

"At his house all he's got is a couple of security men...thinks the high wall surrounding the property and the bars on the windows make him safe."

"And where is this house?"

"It's just on the outskirts of El Monte...I can draw you a map."

"Who's he live with...who would be there any given night?"

"That's the thing, he lives alone...only the occasional girlfriend and a live-in housekeeper sleep there."

"He's not married?"

"Used to be, but his wife left him when he resigned from the military...she's the daughter of a high-ranking army officer and counted on having a husband who'd make the army his career... just like her father."

"Any kids?"

"Yeah, two, but they live with the mother."

"This is good stuff, Fernando...let me think about it," I said getting up from my squatting position. "Let me get you some paper and a pen so you can draw that map. It'd also help if you could sketch the layout of the property and the house, and indicate where the two security men usually position themselves at night."

"You won't tell him any of this...how I helped you...Christ, he'd murder me!"

"He won't learn a thing from us, that I promise...unless, of course, the info you've provided turns out to be misleading."

He nodded then went back to his meal. I walked to the side door and let myself out.

* * *

Jack arrived a little after six o'clock, just as I was putting through a call to Kingstone. I gave him a wave then moved into the breezeway separating the house from the garage to avoid the commotion.

"Have you heard back from the kidnappers?" I asked Kingstone, after Jackson finally extricated him from some sort of family conference and handed him the satphone.

"Yes, they called about an hour ago…wanted to be reassured the money was now in the country."

"It is…Jack just arrived."

"So it's safe then…it's all there?"

"I haven't actually seen it but Jack gave me a thumbs up as he entered the room."

"Excuse my nervousness, Mr. Church, but the man on the phone became dreadfully specific about what would happen to Matt if the ransom was not precisely in accordance with his instructions."

"What I really need to know, Mr. Kingstone, is whether you were able to persuade the kidnappers to supply you with a phone number for me to use in contacting them?"

"They didn't like that business at all," he replied, "gave me the devil of a tongue lashing!"

"I suppose they preferred to learn my identity and initiate the contact themselves?"

"That they did, and it was only after I pleaded to being powerless to alter the situation…that you now possessed the ransom money and were currently in the capital but too scared to stay very long, worried they'd find you, take the ransom and kill you."

"So, did you get the number?"

"Yes, finally he gave it to me…told me to have you call between eight and ten o'clock tonight."

"Did you remind him I'd need to be reassured Matt was still alive and okay?"

"He said such assurances were routine and that you would be allowed to talk with Matt."

"Did he say anything else?"

"Only that this would be my last phone contact with him… that all further matters would be between him and yourself, and if you proved an unreliable link the boy would be found dead—with unspeakable signs of torture."

"Okay, I get the picture…just give me the number and let me get to work."

Kingstone dictated the number and urged me to let him know just as soon as I'd made contact with the kidnappers and learned Matt was all right. I assured him I would, then broke the connection.

I stepped back into the living room where Jack and Boris were engaged in spirited conversation and Elena was curled up on the couch. The conversation stopped as soon as they spotted me.

"What did you learn?" asked Boris.

"That the ransom package had better be configured just as they requested…assuming of course they ever get their hands on it."

"Well, it's still just as it was when it left the bank—in two aluminum attaché cases that I swear weigh over twenty pounds each," said Jack, "if it's screwed up there's nothing we can do now."

"Not to worry," I said, "if they get close enough to the ransom money to complain then they're close enough to suffer the consequences."

"Good to see you haven't lost your perennial optimism, Church," said Jack as he came up and embraced me. "So, Boris and Elena tell me you've got a guy on ice who I'm supposed to babysit?"

"Yeah, though I don't think he'll be a problem…in fact he's supplied me with some useful intelligence that just might make our takedown of Captain Alvarez a little easier."

I briefly filled Jack in on the strategy suggested by Fernando— one that Boris and I had already agreed made sense.

"El Monte is about an hour's ride from here," I said, "I'm thinking we saddle up the bikes and head out just after midnight."

"You planning to neutralize his security with one handgun?" asked Elena skeptically.

"Watch and learn," I said with a smile.

* * *

At nine o'clock sharp I put through a call to the kidnappers. A man speaking heavily accented English answered on the third ring. "You the guy with the money?" he asked in a deep menacing voice.

"Yeah," I replied.

"How come you force the old man to jerk us around, huh?"

"Maybe 'cause I'm just as much a bastard as you and all your friends," I said.

"A wise guy, huh?"

"Listen, asshole, why don't you stop the tough guy routine and get on with business. I'm tied up until later tomorrow at the earliest…that work for you?"

"You got it all wrong, *gringo*, I call the shots…either that or the boy don't show up in real good shape."

"Well, you've got a forty-eight hour window in which to schedule the swap. After that I'm gone and so is the ransom."

"Like hell! That boy means too much to the old man…and you're on his payroll. You'll do whatever we demand or you'll be the one the old man blames for the death of his grandson."

"This ain't a pissing contest," I said, "so why don't you settle down and tell me what works for you?"

"The drop off will occur somewhere on the road leading to the village of San Miguel."

"Where the hell is that?"

"It's a village some distance from the capital…maybe sixty kilometers. The road is narrow but paved, you should find it easily on a local road map."

"What do you mean 'somewhere'?"

"Exactly that…I'll give you more precise instructions just before the swap. You'll arrive at the designated location, get out, hand over the ransom, we'll check it and if it's okay we'll release the boy."

"How are you going to know it's my vehicle?"

"You're going to supply us with a description…and the license plate number."

"That'll work, I guess…so when do you want this swap to occur?"

"Tonight."

"It's not going to happen tonight, I've already told you I've got other plans. If you want it to be a night drop you'll have to settle for tomorrow night or the night after."

"You're a real pain in the ass, *gringo*, maybe I kill you and the boy after taking the money."

"Let's not get stupid, asshole, going around threatening people who plan on bringing you money is a real quick way to get the deal undone and the money well out of your reach!"

"Okay, okay, we'll do the swap tomorrow night. I'll tell you where on the road you're to stop when I call you earlier in the evening, so give me your phone number."

"Not a chance, mister, I'll call you at this number tomorrow evening at this same time. You can tell me then where I'm to go."

"Why you so scared to give me your phone number?"

"Because the less you know about me prior to the swap the safer I feel…so don't ask me for the description of my vehicle either. I'll supply it when we talk tomorrow night."

"So, we done now?" he asked.

"There's just the matter of my speaking to the boy…making sure you've still got something worth exchanging for a ransom as large as this."

He grunted then put down the phone. After a short pause a boy's voice came on.

"Hello, hello?"

"That you Matt?" I asked.

"Yes, who's this?"

"It's the man your parents and your grandfather have commissioned to bring you home."

"When are you coming to get me?"

"Real soon…you all right?"

"Yes, I'm okay…they haven't hurt me or anything, though the food is pretty bad."

"You hang on for another day or so and we'll get this thing done."

"They're pretty scary but they've told me they won't hurt me as long as my family pays them."

"I'm bringing the money they demanded so don't worry…it'll turn out all right."

"You'll tell my mom I'm okay?"

"She'll see that with her own eyes real soon."

"Okay, you've had your talk," said the kidnapper who'd taken the phone away from the boy, "just don't try no funny business between now and the time of the swap…for your sake and the boy's."

DAY 6

"EVERYBODY UP AND AT 'em!" I shouted as I poured coffee into the mugs sitting on the dining room table. It was a little after two o'clock in the morning and we'd all managed about five hours of sleep. It wasn't much of a breakfast but it would have to do—wholewheat toast, butter and strawberry jam, a container of orange juice and a hot skillet piled high with scrambled eggs. I'd set the alarm on my smartphone for a few minutes before the hour knowing it was up to me to volunteer for kitchen duty— hell, it was me who decided on an early morning launch of what I anticipated would be an eventful day and the least I could do was to give the team a few extra minutes of shuteye. But the irony didn't escape me. I was probably the last person to identify with culinary pursuits—living as I do the life of a bachelor in a city rich in fine restaurants. Still, I can manage breakfast and felt a little smug about the spread I'd laid out for the gang.

"God, Church, did you have to shout?" complained Elena who'd spent the sack time curled up on the living room couch.

"Sorry about that," I said, "probably got a little carried away knowing the eggs will grow cold if all of you don't make it to the table promptly."

"I bet you decided on scrambled eggs just to justify putting the rush on us," said Jack sleepily as he came out of his bedroom.

"Well, we've got a lot to do before dawn so let's not argue...by the way, did anyone notice whether Boris is up?" I asked.

"He's in the head," said Elena as she sat down at the table and began applying butter to a piece of toast.

While the three of them fortified themselves with food and coffee I took a plate out to Fernando who'd spent a miserable five hours cuffed to the pipe in the garage, still blindfolded and with his hands bound behind his back.

"Change of plans, Fernando," I said as I untied his hands and placed the food and a cup of coffee on the floor beside him.

He looked up enquiringly, rubbing his hands and wrists. I untied the blindfold and handed him a knife and fork. "You're going for a ride just a soon as you finish eating."

"Where are you taking me?" he asked after taking a big gulp of coffee.

"Out to see your uncle."

"What! Are you crazy?"

"It may seem that way but the truth is I can't spare anyone to keep an eye on you...besides, I need you as a prop...as leverage... to get your uncle to cooperate."

"But you promised he'd never know!"

"Yeah, but in the real world all promises are conditional...you of all people should understand that, given your professed concern for your clients' safety."

"You're a real bastard, you know?"

"Yeah, Fernando, I guess I am, especially when it comes to punks like you who prey on hapless tourists. Eat up, we'll be bundling you into the back of a vehicle before long." With that, I turned and walked out, leaving the connecting door to the breezeway between the garage and the house open so I could keep an eye on him.

* * *

Everybody had showered and changed clothes before hitting the sack earlier that evening so there wasn't much to getting ready once breakfast was over. Elena had removed two AR-15 rifles from the embassy's armory for use by herself and Jack should they need something with more firepower than that provided by their sidearms. They broke the AR-15s down and inspected them before heading for the SUV, a satchel full of extra clips in Elena's hand, the two aluminum attaché cases in Jack's. Boris had taken charge of putting Fernando in the back of the SUV—all trussed up and blindfolded. He was not to catch a glimpse of Jack or have a chance to become more familiar with Elena—aside from their brief encounter at the hotel. As for myself, I secured the house then headed for the garage where the motorcycles were stored.

The air was crisp but not cold this time of the morning, still Boris and I put on leather gloves before starting up our engines. The tanks had been topped off the previous day so nothing stood in the way of our heading straight for El Monte. I signaled Elena who would be following in the SUV then throttled up and swung out onto the road, with Boris right beside me.

El Monte was up in the hills—about an hour's drive according to Elena. The road was paved but with lots of twists and turns. We had to proceed cautiously, especially as it was still dark and we had to be watchful of locals trudging along the narrow road or herding livestock from one grazing field to another.

Fernando's instructions placed the home of Captain Alvarez two kilometers north of the town, on a dirt road we would encounter if we drove to the town's central square, turned left then followed the street that ran along the fenced side of the church. It was almost four o'clock in the morning by the time we reached El Monte and spotted the road. We advanced slowly, trying to get a feel for the neighborhood and hoping not to make any unnecessary noise. It was easy to spot the Alvarez residence given Fernando's sketch: a compound somewhere between a third and a half acre in area surrounded by a nine-foot high cinderblock wall, with the house some seventy-five feet back from the main gate.

Elena pulled over, headlights switched off, some distance short of the main entrance, while Boris and I continued forward, passing the gate and verifying the layout. A wooden guard's shack stood just inside and to the left of the gate. Fernando had indicated one of the two night security guards would be stationed there, the other would be just inside the front door of the house.

We doubled back after going about a half-kilometer, but this time I shut off my engine and glided to a stop just short of the farthest corner of the perimeter wall, walking my bike to a point along the wall about fifty feet from the gate. Meanwhile, Boris motored past the gate, coming to a halt where the SUV was parked then quietly walking his bike back to a point along the wall just short of the guard shack. We'd rehearsed the next set of moves the day before: both of us leaned our bikes against the wall, making sure they were firmly wedged, then carefully stepped up on to the rear wheel rack and used the extra height to enable us to grasp the top of the cinderblock wall and pull ourselves up. I could hear the two guard dogs Fernando had warned us about pacing nervously back and forth near the front entrance to the house. They clearly had sensed our presence but weren't sure how to react.

After pausing long enough to be reasonably certain Boris was in position I dropped down inside the compound. Instantly, motion sensors activated powerful floodlights, placing me in stark relief. The dogs attacked. I was waiting, crouched in a two-handed firing position, my semiautomatic pointed directly at their line of attack. They came at me shoulder to shoulder, both anxious to be the first to lunge. I waited until they were no more than ten feet away then squeezed off two quick shots, aiming for their broad chests. They went down.

The guard at the gate, momentarily disoriented by the bright white lights, finally rushed out of the small wooden building, an assault rifle in his hands and began to take aim at me, but before he could get off a burst two large gloved hands violently twisted his head, breaking his neck and killing him instantly. It was Boris. He had dropped inside the compound just as the dogs initiated their attack and had come from behind the guard shack to subdue the guard before he could pose a serious threat to me.

The second guard came out the front door of the house at the sound of gunfire, saw the body of the guard near the gate and what he must have thought was the carcass of one dog. Assuming I was the perpetrator of both killings, he shouted at me to drop my gun and put my hands up, pointing his assault rife menacingly in my direction. I complied without hesitation. But just then Boris, who had scooped up the first guard's assault rifle and had concealed himself in the guard shack, crawled out from the shack, assumed a prone firing position and let off a burst of gunfire—killing the second guard.

As soon as the second guard was down I picked up my gun and raced for the open front door. I managed to make it through the door just as a bare-footed, shirtless guy dressed in an unbuttoned pair of pants came rushing down a long corridor that must connect the bedroom wing to the front hall. He was carrying a handgun in one hand but not moving guardedly—certainly not anticipating any imminent danger, at least not in the house.

"Drop your weapon!" I shouted in Spanish, pointing my gun directly at him.

He looked surprised but did as instructed. I moved quickly to where he stood, kicked the gun away and marched him through the front hall and into what I took to be the living room. A lamp on one of the side tables was lit, casting enough light to allow me to confirm no one was in there.

"Who else is in the house?" I demanded, shoving him roughly into an upholstered armchair.

"Only my housekeeper...who the hell are you?"

"We'll get to that shortly, right now I want you to shut up."

Boris came in moments later, carrying the guards' two assault rifles.

"His handgun is on the floor in the side corridor," I said to Boris, "and he says only the housekeeper is in the house."

"I'll check it out," said Boris returning to the front hall.

I stood over him, my gun still out, waiting for Boris to secure the rest of the house. After a few minutes he came back in dragging a middle-aged woman dressed in nightclothes. "She's the only one I could find," he said.

"She your housekeeper?" I asked.

He nodded.

"Put her in one of the bathrooms…make sure it doesn't have a phone."

"You heard the man," said Boris in Spanish to the woman, "get into the bathroom just off the front hall and remain there with the door shut. If I see you peeking out I shoot—you understand?"

"*Si, señor,*" she said as she rushed out of the room, Boris following closely.

"Now, what's this all about," demanded the man.

"You Captain Alvarez?" I asked.

"Of course I am…this is my house!"

"You know Colonel Felipe Cruz?"

"Why…what does he have to do with this?"

"We're here to tell you the colonel wants possession of the American boy your gang kidnapped a week ago."

"What are you talking about? I don't have a gang…and for Christ's sake I'd also like to get my hands on the men who took that boy…after all, it happened in my jurisdiction!"

"You misunderstand, the colonel isn't interested in seeing justice done, he's interested in collecting the ransom your people negotiated with the Americans."

"Why do you keep referring to 'my people'... as if I had something to do with the kidnapping?"

"Come now, Captain, you don't really believe you can run a criminal operation without the head of counter-intelligence learning of it, do you?"

"Who the hell are you two...you aren't from here, that I know?"

"It doesn't matter who we are...just that we're working for the colonel."

"This doesn't make any sense. Who is it that accuses me of being involved in this alleged criminal enterprise?"

"Bring him in," I shouted to Boris.

Boris entered the room, gripping Fernando by the arm. He was still blindfolded and his hands were bound behind his back.

"Your nephew has been very talkative, explaining in considerable detail the sweet arrangement you put together—him leading gullible tourists to a spot on the road where armed men stop his car, rob your clients then disappear. He dutifully reports the robbery to you, where the report is buried and no pursuit of the gang is initiated—all in exchange for a healthy share of the takings."

"They made me tell them," cried Fernando, "they beat me until I couldn't take it any longer."

"Shut up!" ordered Alvarez. "Let me think!"

Everyone was quiet for some moments then Alvarez wagged his finger dismissively, "No," he said firmly, "the kidnapping was not of my doing...this I can say in all honesty. Okay, my nephew and I would on occasion arrange for the robbery of some wealthy tourists but never was there any harm to come to them...that I insisted!"

"You saying you don't expect to receive any portion of the ransom money...you expect the colonel to believe that?" I asked skeptically.

"I didn't say that...I said I had nothing to do with the kidnapping...it was the men doing the robbery that got greedy and took the boy."

"But once the kidnapping was a fact you expected your cut... isn't that right?"

"Yes, that's correct, though I'm not sure I'll ever see it...these men are out of control!"

"You mean they're out of your control?"

"Yes."

"Well, we're here to correct the situation," I said, "just tell us where they're keeping the boy and we'll take over the operation and see you're properly compensated."

"What colonel is he talking about?" asked Fernando, clearly confused. "I thought these guys were Americans from San Francisco...here to rescue the boy."

"Shut up, Fernando!" said Alvarez harshly, but it was clear the tour guide's confusion had sunk in. Alvarez looked up at me defiantly. "Prove you represent the colonel and are not just some *gringo* mercenaries on the payroll of the boy's family."

I didn't say a word, just holstered my gun and threw a haymaker punch right in the center of his face with my gloved fist. Blood splattered all over his face and dripped down onto his bare chest. He brought his hands up to clear away the debris of broken teeth and a flattened nose. I gave him time to work through the pain and shock.

"I don't really care whether you believe me or not," I said. "What I do care about is getting an answer to my question."

"Go to hell!" he said, gripping the arms of the chair and bracing himself for another punch.

I shook my head in disappointment then reached for my gun, aimed it carefully and shot him in the fleshy part of his right thigh—not too far from his crotch.

"Jesus Christ," he shouted in panic, "you're a Goddamned maniac!"

"You're wasting my time," I said quietly. "If you truly don't wish to cooperate we'll finish this little visit, but you and your nephew will be left behind just as dead as the two security guards out front…that what you want?"

"Okay, okay, I'll tell you…but don't blame me if they're no longer there."

"No longer where?"

"They've been operating out of a small ranch some ten kilometers off the road to El Monte."

"How would we find it?"

"You won't find it at night that's for sure, the turnoff's too difficult to spot."

"How far is the turnoff from the edge of town?"

"Maybe twenty kilometers…the turnoff is only marked by a jury-rigged shrine to some poor sap who got run over by a car a few years back."

"Hell, there must be a whole slew of such markers along the highway."

"Yeah, but this one's always got fresh flowers on it…seems someone still cares about him."

"Once we're on the side road how will we recognize the ranch?"

"It's the only outfit after you've driven beyond the first five kilometers, but like I said don't blame me if they've moved out."

I nodded then walked over to the phone sitting on a side table and dialed a number. "Let me talk to the colonel," I said, pretending to be in contact with someone on his staff. "Colonel, we've persuaded the captain to cooperate and are about to leave. What do you want me to do with the two of them?"

Alvarez looked up fearfully, pleading with his eyes for me to resist giving the colonel such authority.

"As you wish, Colonel," I said then hung up. I looked over at Alvarez who was steeling himself to handle the verdict. "Colonel says you and your nephew are to be left alive but with the understanding that neither of you make any effort to alert the kidnappers…and under no condition should the colonel be implicated in the events that transpired here this morning—you clear on that?"

Both men nodded vigorously. I signaled to Boris who untied Fernando and removed his blindfold.

"Once we're gone you're free to seek medical care for your leg and face," I said to Alvarez, "but don't even think about mobilizing your police to hunt us down…you'd be facing a couple of truck loads of armed troops with orders to seize you and to confiscate all your property."

We walked out of the house each carrying one of the guards' assault rifles and headed for the gate. Once we reached the gate Boris, who had also taken possession of the captain's nine-millimeter semiautomatic handgun, searched the first guard's pocket and came up with the key. He unlocked the gate and we walked towards our respective motorcycles.

"Everything all right, Church?" said a voice that sounded very much like Jack emanating from the dim early morning light no more than ten feet from where I was. "That you, Jack?" I asked.

"Yeah, Elena and I moved up to a point near the gate to provide cover," he said as he stepped away from the wall and came up to me, "look's like we weren't needed."

"The day's still young," I said, continuing towards the place next to the wall where I'd left my bike.

Boris and I rode our bikes to the open gate, the engines revved up, counting on Alvarez and his nephew to be monitoring the brightly illuminated front yard watching for our final departure. I wanted to ensure they got a good glimpse of the motorcycles—an added piece of evidence our claim to be working for the colonel was valid. Meanwhile, Elena and Jack had returned to the SUV and were in the process of stowing their AR-15's on the back seat when we pushed off from the driveway with one final blast of the mufflers.

"I see you guys have acquired a little more firepower," said Elena as we came alongside the SUV.

"Thought we'd take advantage of the hospitality of our recent acquaintances," said Boris with a smile.

"You think to get some extra clips?" she asked.

"Found them obliging in that regard as well," he replied pointing to an ammo canister strapped to the side of his bike's rear storage rack. "Half a dozen clips for the rifles and two loaded clips for the nine-millimeter."

"Well done," said Elena admiringly, "what's next on our schedule?"

"We've got the location of the kidnappers' camp," I replied, "but I'm thinking the captain will be phoning the gang as we speak, telling them to clear the hell out...so we've got to make a real quick dash for their base camp and intercept them if we can."

"You anticipated this?" asked Jack.

"Yeah, it's a calculated risk, I know, but it seemed important to let Alvarez make the case any hassles the gang has with people shooting guns can be placed at the colonel's doorstep...keep our dealings with the gang free from that sort of suspicion."

"Well, why don't the two of you take off," said Jack after I gave him the directions to the ranch. "We'll follow as quickly as we can."

I nodded, waved goodbye and roared off, with Boris fast on my heels.

* * *

It was after six o'clock in the morning by the time Boris and I reached the roadside shrine Alvarez had described. Sure enough, there was a narrow dirt road leading off from the highway just next to it—probably the poor guy being memorialized had come from this road when he got hit. The sun was well above the horizon by this time and we were able to keep up a good clip as we raced down the road, hoping we wouldn't be too late. As we approached the ranch we throttled down, becoming cautious knowing whoever was there might have close to a thirty-minute edge in setting up an ambush.

The ranch consisted of a spread of weed-infested pastures surrounded by rotted-out wooden fencing. Three buildings in various states of disrepair comprised what was at one time the operational center of a working ranch. One of the buildings looked like a single-story barn or stable with the remains of an old corral attached, another like a bunkhouse for ranch hands. What appeared to be the principal residence was the only building that looked somewhat habitable, with intact windowpanes, a functioning doorway and no obvious holes in the metal-sheeted roof. A recent vintage pickup truck was parked next to the wooden staircase leading up to the front porch. Cardboard boxes, their flaps open, took up about half the area of the truck bed. The rear gate was down suggesting loading was still in progress.

"I'll ride down and see what's going on," I said, "you take up a concealed firing position, getting as close as you can."

"I should be able to make it to the fence…their attention will be drawn to your approach," said Boris as he dismounted from the bike and grabbed a couple of clips from out of the ammo canister.

I left my assault rifle strapped to Boris's bike and made sure my 8-caliber piece was securely hidden under my shirt then slowly motored down towards the ranch house.

"*Hey, hombre, donde se cree que va?*" shouted a lean, dark-haired man who couldn't be more than twenty who'd rushed out the front door, a pistol in his hand.

"Take it easy, friend," I said in Spanish as I glided to a stop, the engine off. "You the guys who've got that American kid…Matt I think his name is?"

"Who the hell are you?" demanded the young man, his gun now leveled straight at me.

"I'm here to parlay," I said, keeping my hands loose at my sides. "I believe Captain Alvarez told you I'd be coming…now didn't he?"

"You the guy who works for Colonel Cruz?"

"Yeah…your sergeant in the house?" I asked.

"Nobody's here but me."

"You mind if I look for myself?"

"Suit yourself," said the young man as he shoved the gun into the waistband of his pants, "I've just got a couple more boxes to load then I'm out of here."

"Where you boys hold up at?" I asked as we walked together into the house.

"None of your Goddamn business!" he replied belligerently.

"Well now, don't think the colonel's going to be too pleased to learn some half-grown *pistolero* thinks he can disregard a legitimate inquiry."

"Legitimate, my ass! The captain told us your guy only wants to steal the ransom money from us, not enforce the law."

"Can't argue with you there, friend," I said as I checked out the rooms of the house. "You want some help with that last box?"

"Don't screw with me!" said the young man as he walked out the front door with a large cardboard box that looked to be full of clothing. "There ain't no way you're going to get me to tell you where we're based...and don't try to follow me—I see your bike or your buddy's bike in my rearview mirror I'll take you on a joy ride over roads that'll make your kidneys ache for a week!"

"I hear you," I said, following him out with the last box, "but you gotta know the colonel's not going to take no for an answer... he'll find you and when he does he'll probably shoot the whole lot of you...unless of course somebody on the inside—like you—were to cooperate. That somebody would be let go...and with a sizeable amount of the ransom money to boot!"

"We've got protection...can't do better than the National Police...so don't try to scare me into giving up the location. And you better tell your boss to get cracking if he's really going to make a move...swap's going down real soon."

"I'll be sure to tell him," I said with a chuckle as I slid the box onto the truck bed and helped the young man shut the rear gate.

I stood there, with my hands in my pocket, as the guy started up the engine, made a tight turn on the dusty clearing and roared off down the road we'd just come from. I signaled to Boris to let him pass. Once the truck was out of sight I ran over to where Boris was lying.

"I'll explain later," I said to him as I kept going to where our bikes were parked. "First off, I've got to get hold of Elena and Jack."

I grabbed the satphone from my pack and punched in the number of Elena's phone. She picked up immediately.

"What's up?" asked Elena.

"Get off the side road leading to the ranch as fast as you can and return to the main highway. Drive slowly in the direction of the capital. After about fifteen minutes or less a green pickup driven by a young man will overtake you. The bed of the truck will be full of cardboard boxes—most of them with their lids open. He's one of the kidnappers and he's heading for their new base of operations. The kid's pretty dumb so it shouldn't be hard to keep a tail on him. Don't be surprised if he seems to be looking in his rearview mirror a lot—it's not that he's suspicious of you, rather he wants to reassure himself Boris and I are not following him on our motorcycles."

"How the hell did you get all that out of him?" asked Elena as she began to execute a U-turn and race for the junction with the main highway.

"Just pretended to be a hired hand...like him...but with different bosses. Let the kid play the tough guy...allow him to brag a little about how his team will prevail."

"Okay, we'll stick with him once he gets here," said Elena. "You have any idea of roughly where he'll be heading?"

"The swap scheduled for tonight is supposed to happen somewhere along the road to the village of San Miguel. I'm betting the gang is holed up somewhere in the immediate vicinity of the village or along the road leading there."

"What do you want us to do once we've located the place?"

"Give me a call…we'll join you as soon as we can. Oh, and try to maintain surveillance…don't want them getting nervous and shifting location once again without our knowing about it."

"Will do," said Elena before hanging up.

* * *

The highway held a lot more traffic now that the morning was in full swing—commuters driving to the capital, pickups loaded with produce for the central market, and government officials shuttling back and forth between ministry offices in the city and municipal headquarters in the outlying towns. It was the latter cohort that was to prove troublesome. Boris and I were cruising along at the prevailing speed—not anxious to overtake the guy in the pickup truck and in no particular hurry—when a black sedan maneuvered to a spot right behind us and switched on a pair of flashing red lights. Boris and I looked at each other, gauging our respective inclination to make a run for it but indicating with a shrug of the shoulders we might as well pull over and see what we were up against.

We pulled over, shut off the engines and climbed down, taking a position to the rear of the bikes we hoped would block from view the sight of the assault rifles strapped conspicuously to the top of our storage racks. The sedan had pulled to a stop about twenty feet behind us. For some moments nobody emerged from the vehicle, then all four doors opened simultaneously and four men climbed out.

None were visibly armed but it didn't take much imagination to speculate each had a handgun concealed somewhere under their suit jackets. These were not members of the National Police—that seemed certain, making it likely we were about to finally meet up with some of Colonel Cruz' agents. We were not disappointed.

"You boys have been busy," said a heavy-set guy I took to be the man in charge of the team. "Impersonating a member of the military, kidnapping, homicide, criminal trespass and assault... did I leave something out?"

"It seems your informants in the National Police are extraordinarily good at their job," I said, "particularly since some of what you allege transpired less than a few hours ago".

"Yes, they are good but we're not here to discuss the finer points of counter-intelligence but to inquire what warrants such unlawful behavior on the part of a couple of *gringos* from the States?"

"And who might you be?" I asked.

"My identity isn't in question here...rather that of you and your friend. You will hand over your identification papers," ordered the man, his hand extended.

"I'm afraid we neglected to bring them along...this being simply an early morning excursion. But if it's important perhaps you'll advise us as to where we should present ourselves and our passports once we return to the capital."

"You talk nonsense," said the man disgustedly, 'you know perfectly well there's a strictly enforced law requiring foreigners to have their papers in their possession at all times."

I shrugged and looked inquiringly at the man while maneuvering slightly in front of Boris who I'd noticed was edging closer to his assault rifle.

"Very well, you are hereby under arrest...both of you. We will continue this conversation at a more appropriate location...the headquarters of Colonel Felipe Cruz."

As two of the men stepped forward to place us in cuffs I held out my hands as if to cooperate but once the man approaching me was within reach I grabbed his left hand with both of mine and wrenched his arm behind his back, pivoting him so he faced away from me and finishing the maneuver by placing him in a choke hold. The violence of my moves distracted the other three who began reaching for their guns. But it was too late. Boris had his assault rifle leveled at the leader and the unnerving sound of a round being chambered made them all freeze.

"All of you, drop your guns...on the ground," commanded Boris.

"You can't expect to get away with this!" shouted the exasperated leader. "Look around, there are dozens of vehicles passing by—all filled with citizens who see what is going on!"

"Do it!" said Boris, who moved menacingly closer to the leader.

The three did as instructed, letting the weapons they'd just drawn fall onto the dirt. I pulled the weapon of the guy I was holding from its holster and let it drop while at the same time pushing him away from me. I then turned my attention to the storage racks on the bikes—freeing my assault rife from its straps then untying my pack, as well as the one Boris had brought along. Lugging both packs, together with the assault rifle and the ammo canister, I walked over to the sedan, whose red lights continued to flash, and dumped all the gear onto the rear seat. Returning to where Boris was covering the four men, I picked up the four guns from the ground and headed back towards the sedan.

"We're going to borrow your car for a while," I said as I tossed the guns onto the back seat, slamming the door shut. "Believe me," I added as I returned and faced them, "we're both working for the same guy—your colonel. The only difference is he's commissioned us to collect a whopping pile of money from some unscrupulous countrymen of yours and not to be too concerned with the niceties of the law if that should prove necessary. So when you report to him…if you've the temerity to do so…keep in mind the fact that if you'd succeeded in placing us in custody you would have deprived him of a fortune in U.S. currency."

"Now if you'll all just step away," I said, pulling out my 38-caliber semiautomatic, my companion here will render the motorcycles inoperative."

At a nod from me Boris turned and aimed the assault rifle at our two bikes, letting off a burst that shattered them into a scattered pile of metal fragments, with the remnants of the fuel tanks spurting flames.

"You drive," I said to Boris as we backed away from the wreckage and the spot where the four men stood.

Boris nodded, keeping his weapon pointed at the men as he made his way to the driver's side door, which was still open. When he reached it he quickly slid behind the wheel and started the engine. I slammed shut the rear door on my side and jumped into the front seat on the passenger side. Boris put the car in gear and we roared off.

"Where to?" asked Boris once we'd put a few miles between the counter-intelligence agents and ourselves.

"Let's head for the safe house," I replied, "we can get the car off the streets while we wait for word from Jack and Elena."

"You don't think we've been a little rash...you know...taking the car from one of the colonel's team of agents?"

"Yeah...a little rash, I admit, but honestly, Boris, I couldn't figure any other way of getting us out of there...especially since staying with the bikes after the altercation with those guys seemed really out of the question."

"Yeah, I guess you're right, though maybe now would be a good time to switch off the flashing red pursuit lights."

"Jesus, I forgot all about them...yes, shut them off!"

"Still, I've got to believe the colonel won't be real anxious to spread the word his agents lost their vehicle," said Boris as he flicked the switch. "Chances are good he'll restrict such information to his own people and if so that'll limit the number of patrols we'll need to worry about."

"Also helps the car is in all other respects no different than any other black four-door sedan," I added.

"Yeah, except for the license plate...I suppose it's a giveaway among all law enforcement types," said Boris thoughtfully.

I nodded, then settled back as Boris drove the remaining distance to the capital.

* * *

It was half past eight in the morning by the time Boris pulled the car into the safe house garage. We spent a few minutes sorting out what gear we wanted to keep close at hand—like our packs—and stowing the rest in the trunk. The rest included the assault rifles, the agents' handguns and Boris' ammo canister. I headed for the house while Boris made sure the garage door was securely closed, as well as the main gate at the street.

Elena called at nine o'clock.

"Sorry it's so late, Church, but the guy stopped to pick up some food and other things before finally making it to the gang's location."

"You sure they're where he's at?" I asked.

"I think so. Two guys came out of the house to help him unload the truck."

"So where are you?"

"It's like you said, the place is right on the road that leads to the village…about fifteen kilometers out from the capital."

"Can you maintain surveillance without being spotted?"

"Yeah, we're parked about a hundred meters away with a clear view of the two vehicles parked out front of the place."

"We'll be there shortly."

"Bring some food…Jack's complaining of hunger."

"Will do...oh by the way, we'll be showing up in a black four-door sedan, courtesy of four counter-intelligence agents who stopped us on the way back to the capital."

"Christ! Anybody hurt?"

"Nope. But the motorcycles are history."

"Jesus, the colonel's really going to be after your ass after a stunt like that!"

"My thoughts exactly," I said, "and he'll now know there's a whole lot of U.S. cash driving the whole operation...something he may decide rightly belongs to him rather than to us or to the kidnap gang."

"Yeah, especially since you've been spreading the word he's behind all the mayhem."

"Point well taken...we'll see you soon."

I broke the connection and slipped the satphone back in my bag.

"Everything all right?" asked Boris, who'd just come into the room from the kitchen where he'd been raiding the fridge.

"Yeah, they're on stakeout, but Elena says Jack's getting hungry. You didn't happen to spot a place that serves food during your walk through the neighborhood did you?"

"There's an outfit about a block away that sells takeout...you want me to pick something up?"

"See if you can't get something that's easy to eat but filling... for all four of us...and some cold beer."

"Will do," said Boris as he headed for the front door.

While Boris was gone I tried to come up with a game plan for extracting the boy from the hands of what I'd been told was a well-disciplined and dangerous gang. According to what we'd learned it seemed likely there were five of them: a leader, the sergeant, who still went by his military rank and four from his old squad. They were hold up in a house—at least until tonight when the swap was to take place. Storming the house in broad daylight, even with four of us, would risk injuring the boy as well as making it likely some of us would end up casualties. On the other hand, counting on the kidnappers to allow Matt to go free once we'd turned over the ransom was precisely what old Kingstone didn't want to have to rely on. He simply didn't trust them and neither did I. That left only one option: to extract the boy during the swap. As I waited for Boris to return I began to flesh out a possible way that could be done.

"Got some chicken *tamales*," said Boris, holding up a paper bag as he entered the house, "and some local beer."

"Well, let's get going before they turn cold," I said, grabbing my bag containing the satphone and heading for the door leading out to the garage.

As Boris backed the car out of the garage he powered down the side window, "Maybe we should think about changing the license plate."

I was standing off to the side of the garage, waiting for him to clear it so I could put down the door. I nodded, "Good thinking… but switching plates in broad daylight without getting caught isn't easy."

"Well, we should keep it in mind…see if an opportunity presents itself," said Boris.

"Okay, I'll keep an eye out," I said as I hopped into the car after closing the driveway gate.

But no convenient set of circumstances for making the switch came to my attention during the drive out to where Elena and Jack were on stakeout.

* * *

It was approaching ten o'clock by the time we reached the location. The building was a plastered cinderblock structure in a washed-out yellowish-gold color with a broad horizontal band of burnt orange at its base. The paint exhibited extensive peeling, testifying to years of neglect. The front door was set deeply within the unpainted cinderblock threshold and had lost most of its paint—a dull forest green color, at odds with the hot, bright colors of the walls. I could see a padlock hasp securing the door had been dislodged, leaving the padlock hanging uselessly. The gang seemed to have gained entry by means of force. The green pickup Elena had tailed was parked outside, along with a nondescript four-door sedan.

We pulled up right behind Elena's SUV, climbed out and walked over. Boris was carrying the bag of *tamales* while I lugged over a carton containing bottles of the local beer.

"Just in time," said Jack, reaching for the bag Boris was holding.

"Any new developments?" I asked as I handed out the bottles of beer.

"No, there's been no activity outside the building," replied Elena, "seems they're intent on keeping a low profile until time for the swap."

"As should we," I said. "Listen, I think the best time to move will be when the swap is underway and the kid is out in the open."

"You got a plan?" asked Elena.

"Yeah, I think so," I replied, laying out the details of the extraction maneuver I'd worked out while waiting for Boris.

I let them think about the plan as we ate our food, hoping whatever flaws the plan might have would become readily evident to at least one of them. After all, they'd all had tactical police or military training and I was pretty sure even Elena had participated in comparable operations.

"The big variable is whether the exchange is to take place within walking distance of the building or somewhere requiring cars to take them there," said Jack. "Your plan needs to factor in that unknown."

I agreed, and we bounced several ideas around that might accomplish that objective. Eventually we agreed on a contingency option and settled into what was likely to be a daylong surveillance operation. We split up into two teams: Elena and I would take the first shift, using the black sedan as our stakeout vehicle, while Jack and Boris returned to the safe house in the SUV—to get some rest and freshen up. Each team would do a three-hour shift.

"Why'd you decide on keeping the sedan here and not my SUV?" asked Elena after Jack and Boris had driven off.

"I've got to think there's a higher chance of running into the colonel's agents in town than out here along a rural highway. I worried that if we used the agents' car to make the run between here and the safe house we'd increase the likelihood of being pulled over."

"You're probably right," said Elena, absentmindedly picking at the upholstery of the front seat. "By the way, William, you haven't told me much about yourself...seems only fair you'd shed a little light on the matter given your push for details of my life."

"What do you want to know?" I asked, not looking at her—still absorbed with watching for any movements of people in the immediate vicinity of the building the kidnappers had taken over.

"Other than the fact you've done a stint in the Bureau and that you've carved out a neat little niche in freelance recovery work I don't have a really good handle on what makes you tick."

"I thought we'd settled that...agreeing we're both wired to seek action and to demand a fair measure of autonomy in our dealings with the world."

"Well, that part's pretty clear...what I don't know is how that manifests itself in your day-to-day living—you got a steady girlfriend or wife, for example?"

"Neither," I admitted, "though I'm not averse to such a prospect...just doesn't seem to be in the cards...at least for now."

"Come now, a tall, big-shouldered guy like yourself can't help but attract the attention of highly eligible beauties, especially in a town like San Francisco. You telling me none put the full court press on you?"

"Okay, maybe I'm a little more inclined to push off when confronted with an intanglement than I've admitted but what man isn't at my age."

"And what age is that?"

"Christ, you don't give up! Okay, what the hell...I turned thirty-one last November."

"So we're about the same age."

"Yeah, and I don't see any wedding ring on your finger!" I said with mock indignation.

"Okay, I'll behave," she said with a smile, "but seriously, tell me a little about your life in San Francisco."

I did, telling her about my tiny apartment in the modern hi-rise overlooking the Oakland-Bay Bridge, about the sailing boat Jack and I jointly own, about my morning runs down at Crissy Field, about Chelsea, and about all the other people and venues that make the city such a special place for me. By the time I'd finished, our three-hour shift was almost over.

"That was lovely," she said, taking my hand in hers and giving it a squeeze. "It was almost like having a really successful date." She then climbed out of the car and walked a ways down the street, seemingly deep in thought.

* * *

Jack and Boris showed up at the appointed hour—fresh and clean-shaven. After a few minutes of conversation Elena and I climbed into the SUV—Elena behind the wheel—and headed for the safe house. The sky was overcast as billowing gray clouds began to assemble off to our left, promising a heavy downpour over the capital later that afternoon.

"Think the rain will complicate things?" asked Elena.

"Don't think so…the storm should just pass through…probably be dry as a bone by sunset," I said as we approached the outskirts of the capital.

We entered the safe house through the side door next to the garage.

"The boys left the place pretty ship-shape," commented Elena as she inspected the kitchen and living room.

"For your benefit I'm sure," I said with a laugh.

"Well, just as long as they spruced up the bathroom," she added, approaching the door to the bathroom somewhat apprehensively.

"Well?" I asked.

"Clean as a whistle!" she shouted. "You don't mind if I monopolize the bathroom for a bit, do you? A shower will feel real good just about now."

"No problem. I'll take one after you're done."

I settled back in one of the armchairs in the living room and closed my eyes, hoping I'd be able to get a little shuteye while Elena was otherwise occupied.

* * *

"Wake up, William," whispered Elena, who'd come out of the bathroom only to find me sound asleep.

"What…what is it?" I asked, trying to shake the sleep out and gain some clarity.

"Nothing to worry about," said Elena softly, "just thought you'd want to hit the shower now that the bathroom is free."

"Yeah, I said sleepily, putting my hands around her waist and drawing her closer. God, you smell good."

"You need to get up now," she said, offering no resistance as she slipped down on top of me.

"I know," I said softly as I brought her lips close to mine.

"What are you doing, William?" she asked tentatively, her eyes closed.

"Something I've been aching to do ever since I laid eyes on you," I said as I lifted my head up, bringing our lips together in one long passionate kiss.

I held her close, feeling the warmth of her body and slipping my hand underneath her cotton blouse to caress the exposed skin on her back.

"I'll wait for you in the bedroom," she said gently as she extricated herself from my embrace.

"I'll be quick," I said, rising from the chair and taking her once again in my arms.

We kissed again, this time at her urging.

* * *

I entered the bedroom wrapped only in a large bath towel. She lay on my bed, covered by the top sheet—with her long dark hair spread luxuriantly across the pillow. She was smiling as I leaned over and gave her a chaste but intimate kiss. As I let the towel fall to the floor she flung the sheet aside, revealing a perfectly formed figure of breathtaking beauty.

* * *

The rain began as we lay in bed—spent by the labors of love making. It was tropical in its force—coming down in a continuous sheet and punctuated by claps of thunder. We pulled the covers up, seeking the comfort they provided, and drifted off into a deep sleep.

* * *

"William, we've got to get up!" said Elena as she shook me vigorously, "It's almost time to relieve Jack and Boris."

"Okay, I'm up," I said as I swung my legs off the bed and prepared to standup.

"I'm going to take a quick shower," said Elena as she scampered out of the room, grabbing the pile of clothes she'd left on the bureau next to the door.

I dressed quickly, putting on a fresh pair of jeans, canvas shirt and my lightweight waterproof shell. I was pretty sure the storm had passed but at this time of the year another could materialize without much notice.

I drove while Elena combed her hair and put the finishing touches on her makeup. The rainstorm had indeed come to a halt, leaving the capital smelling fresh and foliage glistening with moisture. The sky had cleared, but since it was almost five o'clock the sun was relatively low on the horizon and bold shadows dominated the streets—cast by the many Spanish-styled buildings along the way.

"Are we going to talk about what just happened?" asked Elena as we turned onto the highway leading to the village of San Miguel.

"Depends."

"On what?"

"On what the issues are…from my perspective the most important issue is finding a way for us to spend some more time together."

"Well, let's stick with that issue…do you have something in mind?"

"Not yet but I'm working on it."

She gave me a smile then returned her attention to the road, trying to familiarize herself with its layout in the event the place chosen for the exchange should be along this stretch.

* * *

Boris and Jack were standing beside their car as we drove up.

"What's up?" I asked after swinging around and coming to a halt just back from where they were standing.

"One of the guys came out for a smoke about ten minutes ago…thought we should look like we've business out here in case he spots us," said Jack.

"He go back in?" I asked.

"Yeah…everything all right with you two?"

"We're ready to take over," said Elena, "and thanks for leaving the house in such great shape."

"We'll expect you back about eight o'clock," I said to Boris who'd climbed in behind the wheel of the SUV.

"Not to worry," he said with a smile, "we'll be on time."

Elena and I watched as the SUV pulled out onto the highway and picked up speed. When it was well past the gang's hideout we climbed into the black sedan and resumed the stakeout.

DAY 6 – THE EXCHANGE

EIGHT O'CLOCK CAME SURPRISINGLY swiftly. It was dark now and Elena and I could see lights on in the building under surveillance.

"Should we attempt to get closer...maybe find a window not fully covered?" asked Elena.

"I'd like to but seeing how close it is to the time for the swap I'm betting the guys inside are restless and more apt to do something unexpected like burst through the front door looking for some fresh air or just to get a smoke."

Elena nodded then pointed at a pair of headlights advancing from the direction of the capital, "I think that's them."

Sure enough, it was the SUV with Jack and Boris. They cruised quietly past the building, swung around and came to a stop behind the black sedan. I got out and walked over to them.

"Let's go over the maneuver," I said, motioning for Elena to join us at the SUV.

"Jack, you've got the cases with the ransom money. You keep them and drive the SUV to where the road to the village begins… at the outskirts of the capital. Wait there until I call you with instructions regarding the location of the swap. The rest of us will wait in the commandeered sedan…prepared to follow the gang when they make their move."

"You sure you want me to actually hand over the ransom?" asked Jack.

"Play it by ear," I replied, "if it looks like they'll get nasty if you don't move on it right away let it go, otherwise stall for time."

Jack nodded.

"Okay, we all know our respective roles so let's get positioned… this thing's going to happen real soon," I said.

Boris climbed out of the SUV after grabbing Elena's AR-15 from the backseat. He handed it to her along with a couple of extra clips he taken from the bag she'd left in the vehicle.

Jack checked his government issue nine millimeter semiautomatic then returned it to its holster on his belt. He then reached back and retrieved his AR-15, placing it in easy reach on the seat next to him. The aluminum attaché cases with the ransom were already stashed on the floor on the passenger side. Okay, I'm ready," he said.

"Good luck," I said as he backed the SUV away from the sedan and pulled out onto the highway. We watched as his tail lights disappeared into the night.

"Let's pull the car back another fifty meters," I said, opening the door of the black sedan and sliding in behind the wheel.

"Let me get our weapons out first," said Boris who approached the rear of the vehicle. "Pop the trunk lid," he shouted. With the trunk opened, he removed the two assault rifles we'd picked up from the dead security guards at the Alvarez house together with the ammo canister containing extra clips. He left behind the four handguns taken from the counter-intelligence agents since we had our own.

All right, let's go," he said as he climbed into the back seat with the weapons.

I put the car in reverse and slowly but steadily backed up, counting on the low-slung backup lights to provide sufficient illumination to ensure I didn't run into anything in the process.

I doused the lights and settled back to wait the forty minutes or so before making the call. Elena sat next to me, holding her AR-15 on her lap. No one was in the mood for conversation and time seemed to move slowly. But finally nine o'clock came around and I pulled the satphone from my bag and punched in the number.

"It's me," I said as soon as the guy with the tough-sounding voice answered the phone.

"You still got the cash?" he asked. "Seems another party's been after that ransom since we talked this time last night."

"Yeah, it's here…right beside me," I said, "so where you want to meet?"

"You coming alone?"

"That's the deal…nobody but me."

"What are you driving?"

"A tan SUV…late model."

"You armed?"

"Christ, you're as nervous as a girl on her first date. Use your imagination, I'm driving alone on a rural highway, a ton of money under my care, about to meet up with guys that are armed and not too particular about whether their behavior is lawful or not. What do you think?"

"Okay, wise guy, have it your way…but listen real good…we see any sign of a gun when the swap's going down you'll be a dead man…and the boy as well!"

"Spare me the threats and just give me the directions…can you do that, or do you need to spend a little more time trying to convince me you're a real tough *hombre*?"

"Go to hell!"

"I'm waiting."

"Take the road to the village of San Miguel, stopping when you see the white-washed concrete marker reading 'Kilometer Ten'. It'll be on the right side of the road. My men have cleared the vegetation around it so it should be easy to spot in your headlights."

"What then?"

"Douse your lights and wait…we'll give you further instructions once you've been checked out."

"And when is this thing going to happen?" I asked.

"I'll give you twenty minutes to get there…starting now. You got that?"

"Don't want to give me time to call out the cavalry, huh? That's all right…but I gotta tell you, it's a good thing I'm a fast driver."

"You'll make it or the kid dies," he said menacingly then hung up the phone.

I relayed the information by phone to Jack, cautioning him to delay moving out from his position for about ten minutes so as to give the impression he'd started from somewhere in the capital.

"Okay," I said, "we're on. They should be heading out any minute now."

Sure enough, the two vehicles parked in front of the hideout showed signs of activity: headlights came on and doors were being slammed shut. I started the engine and let it idle, waiting for them to make their move. The sedan moved out first. I couldn't see who was in it but I figured since it was the first vehicle it would be the one handling the swap. That meant the sergeant and maybe a couple of his men were in it. The pickup truck followed but at a slower speed.

"Probably trying to delay his arrival at the swap location," said Boris, reading my mind.

"That's where the boy is," said Elena.

"Yeah, I'm counting on that," I said, pulling in behind the pickup, my headlights off.

The drive to the ten-kilometer marker took just minutes, even at the slower speed of the pickup. I pulled over and stopped—close enough to monitor the action but back far enough to avoid coming to the attention of the gang. It helped the area was rural: no street or house lighting, and virtually no road traffic this time of night. I had to guess it was one reason the kidnappers chose it for the swap.

The first car had pulled over just short of the marker and three men had climbed out, leaving the headlights on. Two faded into the tree line on either side of the road. The third took a position behind the car. The pickup was parked about fifty feet back from the sedan. Nobody got out.

Right on time, Jack approached the marker, letting the SUV glide to a halt about twenty to thirty feet from the sedan. As instructed, he shut off the engine and doused the lights.

Nothing happened for about five minutes.

"Probably checking to see if any backup is on his tail...or whether there are others concealed somewhere in the SUV," whispered Boris.

Sure enough, the two men who'd taken up positions along the tree line approached the SUV cautiously, weapons at the ready. When they reached the vehicle one of the men directed a powerful flashlight beam into the vehicle, probing for any sign of someone hunkered down out of sight. Satisfied Jack was alone, they ordered him to climb out, hands over his head. I could see him shaking his head—refusing to comply with their demands.

The two men came around to the front of the SUV, gesturing with their handguns for Jack to comply with their commands. Again he shook his head while at the same time putting down his side window.

"I'll come out once you bastards step way back and lower your weapons," he shouted through the open window.

The two men turned towards the guy behind the sedan—obviously waiting for instructions. The man—whom I took to be the sergeant—stepped out from behind the vehicle and walked forward, into the glare of the headlights. As he did so he signaled for the two men to move back. They did so, reluctantly, lowering their guns at the same time.

"My men have done what you asked," said the sergeant, "so why don't you come out so we can get on with our business."

I watched as Jack slowly climbed out of the SUV, his AR-15 at the ready.

At the sight of the weapon the two men behind the sergeant quickly trained their guns on Jack—each had a large caliber semiautomatic. The sergeant did likewise, pulling his gun out from beneath his shirt.

"I told you no guns!" shouted the sergeant.

"Yeah, I know you did but until I see the boy is here and in good condition it's my job to protect the money, , ,you want to see this weapon disappear you'd better hurry and show me the boy!"

"First the money…you show me the money!" shouted the sergeant.

"No way," shouted Jack, "until I've checked out the boy you don't even get a peek at the money!"

I could tell the kidnappers were hesitant to force the issue since Jack had the advantage of a much more accurate firearm; their handguns would not be reliably accurate at the distance separating them from where he stood. If he opened up with a burst it could take down their leader.

"Okay, we show you the boy," said the sergeant, turning and motioning to someone in the pickup.

The doors to the pickup opened and two men climbed out. Then the man on the passenger side reached in and pulled out the boy. He wasn't tied up but the man held him in a tight grip as the three of them came around and stood in front of the truck's lights.

"There, you can see him…you satisfied?"

"I need to talk to him…see if he's still in good shape," said Jack.

"Let's do it," I whispered.

Boris and I opened our doors and climbed out quietly, each holding an assault rifle. Elena climbed behind the wheel and waited for us to get into position. We moved swiftly down the road towards the pickup truck. When we were near enough, I signaled Elena who started the engine and put the car in gear. She turned on both the headlights and the red flashing lights and raced forward, swinging wildly around the pickup and screeching to a halt broadside—between the pickup and the kidnapper's sedan.

As the kidnappers' attention was riveted on the sudden appearance of what looked like an official vehicle, Boris and I aimed our weapons and shot the two men standing next to Matt. Elena, hearing the gunfire, leapt out of the car and ran towards Matt just as the sergeant and his two men turned their gunfire on the now empty black sedan with flashing lights.

"I've got you, Matt," I heard her say as she grabbed his hand and urged him to hurry.

Meanwhile, Jack took cover behind the open door of the SUV and began firing at the three men whose attention had been drawn to the official car. The first burst took out the sergeant. The other two seeing their leader lying in a bloody heap on the road ran back towards their car. A second burst from Jack's AR-15 dropped the one farthest out on the road and in the full glare of the pickup's headlights. The last man made it to the non-descript sedan but before he could open the door on the driver's side a shot from Boris' assault rifle brought him down.

Jack climbed into the SUV, started it up and pulled forward with the headlights on. He stopped next to the pickup, where Elena and the boy were crouching. Elena quickly opened the door on the passenger side and pushed the boy in, then climbed in beside him.

As Boris checked each of the downed kidnappers, verifying they were dead or soon would be, I climbed into the black sedan and turned on the two-way radio linking the vehicle to military headquarters. "This is Patrol Car Thirteen reporting in," I said in Spanish. "It's been involved in a shootout at the KM 10 marker on the San Miguel highway. There are five bodies at the scene—all male. Urge immediate activation of a rapid response team." As the operator demanded to know whom he was talking with I turned off the radio and exited the car.

"Let's get out of here," I shouted.

Boris nodded, dropped the assault rifle and began to run to the SUV. I followed. We both jumped into the back seat and signaled Jack who turned the vehicle around and sped off in the direction of the capital.

"Let's hope we get off this road before the troops arrive," said Boris.

"Can't believe they'll reach the highway in the ten minutes it'll take us to disappear," said Elena. "But just in case you might want to step on it, Jack."

"Will do," said Jack as he pressed the accelerator and brought the vehicle to speeds well above what would be prudent on a road like this.

"So, how's our kidnap victim?" I asked as the vehicle bounced wildly down the highway.

"I'm all right," said Matt, who was clasped protectively by Elena.

"You see those two metal cases at your feet?" I asked him.

"Yeah, I see them," said Matt.

"Well, each one contains one million dollars in cash…that's the money your grandfather raised to get you released."

"You going to return it to him?" asked Matt.

"Absolutely," I said.

"First things first," said Elena, "we've got to get Matt to the embassy where he'll be safe.

"Why don't you and Jack drop us off at the safe house then the three of you can head for the embassy," I said.

"What about the ransom money?" asked Jack.

"We're getting ahead of ourselves," said Elena, "we'll need to secure a green light from the embassy before we drive up there… can't know whether Colonel Cruz or Captain Alvarez has caught on to the role of the embassy in this operation and set up an intercept point."

"Good thinking," I said, "why don't we all head for the safe house where Elena can make her call."

Jack nodded, keeping a tight grip on the wheel as the SUV hurtled through the darkness.

* * *

We made it to the safe house in record time. I climbed out of the vehicle and hurriedly opened the gates then ran and opened the garage door. As soon as Jack pulled the SUV into the garage I closed the door and went over to give Jack a hand carrying the two attaché cases into the house. Meanwhile, Elena ushered Matt through the side door and into the breezeway.

It was going on eleven o'clock by the time the five of us were seated comfortably in the living room, with Boris passing bottles of beer around and Matt contentedly munching a candy bar Elena had thoughtfully supplied.

"Make the call," I said to Elena.

She nodded, took out her satphone and called the embassy. At this hour only the night duty officer would be monitoring phones but she assured us the call could be routed to whoever was tasked to deal with a problem like this.

"Is that you, Thomas? This is Elena, put me in touch with the consular officer handling off-hour referrals…it's who…fine, put me in touch with him."

"Brady, it's Elena Bolinas. I've got the boy…you know, the Kingstone kid who was kidnapped about a week ago. I need you to get back to the embassy and let me know if it's okay for me to bring him in…sure, I know the duty officer will let me in…that's not the issue…the problem is I need to know whether there's a military or police cordon around the embassy intent on intercepting me and the boy. Why? Because I think certain key higher-ups in the government have gotten it in their heads they're entitled to the ransom money…thanks, Brady…call me back on the satphone—you've got my number."

"Okay, the consular officer on duty this evening will do a drive-by and let us know what he sees," said Elena, "in the meantime, young Matt here should probably get some sleep."

"I'll put him up in my room," said Jack, "come on, Matt, let's get you settled down."

Matt didn't put up any resistance. Clearly, the night's events had put a real strain on him. He got up from the couch, grinned sheepishly then quietly followed Jack down the hall leading to the bedrooms. The rest of us tried to relax as best we could.

* * *

Elena's satphone rang thirty minutes later. It was Brady. "Yeah, Brady, what's happening?"

Elena listened attentively to whatever Brady was saying, a worried look on her face. "Okay, I've got the picture…we'll stay away…but make sure you persuade the ambassador to meet us at the airport tomorrow morning…thanks." Elena hung up and looked at us. "He reports a cordon has been set up around the embassy…staffed by agents of the office of military counterintelligence, according to the officer in charge with whom he talked. They've been instructed to take into evidence any large amounts of American currency found in vehicles heading for the embassy."

"What about Matt?" I asked.

"Their orders aren't clear on that…seems they're likely to take the boy and whoever is with him into custody…as leverage should the ransom money not be found."

"Can't we just insist the money was given to the kidnappers in exchange for the boy?" asked Boris.

"That'd be hard to do seeing as we've tipped the military to the shootout on the road to San Miguel…they're not likely to believe those dead bodies are anybody but the kidnappers," I said.

"And thus the ransom money should still be in the hands of agents of the Kingstone family…who probably were responsible for the bloodshed…I get it," said Boris, "but still they don't know for sure what actually went down…maybe we can bluff it."

"It's too dangerous," said Elena. "Our best bet is to ensure Matt gets out of the country quickly…we can worry about the ransom money later."

"What's your plan?" I asked.

"Tomorrow morning Jack and I take Matt directly to the airport where Brady will have arranged for the ambassador to meet us…with a full complement of the international press in attendance. Brady will have booked Jack and the boy on a non-stop flight to the States. I'm betting Colonel Cruz won't try to stop us…at least as long as he can verify no money is being repatriated at the same time."

"How's he going to verify it?" asked Boris.

"We'll simply step away from the SUV once we've reached the airport, making it clear neither Jack nor I are carrying anything that could be suspected of containing that much cash. The colonel's agents can check out the car while we're talking with the reporters…reassuring themselves the money isn't stashed somewhere in the vehicle."

"Okay, the plan makes sense," I said, "but Elena you've got to realize Colonel Cruz is most likely going to try to take you into custody in hopes he can pressure you into revealing the location of the Kingstone ransom."

"I've thought about that…the best way to avoid him will be to catch a ride back to the embassy with the ambassador…you know, let someone from the embassy drive the SUV back."

"You can't stay in the embassy forever," I said, "what'll you do to protect yourself in the days ahead?"

"I'll phone the colonel and give him what he wants…you and Boris."

"What the hell?" exclaimed Boris.

"Hear me out," said Elena, "the colonel already knows he's dealing with two unidentified guys who've been pretending to work for him and who've been linked to multiple homicides and a host of other crimes. I'll simply report it was these guys who turned Matt over to Jack and myself, and when I asked them to turn over the ransom money they protested…saying they didn't take down the kidnappers just for fun…they feel entitled to keep the money for themselves."

"That'll work," I said, "especially since they'll have connected us to the killings by the presence of the commandeered agent's car at the crime scene."

"That means we'll have to somehow manage to take the ransom money out of the country ourselves," said Boris.

"Yeah, and get ourselves out while we're at it," I added.

"Well, let's get some rest…tomorrow's a busy day," said Elena.

"You take my bed," I said, "I've got a couple of phone calls to make…once I'm done I'll crash on the couch."

"You sure?" she asked.

"Yeah, I'm sure."

"What about Jack?" asked Elena.

"I'll hang out with Church," said Jack who'd settled comfortably into one of the easy chairs next to the couch.

Once Elena and Boris had disappeared into the bedrooms, I pulled out my satphone and pressed the quick dial for the Kingstone residence.

"You going to give them the good news?" asked Jack.

"Yeah, haven't wanted to call them until the thing was done… they're probably pretty stressed out by now."

"Yes, Jackson? It's Church. Is the family still up? Okay, could you bring him to the phone…Mr. Richmond it's Church…just wanted to give you the good news…we've rescued Matt. Yes, your son is in good health…a little shaken up by all the excitement but otherwise unscathed. You'd like to talk to him? I can understand that…but listen Matt's sound asleep…should I wake him up? Okay, I'll let him sleep…you know, he's got a busy day tomorrow…meets up with the U.S. Ambassador and a whole bunch of reporters then takes an early flight to the States in the company of Agent Barker. Yes, Agent Barker will accompany him all the way back to San Francisco and will personally escort him to the Kingstone residence where I imagine you and the rest of the family will be standing by. He's on his way to the phone? Well, put him on."

A lengthy paused ensued. I could here Jackson talking with someone in the room. Then a voice came on the phone.

"Church, it's Kingstone, Henry filled me in…just wanted to tell you how grateful I am you've accomplished this difficult and dangerous task."

"We're pleased it turned out well, Mr. Kingstone, and I'm also happy to report the ransom money is still in our possession."

"Splendid! Will Jack be bringing it back…along with Matt?"

"No, there's been a complication…a powerful man in the military has persuaded himself he's entitled to the money…and unfortunately he's got sufficient influence to arrange its seizure should Jack show up at the airport with it."

"So what do you plan to do?"

"I'll figure out something…the problem just came to light within the last hour."

"Well, do take care of yourself…again, I'm awfully grateful for everything you've done."

"Thank you, Mr. Kingstone, I'll get back to you once I've worked out a way to return the money."

"Yes, please do…good bye."

He hung up. After a moment of indecision I dialed a second number.

"Dora, it's Church."

"William, are you all right?"

"Yes, I'm all right…and I'm sorry to call so late but I've got to ask a big favor of you."

"It's okay, William, I wasn't asleep…what is it you need?"

"Before I get to that let me reassure you I've been able to effect a rescue of the kidnapped boy. He's scheduled to leave the country tomorrow morning…the press will be in attendance so you should see something of the departure on television and in the papers."

"That's wonderful news, William, will you be flying out with him?"

"No, for two reasons…and that's why I need your help… first, since I entered the country illegally I'll need to leave it in a similar fashion and second, there are powerful men high up in the country's security forces who are bound and determined to seize the ransom money before it can be repatriated."

"You mean you didn't have to give the money to the kidnappers?"

"No, and the prospect of gaining possession of two million dollars in cash has wet the appetites of two powerful men: Colonel Felipe Cruz of the military's counterintelligence agency, and a captain in the national police based in El Monte—Captain Alvarez."

"So how can I help you?"

"You once mentioned the valuable work of an Italian archaeologist who's conducting a site survey in the border region."

"Yes, Professor Carlo Sassari, how is that relevant?"

"Is he currently in the field?"

"Yes, I talked with him just yesterday…he's planning on bringing a shipment of artifacts to the institute on his next visit."

"You also mentioned his preference for flying his own plane when commuting to the capital from his base of operations, and for aerial reconnaissance prior to land-based traverses."

"Yes…but I'm still not getting the connection."

"Does he ever make long distance flights?"

"I suppose so…though I'm not sure what you mean by 'long distance'."

"What I'm driving at, Dora, is approaching Professor Sassari with a proposal: in exchange for him piloting myself and another American to Grand Cayman Island I'd donate ten thousand dollars in cash towards his field expenses."

"Ah, now I understand," said Dora. "You want me to get in touch with him and sound him out."

"Yes, and also urge him to schedule his trip to the capital as soon as possible."

"Shall I have him call you…that is if he's interested?"

"Yes, I'm sure he'll be curious…especially since what I'm asking could get him into all sorts of trouble with the authorities."

"Are you safe where you are now, William?"

"I believe so…but given the heightened interest of the security services in getting their hands on the money I can't be confident our whereabouts won't be discovered soon."

"Okay, I'll make the call. If you don't hear back from me it means Professor Sassari is willing to consider the proposal and will call you back himself."

"Got it. I have to say, Dora, you're a real angel."

"Just to satisfy my own curiosity, William, did you have to resort to bloodshed to effect the release of the boy?"

"Best for you not to know any details, Dora, although I suppose you might read some typically sensationalist stories in the press in the next day or so that point the finger at a couple of unidentified *gringos*."

"I understand...still, I probably should alert Professor Sassari to the possibility he'd be dealing with a fugitive wanted for something a little more serious than illegal entry and attempting to smuggle legitimate cash out of the country."

"Probably a good idea...let him know the full import of what he's being asked to do."

"Well, I'll call him right away...and ask him to contact you this evening if he's interested."

"Thanks, Dora, I'd appreciate it."

As I hung up I could see Jack had been attentively listening in to my side of the conversation.

"Clever," he said. "You think he'll go for it?"

"My experience with Italian archaeologists is they've got a real taste for adventure...I'm hoping this guy is no exception."

* * *

It was just before midnight when a call came through to my satphone. It was the professor.

"Carlo Sassari here, am I talking with William Church?"

"Yes, this is Church...Dora fill you in?"

"Yes, but I'd like you to go over it in detail...not just your need for a lift to Grand Cayman but what's led up to it."

"I trust what I tell you will go no further...even if you choose not to become involved."

"You have my word."

I gave him a blow-by-blow account of the sequence of events, starting with our illegal entry by boat and including our efforts at locating the kidnappers. I finished up with a brief account of the shootings that took place in connection with our rescue of the boy and the fact both a captain in the national police and a colonel in the military are out to grab the two million dollar ransom for themselves.

"You say the FBI is fully aware of your actions and has in fact participated in some of the incidents?"

"That's correct. The boy will be escorted out of the country tomorrow morning by a Special Agent of the FBI who happens to be sitting next to me as we speak."

"So from the standpoint of your country nothing you or your associate have done would be regarded as criminal…given the circumstances."

"Yes, and once we're outside this country's jurisdiction whatever charges certain individuals in the security services might wish to press would not hold up to scrutiny given the criminal actions of the purported victims."

"But since you've taken pains to conceal you identity and that of your associate I take it no charges could actually be filed…assuming of course you don't fall into the hands of your adversaries."

"You've summed up the situation with enviable clarity. Are you interested?"

"Yes, very much."

"When can you make it to the capital?"

"I'll fly in tomorrow morning…can you get to the airport's general aviation terminal by ten o'clock? I'd make it earlier but I've got to get a load of artifacts down to the Archaeological Institute and pick up a few things at local shops before starting back."

"Yes, we can be there by that hour."

"Oh, and I assume you know I can't have any unlawful firearms on the craft."

"I understand...the only firearm will be my handgun...which I'm duly licensed to carry under Interpol regulations."

"Very well, then I'll see the two of you tomorrow morning."

And with that he signed off.

"He seemed pretty eager to get involved," said Jack who'd been listening, "especially after reassuring himself you and Boris aren't some international criminals."

"As I said, Italian archaeologists are an adventuresome breed."

"And I gather he didn't even raise the issue of the donation."

"No, and that's rather surprising. I can only guess the amount I've offered is generous in comparison to the modest size of his fieldwork budget."

"How are you going to pay him?" asked Jack.

"I'll take one of those ten thousand dollar packets of one hundred dollar bills out of one of the attaché cases."

"Shouldn't you get Kingstone's authorization?"

"Ideally, but I'll take responsibility...if he objects I'll tell him to deduct it from what he owes me."

"Can't imagine he'll object," said Jack, "with the most likely alternative means of leaving the country posing a far greater risk of the entire ransom falling into the hands of the good colonel."

"I may call upon you to repeat that assessment should old Kingstone put up a fuss."

"You can count on it, buddy, but seeing there's nothing more we can do tonight why don't we try and get some sleep."

"A good call...until the morning then," I said as I turned off the light of the table lamp next to the couch and pulled the blanket Elena had left there up over my stretched-out frame.

DAY 7

Morning came around eight o'clock when Boris returned from a neighborhood cantina with a cardboard tray filled with fresh *tamales de elote* and a large container of coffee. "Didn't want us to encourage Church's new-found enthusiasm for kitchen duty," he said as he set the food on the table.

I rolled my eyes but eagerly snatched up a *tamale* as did the others.

Matt seemed more the spunky eleven-year-old boy after a night's rest and joined in the friendly ribbing at my expense. The nightmare of last night's shootings seemed not to have affected him, at least that was the impression he gave. I could only hope all the experiences of the past week would remain equally manageable once he returned to the States.

A phone call from the embassy interrupted the morning chatter at the dining room table. It was for Elena.

"Yeah Brady, what's up...okay, we can manage that...see you at nine."

She put down the satphone and looked at all of us. "The meet at the airport is set for nine o'clock. The ambassador and the press will be stationed off to one side of the departures section... we're supposed to pull up right in front of that section and allow ourselves to be escorted into the building by embassy personnel... no hesitation."

"Any word on what we can expect from the colonel's men?" asked Jack.

"Nothing solid...just that they'll try to capitalize on any sign of confusion or indecision on our part...part of the reason the embassy wants to control our movements."

"When's the flight?" asked Jack.

"An hour later...should give us time for a brief press conference and still get you and Matt through security and safely into the departure lounge in time for boarding."

"But I don't have a passport," said Matt, "or any kind of identification...will they let me leave?"

"The embassy's prepared a duplicate passport for you, Matt," said Elena, "no need to worry."

"Okay, Matt, let's get you polished up real good," said Jack, taking Matt by the arm and ushering him out the room, "don't want your parents seeing a scruffy image of you plastered all over the newspapers and video screens."

While Jack supervised Matt's appearance and gathered together his own luggage I pulled Elena to one side.

"I think Boris and I have a way to get to Grand Cayman."

"When did that possibility present itself?" she asked, revealing genuine surprise.

"A friend of mine put me in contact with an Italian archaeologist who's got a private plane. He's agreed to fly us out of San Rafael at ten o'clock this morning."

"How's he going to clear it with the authorities…Christ, every departure from the airport requires approved flight plans…when they see he's heading out of the country with two *gringo* passengers all sorts of alarm bells are going to start ringing!"

"That's the beauty of it…he'll be filing a flight plan to his base camp location…a small village in the border region called Santa Clara…the authorities will justifiably regard his two passengers as fellow archaeologists on a site visit…and their metal attaché cases as containing special analytical instruments."

"Okay, I can see how that might get you out of the capital but how does it get you to Grand Cayman…are you going to cross the border and attempt to fly out from the adjacent country?"

"No, the archaeologist will fly us out to the island from his base camp location…that way no flight plan needs to be filled out and no surveillance on the part of the government is possible."

"They'll see the plane on radar, Church, and scramble a couple of jets fighters to force him to land."

"No way, Elena, there are hundreds of privately-owned aircraft that run quick flights between rural airstrips—not only within the country but into neighboring countries and even to nearby islands in the Caribbean. No, what the authorities are worried about, and what they try to interdict, are airplanes attempting unauthorized entry into the country—like smugglers of illicit narcotics or illegal immigrants."

Elena nodded, beginning to see the logic of the plan.

"Still, there's a hitch," I said, "we'll certainly run into questions from the authorities on Grand Cayman if we try to board a commercial jet to the States carrying all that money."

"I can see that," she said.

"So, what I'm thinking is for you to fly to Grand Cayman and meet up with us...use your formidable influence with the American consulate on the island to smooth the way...you know, having them declare us to be duly authorized couriers...that sort of thing."

"Let me think about it, William," said Elena, "I'll call you later today...once Jack and the boy are airborne and I've had a chance to smooth things over with Colonel Cruz...it'll also give me time to have a word with the ambassador about putting a call through to the U.S. Consul General on the island."

"Okay, we'll leave it open...as a possibility...but perhaps I can come up with an added inducement."

"Like what?" she asked.

"I'll tell you when you call back...still need to put a few things in motion first."

"Being mysterious, huh?"

"Perhaps a little...but for a very good cause...as you'll soon see."

She just shook her head and got busy pulling her gear together. Boris, who'd been sitting at the table watching us, smiled.

By quarter of nine the three of them were ready to leave. Elena was in the driver's seat, Jack next to her, and young Matt in the back. Boris and I handled the garage door and the driveway gate as Elena backed out. She gave us a smile and a little wave as she took off down the street.

Boris and I headed back to the house; once inside I pulled out my satphone and put a call through to Chelsea.

"Hey, Chelsea, Church here, need to have you handle some logistics."

"Whoa…fill me in first…where are you and what's happening… did the rescue take place?"

"Yeah, the boy's just about to catch a plane for the States…in the company of Jack."

"Won't you be on it?"

"Hardly, Chelsea, you'll remember Boris and I came into the country in a rather unconventional manner…we'll need to leave in a similarly stealthy fashion."

"But you're all right…no bullet holes or anything like that?"

"We're all fine, Chelsea, including the boy, now about that task I need you to handle."

"Okay, what's up?"

I told her what I had in mind. She took notes and said she'd get right on it.

"Let me know what you've worked out as soon as you can," I said just before breaking the connection.

"You've really got a thing for Special Agent Bolinas, don't you?" said Boris who'd been listening.

"Well, let's just say she's one in a million and anyway I promised her I'd think of a way for us to spend some quality time together.

* * *

We were in luck, most security personnel were concentrated around the departure section of the main terminal as our cab approached the kiosk handling access to the general aviation area of the airport—a consequence no doubt of the commotion arising from the highly public send-off given to Matt. Still, the cab was instructed to come to a halt. A uniformed agent stepped out of the kiosk, a clipboard in hand, and approached the vehicle.

"We're here to deliver some archaeological equipment to Professor Sassari...is he here yet?" I asked in Spanish, trying to convey a sense of urgency.

"Came in about twenty minutes ago, you'll have to hurry...he mentioned he'd be taking off right away."

"Christ, I hope we're in time...he said he really needs the equipment for the next phase of the survey...you know about his work don't you?"

"Yeah, we all do...he talks a lot about it...a strange guy."

"Could you call ahead and let him know we're on our way?"

"Can't contact him directly but I could let the traffic controller's office know to delay his take off until you've reached him."

"That would be great! How far is it to where his plane is parked?"

"Not far...just take this road until you see the main entrance to the general aviation section...there'll be a sign. Once past the gate turn left and swing by Hangar B. His plane should be parked just out from the hangar."

"Many thanks…what's your name by the way…Professor Sassari will want to know who it was who expedited our arrival."

"Just tell him it was Agent Mendocino…the guy with all the Pavarotti records…he'll know who it is."

"Will do…drive on cabbie!" I said, waving a thank you to the agent as the cab took off down the road.

"Nice piece of misdirection," said Boris under his breath.

"Didn't want to give him a chance to demand to see our papers…but he'll have a lot of explaining to do when the cab comes back empty."

"Probably should pay the cabbie to remain out here until he sees our plane has taken off," said Boris.

"Yeah, and instruct him to inform Agent Mendocino the professor requested we accompany him to the survey camp to demonstrate the proper use of the new equipment," I added.

"That should work…gives Mendocino a plausible explanation for our disappearance," said Boris.

"Now, let's hope the professor agrees to take us with him," I said as the cab passed through the gate and headed for Hangar B.

* * *

Dr. Sassari was standing by the open door on the co-pilot's side looking expectantly in our direction as we drove up. I stepped out of the cab and went over to him as Boris settled with the driver.

"Dr. Sassari, I'm William Church and my companion over there is Boris. I hope you haven't changed your mind about giving us a lift."

"Please call me Carlo," said the professor as he shook my hand. He was an athletically built man about my age with a head full of curly dark hair and an engaging smile. I took to him immediately. "No, the flight's still on…any trouble getting through security?"

"We were able to secure the cooperation of Agent Mendocino and passed through without having our identity papers examined. His records will show we're two men bent on delivering analytical equipment for your archaeological survey. We've arranged for the cabbie to report you insisted on having us accompany the equipment so we can show you how it should be operated…a spur of the moment kind of thing."

"Perfect…that'll resolve the question of why my flight plan doesn't make any reference to two passengers. Chances are the flight controllers in the tower won't notice your presence…keeping the whole issue thoroughly ambiguous. With any luck no one will pursue the matter."

"You must be Dr. Sassari," said Boris coming up to where we were standing.

"Please to meet you, Boris…and do call me Carlo…under the circumstances I think a little informality is called for."

"Very well," said Boris shaking his hand, "where do you want me to stow our gear?"

"There's a stowage compartment over there," said Carlo, pointing. "It'll hold all your gear…including the two aluminum cases."

Boris opened the cargo hatch and carefully rearranged the items Sassari had already stored there—making room for our gear. He then placed the attaché cases inside, making sure to surround them with the soft luggage he and I were carrying. While Boris was busy handling that task I took the opportunity to examine the airplane more carefully. It was a common enough craft: a fixed-wing four-seater with a single engine and a tricycle landing gear. It looked to be in good shape.

"Let's get moving," said Sassari once he checked to see Boris had secured the cargo hatch correctly. He climbed on to the wing and stepped into the cockpit through the open door. Boris followed, placing his large frame into the seat behind the pilot's. Finally, I climbed gingerly into the co-pilot's seat and closed the door. Sassari started up the engine and began going through his preflight check. He spoke quietly into the mike, listened for a reply then gave thumbs up.

"We've got clearance for take off," he shouted as he released the brakes and began taxiing towards the end of the runway.

We lifted off into a clear blue sky, rising rapidly to avoid the higher elevations of nearby hills. Once Carlo reached cruising speed and we'd leveled off I threw some questions at him.

"Carlo, you sure this plane can make it all the way to the islands?"

"Not to worry, it's got a range of some six hundred and fifty nautical miles…enough to get to Grand Cayman from most locations in Central America."

"So how many hours of flight time are we talking about?"

"Figure it out for yourself, it cruises at a little less than one hundred and fifty miles an hour…so depending on the precise distance between the point of departure and one's destination it could be anywhere from under an hour to something just short of five hours of flying time."

"And in our case?"

"I haven't worked out the flight plan yet so I can't give you a precise estimate but it'll certainly be well within the plane's cruising range and thus within the time frame that goes with it."

"So if we lift off early in the morning we should arrive at Grand Cayman Island no later than noon that same day?"

"I'd say that'd be a reasonable assumption…why…is it important?"

"I'm trying to work out the schedule of a colleague who's supposed to meet up with Boris and myself."

"If the person plans an arrival at one o'clock on that day I've no doubt you'd be there to welcome him."

"It's a woman friend, actually," interjected Boris from the back seat.

"Ah, the importance of scheduling becomes clearer…one wouldn't want to have a young lady arrive at the airport without some assurance someone would be there to greet her," said Carlo with a knowing smile.

"When do you expect we'll arrive at your camp?" I asked.

"Actually, our arrival will be delayed somewhat since I thought you'd enjoy a flyover of the survey area…get a feeling for the project I've been working on these past several years."

"How many more seasons of fieldwork are you planning on?"

"Actually, this is my last. Come next year I hope to be working the region from the other side of the border. We've documented over a hundred new sites and have conducted exploratory excavations at about three-dozen. But sites attributable to this ancient culture are believed to extend well beyond the border."

"Can't you simply operate out of your existing base, crossing the border as needed?" I asked.

"Theoretically, yes, but for political reasons it makes a lot more sense to set up camp in the new country and employ nationals from that country to help with the survey."

I nodded, then seeing our conversation had come to an end I settled back and directed my attention to the spectacular landscapes below.

* * *

The village of Santa Clara, where Carlo had his base of operations, was a poor farming community of perhaps twenty households scattered about and connected by dirt paths. The airstrip was an improvised one, relying on livestock to keep vegetation short. The landing was bumpy, and despite the grazing efforts of livestock a cloud of shredded vegetation and dust could be seen trailing behind us as we advanced down the runway. An expedition vehicle driven by one of Carlo's students transported us the short distance separating the airstrip from the village. The student pulled up in front of the only cinderblock building in sight—a single-story rectangular structure I was soon to learn was divided into three sparsely furnished sections: a sleeping/lounging area, a kitchen/dining area, and an area devoted to the processing of artifacts recovered during survey. We stepped out of the vehicle and followed Carlo into the building.

"I'm afraid you'll find the facilities somewhat primitive," said Carlo, "but it's all I can offer."

"They'll be fine," I said, as I studied the layout.

"You can put your luggage here," he said as he guided us into the sleeping area and pointed to two metal-framed beds each with a thin mattress and a neat pile of linens stacked on the pillow. "They're not in use right now…the students assigned to them have already gone back to the Italy."

"I'm anxious to see the lab operation," I said, dumping my bags on one of the beds, "did a bit of survey work on Sardinia some years back."

"That so," said Carlo, "you studied archaeology then?"

"As a graduate student…part of my coursework in a joint archaeology/art history program."

"How'd it lead to fieldwork on Sardinia?"

"The usual way…one of my professors was running a dig in the west-central piedmont area of the island…near the town of Macomer…asked me to come along."

"Strange, though I've a family surname linked to the island I've never been there," said Carlo.

"Are your paternal ancestors Sards?" I asked.

"If they are it goes way back…no living relative owns up to having a connection with the island."

Boris, an attaché case in each hand, followed Carlo and myself out to the lab section of the building where a half-dozen students were standing around a long rectangular table sorting pottery sherds and stone artifacts into discreet piles in preparation for cataloging.

"Only a small fraction of the artifacts we've collected are still here," said Carlo as we walked around the table, "the bulk of our finds have already been taken to the institute in San Rafael."

I came alongside one of the students and watched intently as he handled a sherd, carefully examining its paste, color, surface finish and decorative treatment before assigning it to one of the piles before him on the table. I nodded appreciatively then joined Carlo and Boris as they headed for the main entrance.

"Let me show you the village," said Carlo once we stepped outside, "it'll be a while before lunch is laid out and I suspect you both would appreciate an opportunity to stretch your legs after the flight in that crammed little airplane."

* * *

It was early afternoon before Chelsea got back to me. Boris and I had just returned from accompanying Carlo on a visit to one of the newly discovered sites located within easy walking distance of the camp where local villagers employed by him were carefully excavating a test trench under the watchful eye of one of his students.

"Yeah, Chelsea, what were you able to arrange?"

"Locked in a bareboat charter from a local guy…it's a thirty-six foot sloop with retractable sails and all the amenities…he says you can have it for a week."

"And provisioning?"

"Made contact with a provisioning outfit…very upscale… they'll stock the vessel with a week's worth of food and liquor. The owner knows the outfit and promises to give them access to the boat…thinks they'll have it ready for you by first thing tomorrow morning."

"Where's it docked?"

"Alongside the quay at a boat repair facility on the North Sound…not far from the airport."

She gave me directions to the place and also the guy's phone number so I could schedule a walk-through before taking possession of the charter.

"Everything looks perfect, Chelsea, you've outdone yourself once again."

"Thanks, Church, but let's get down to the real business… who's the gal?"

"I told you…she's an FBI agent stationed in country who's been working with us."

"Yeah, I know that, what I don't know is what she looks like and where this thing's headed."

"She's of Cuban descent and gorgeous…handles herself well in tense situations and seems to share a similar approach to dealing with the world."

"That mean the two of you have a special kind of rapport?"

"I guess you could say that."

"So where's this thing going…you're not going to make a bid for her hand are you?"

"Not quite," I said, laughing. "It's just a chance for us to be together in a less professional setting—one that doesn't require assault rifles, tactical maneuvers and bloodshed."

"You sure about that?"

"Yeah, I'm sure…what I'm not sure about is whether she'll go along with the plan."

"You haven't asked her?"

"Just a few hints…thought I'd spring it on her when she calls later this afternoon."

"God, you guys are too much."

"Enough with the sarcasm, so what did you put together for Boris?"

"He's booked on a three o'clock flight to Miami…thought that would give your girlfriend enough time to square it with the Cayman Island authorities…you know,…him carrying all that money."

"Perfect! So give the Kingstone family a ring and let them know they can expect Boris to return the ransom late tomorrow evening."

"Will do…should I also call Boris' wife…let her know?"

"No, he'll handle that once we've arrived in George Town."

"Okay, just give me a call once you've worked out your schedule for returning to San Francisco…I'll have someone give your condo a dusting."

"You're an angel…talk to you soon."

And with that I severed our connection and put the satphone back in his pocket.

* * *

Elena called two hours later. "Are you all right?" she asked.

"Yeah, why do you ask?"

"Well, it's just a feeling I have that something isn't quite right."

"Can you spell it out for me?" I asked.

"It's the phone conversation I had with Colonel Cruz just moments ago...I explained to him how the two men who delivered the boy to me were the ones who claimed to have the Kingstone ransom and were bound and determined to hold on to it. The strange thing was he didn't even question me about it...made no attempt to check for inconsistencies in what I'd told him or threaten to raise hell if what I said proved to be incorrect. It was as if he already knew how to recover the ransom money and to apprehend the two men involved."

"He might have been fed a line by one of his own men or by Captain Alvarez...I wouldn't worry about it."

"But what if he knows where you and Boris are?"

"That's always a possibility...someone at the general aviation section of the airport might have been troubled by the unscheduled transport of two unidentified men by Dr. Sassari...I'll talk to Boris about it and see whether he thinks it might be wise for us to take evasive action here just in case."

"Can't you leave for Grand Cayman right away?"

"Dr. Sassari doesn't want to make the flight at night...too much chance the authorities will be suspicious...locals don't fly at night."

"Okay, but do take my concern seriously."

"I will, don't worry...anyway, how did it go at the airport?"

"No problems…the impromptu press conference kept the authorities at bay and provided Jack and the boy VIP attention… they boarded on time and took off on schedule."

"And you?"

"The ambassador was very gallant…wouldn't let me out of his sight and made sure I was surrounded by a handful of marines in civies so no one would attempt a snatch. It was the marines who drove my car back to the embassy."

"Anything new on the Grand Cayman end?" I asked.

"It seems the state department rep on the island is under the jurisdiction of the ambassador in Kingston, Jamaica, who in turn is a personal friend of the ambassador. He agreed to arrange for the attaché cases to be officially sealed for courier transport. What time is your flight tomorrow?"

"Three o'clock, but only Boris will be on it…carrying the money."

"What about you?"

"I'm hoping you'll agree to take a week off and join me on a cruise."

"What…are you crazy?"

"Here me out, Elena…there's no reason why both Boris and I need to accompany the ransom money…he's more than qualified to ensure no one takes it. And you'll recall I promised to find a way for the two of us to spend some personal time together."

"But, William, getting leave authorized requires enough lead time for the request to make its way through the administrative bureaucracy of the agency. And, anyhow, I've got to prepare an after action report on this whole matter…my boss wants it ASAP."

"All you need to tell him is your trip to Grand Cayman involves not only securing courier status for Boris but also the exhaustive debriefing of William Church."

"But a week's worth? Give me a break, William, he'll smell something fishy if I indicate I need a whole week on a romantic island to have you corroborate my information."

"Okay, you're right, you'll need to suggest something else… maybe that you're stressed out after all the action and would like a few days above and beyond the debriefing to relax and recharge. But the details of what you come up with aren't important, what's important is whether the idea of a week on the Caribbean in a thirty-six foot sloop with me at the helm is something you're up for?"

She didn't reply right away but I could hear her breathing. I didn't prompt her—just let the whole thing settle in. Eventually she spoke.

"I'm sorry, William, for giving you the impression I wasn't interested. I am. You're very sweet to have taken the trouble to arrange such a nice way for us to be together and I assure you I'll be there…with or without my boss's blessing. So what time do you want me to arrive?"

"Sometime after one o'clock would be best, but anytime will do…and Elena, thanks. You've no idea how much I'm looking forward to our time together."

"Just make sure you get out of the country safely, William… you hear?"

"I hear…until tomorrow then."

I hung up the satphone and walked over to Boris who was sitting in the lab. The students were getting cleaned up after their day of field and lab work and were all in the sleeping/lounge area taking showers or relaxing with a beer. Carlo was among them so the lab was quiet. I brought Boris up to speed on what Elena had said—especially regarding the peculiar reaction of the colonel to her attempt at convincing him neither the embassy nor any of its personnel had the Kingstone ransom.

"What do you think?" I asked.

"I think he's on to us," said Boris.

"If so, how's he going to work the take down?"

"I'd guess he'll deploy with helicopters," said Boris, "maybe a dozen or so agents in a couple of recon choppers. He'll land them in such a way as to block any movement on the part of Carlo's plane and then approach the expedition building in force... probably once it's dark."

"Let's say you're right...that would give us maybe two hours or so to take evasive action," I said.

"We'd better get Carlo and his students out of here...don't want them to be involved," said Boris.

'Let me get him," I said as I headed for the lounge area.

Carlo was in the lounge chatting with a couple of the students when I came in. I motioned for him to join me in the other room. When he came in Boris and I ushered him out of the building.

"What's up?" he asked.

"There's a chance Colonel Cruz and his men have figured out we're here and plan an assault on the camp at anytime," I said.

"Jesus, what the hell should we do?"

"You've got to get yourself and your students out of here before they come. They won't believe you don't know who we are and where we're hiding and will lean on you pretty heavily until you tell them what they want to know."

"What about you two?"

"We can hoof it…along with the students…with you flying the plane out…hopefully to a landing the other side of the border that's close enough for us to meet up."

"Yes, that's possible…but better yet I'll have the students head for the capital in expedition vehicles. They can transport the remaining specimens to the institute and arrange for the equipment to be air freighted out then fly out themselves."

"Won't the authorities detain them?" I asked.

"I don't think so…they'll have left the camp before the military arrives and can honestly say they have no idea where we are or who the two strangers are."

"Well, you'd better get to it right away…how can we help?"

There were a total of eight students still in camp and Carlo got them to quickly pack their gear. Meanwhile, Boris and I loaded the two expedition vehicles with bags of artifacts and whatever equipment Carlo identified as in need of shipment. The village women charged with preparing camp meals were asked to put together something for the students to eat while they were on the road. In less than an hour the students were all packed and the vehicles were loaded. I watched as Carlo talked quietly with the students then patted one of the older ones on the back and waved them off. The vehicles took off down the dirt path leading away from the village. Once they were out of sight I came up to Carlo and asked him what he said to them in the way of an explanation.

"Just that some alleged irregularities in how we were handling the specimens was causing the authorities some concern, especially with the unauthorized arrival of two strangers, so our operation was to be shut down immediately. I told the students I was ordered to remain behind along with the two strangers to answer questions and that we would be permitted to fly out once the official visit was over."

"They buy it?"

"I think so…they've all been in Central America long enough to know things like this aren't uncommon…that local authorities can often be unpredictable."

"I sure hate like hell for you and your students to get involved like this…what's it going to do to your project?"

"Don't worry, Church, it'll be all right…we were just finishing up… as long as I can get the project field records and maps out the season's not a bust."

"Well, let us help you load the plane," I said.

He nodded, then led us into the lab and pointed to the shelving where a number of cardboard boxes full of field notes were stashed. Boris and I started carrying them out to the plane. Carlo went over to a rack holding long cardboard tubes, each containing numerous site plans, architectural drawings and topographic maps. He gathered up an armful and carried them out. It took us a good hour to load all the field records and our own gear. While we were working a number of the villagers began to assemble, clearly puzzled by the frantic activity.

"I'm going to have to explain," said Carlo.

"Make it fast," I said, "it's getting dangerously close to sunset."

"I've also got to pay some of them," he added as he retrieved a briefcase from the cabin of the plane and began rummaging through it.

Once the villagers saw those entitled to pay were receiving it the women handling cooking for the project showed up with a basket of freshly prepared food. I stepped up and took the basket, thanking them and expressing a wish I would be able to visit the village again some time.

I could see Boris was getting concerned but there wasn't anything any of us could do except hope the colonel and his men wouldn't show up early.

* * *

Finally, Carlo finished paying off the workers and climbed into the plane. Boris and I followed suit. As Carlo was going through the preflight checklist and allowing the engine to warm up I noticed the villagers were pointing to something in the sky. I opened the door and looked out, trying to see what it was that was attracting so much attention. I couldn't see anything but when Carlo let the engine fall back to an idle I could detect the familiar throb of helicopter rotors.

"They're here!" I shouted, closing the door and locking it.

"Who?" asked Carlo.

"The colonel and his men," I replied. "You're going to have to get this craft off the ground in a hurry or we're in trouble."

Carlo released the brakes, hit the throttle and turned the plane in the direction of the far end of the airstrip. The choppers were still beyond the tree line and hadn't yet spotted our plane. We taxied at a reckless speed, bumping and swerving as the small tires of the landing gear hit agricultural furrows and vehicle ruts. By the time the first chopper cleared the tree line Carlo had reached the end of the runway and was turning into the wind.

"He's landing next to the crowd of villagers," I shouted.

"I don't think they've spotted the plane yet," said Boris.

With the first chopper almost on the ground, Carlo revved the engine and took off down the airstrip. The second chopper spotted us immediately and began to descend directly into our path.

"He's going to try and stop us!" shouted Carlo as he gripped the controls ever more tightly, hoping to keep the plane stable as it raced down the strip.

"It's time for us to play a little chicken," I said, "don't let him spook you, Carlo, keep your run going."

The chopper hovered about twenty or thirty feet above the ground with a man holding an assault rifle at the opening in the cockpit. All of a sudden there was a burst of gunfire from the guy riding shotgun but no evidence we were hit.

"He's just put one over our bow," shouted Boris, "the next burst will take us out."

"Christ, what am I to do!" shouted Carlo as we came ever closer to the chopper.

"Call his bluff," I shouted, "no way they're going to risk destroying the craft and all the ransom money it contains!"

We all held our breath as the airplane raced past the copter and approached lift off speed. Finally lift off. And as Carlo banked in the direction of the border I looked back and saw the copter tailing us.

"Can he keep up?" I asked Boris.

"Not once we've reached cruising speed…but well before then I suspect we'll have crossed the border."

"Is he shooting at us?" asked Carlo.

"Doesn't look like it," I said, "I think he's intent on following us to see where we put down."

"I'm thinking he's read our minds and knows we're aiming for a landing strip just the other side of the border," said Boris.

"Well, Carlo, I know you think it unwise to fly after dark but I'm guessing we'll be a whole lot safer heading out over the Caribbean than hunkering down on some isolated airstrip where the colonel and his men can continue their pursuit."

"They won't cross the border…will they?" asked Carlo.

"Yeah, they will…who's to stop them…you seen any effective border security on the other side during the weeks you've been out on survey? I asked.

"No…you're right," said Carlo as he checked his fuel gage.

"And two million dollars is a hell of an incentive to risk a diplomatic flare up," said Boris.

"Okay, I'm convinced…but we can't head for Grand Cayman Island," said Carlo, "the airport there closes at nine o'clock and there's no way we can make it by that time."

"Where then?" I asked.

"Regardless of the risk it's got to be a nearby airstrip…we've got to put down before sunset or we're in real trouble since none of the rural airstrips have lighting."

"Okay," I said, "but then our only option is to fake them out… set a course as if we're heading for the Caribbean and stick to it until we see the chopper turn back then turn around and head for a strip near the coast."

"Do we have enough fuel for such a maneuver and also to get us to the island?" asked Boris.

"Yes, I had one of the students top off the fuel tanks after we landed. We're carrying more weight than I'd counted on but we should still be all right."

It was only after we'd passed the coast and headed over water that the chopper finally turned back.

"Will they send out fighter jets to intercept us?" asked Carlo as he began the maneuver to return us to the coast.

"I don't think so," I said, "as long as you're flying over territorial waters of the neighboring country they've no legal right to interfere…they would risk a face off with another nation's fighter jets."

Carlo pulled out an aeronautical chart of the region and handed it to me. "We're about here," he said, "try and find an airstrip as close to where we are as possible."

Boris and I poured over the chart while Carlo—consulting his cockpit instruments—tried to estimate how much fuel we'd have left over once we landed. "

"There's an airstrip near what's identified as a food packing plant just up the coast from the village of Santa Cruz," I said, pointing to the spot on the chart.

"How far?" asked Carlo.

"I make it to be about thirty nautical miles," said Boris who'd checked the scale.

"It's going to be tight," said Carlo, "ten minutes to get there and another ten to effect an approach and actually land the plane… let's hope there's still some daylight by that time."

"And that the strip is still operational," added Boris.

* * *

"There it is!" I shouted, pointing down at the jumble of metal-roofed buildings next to a long wharf.

"Do you see the airstrip?" asked Carlo who was busy putting the plane in a controlled dive, wishing to pass low over the complex.

"I think it's that area just back of the loading docks…it's hard to make out with all the shadows."

"I see it," he said as he maneuvered the plane to make a pass directly over what we thought was the runway.

"Keep your eyes on the surface…we need to know if we'll run into any obstructions if we land," ordered Carlo.

"It looks like it was paved once," said Boris. "I can see potholes… doesn't look like it's been used in some time.

"Anything parked on it…any debris?"

"Just weeds, potholes and encroaching vegetation at the perimeter," I said, peering intently out the cockpit window.

Carlo circled back and began to set up his landing approach. Shadows were already obstructing our view of the runway as the sun dipped ever deeper below the horizon. "Hold on tight, it's probably going to be a little rough," he shouted as he began our descent.

The darkened surface of the runway came up fast as Carlo fought the air currents and tried to keep the craft at the right attitude. Contact came with a jolt as the plane hit hard. Carlo worked furiously to keep the plane from swerving towards the overgrown perimeter but finally got it under control. We rolled to a stop just as daylight finally gave out, fully enshrouding us in darkness.

We sat there, motionless, trying to damp down the tension we all felt. Finally, Carlo turned off the engine and gestured for me to open the cockpit door. We climbed out of the aircraft and studied our surroundings. The place looked deserted. No lights, no sign of vehicles or people. As Carlo inspected the plane with a flashlight to see whether the landing had caused any damage to the landing gear or the fuselage Boris and I walked over to the loading docks. I climbed the stairs to the concrete loading platform and tried the doors. All were locked.

"This place hasn't been used in some time," said Boris, coming up beside me. "Think we should walk to the village and introduce ourselves?"

"Let's see what Carlo's found," I said, heading back towards the platform stairs.

"The plane's okay!" he shouted.

"You need help tying it down or something?" I shouted back.

"No, I'll just put wheel blocks on…should be enough for tonight.

Boris and I were just approaching the airplane when we heard the telltale throb of a helicopter. It was coming up fast.

"You think it's local military coming to check us out?" asked Carlo who heard it as well.

"No, it's Colonel Cruz I bet," said Boris. "My guess is he had the pilot hover at the coast waiting to see whether we would circle back…the guy's no dummy."

"But how would he have found us?" asked Carlo.

"Probably consulted the local aeronautical chart just as we did and came to the same conclusion: this runway is the best option given our location and the need to be on the ground before nightfall…didn't even have to tail us," I said

"Okay, what should we do?" asked Carlo, clearly nervous.

"You crunch down and act like you're trying to repair some damage to the landing gear…that'll reassure him we're not going to attempt another takeoff."

"And you two?"

"I'm going to stand here like I'm watching you…Boris, on the other hand, will improvise…right, old buddy?"

Boris nodded then took off at a run.

* * *

Once the chopper cleared the perimeter of the airstrip the pilot switched on powerful landing lights that washed the runway with a white incandescence, illuminating everything in a series of four overlapping pools of light. In no time, our position was caught in the glare. The craft hovered for what seemed like minutes as the team inside evaluated the threat level. Seeing no sign we were hostile, whoever was in charge instructed the pilot to put the craft down—but at a safe distance.

We were once again shrouded in darkness, except for Carlo's flashlight, which he continued to aim at the landing gear—almost as if he was oblivious to the sudden arrival of men bent on doing us harm. The copter's engine was shut down and the landing lights were doused. I could hear boots advancing across the tarmac towards us. Quickly, I removed my gun from its holster, knelt down and wedged it against the back of the tire on the starboard side of the landing gear then stood up and vigorously threw my holster off towards the edge of the runway. I stood there, leaning against the front edge of the starboard wing, when four flashlights flicked on—their beams directed at Carlo and myself.

"On your knees, hands over your head!" shouted the leader as the four men came close enough for me to make out their shapes. All were wearing military fatigues and three were holding assault rifles. The one who barked the command held a semiautomatic. Carlo hurried over to where I stood and the two of us complied with the order. I looked down so none of them could get a good look at my face.

"Well, you've taken us on a merry chase, Professor Sassari," said the leader, "but to no avail…and I guarantee you'll regret having allowed this man to involve you in a criminal conspiracy."

Neither of us said anything, just knelt in front of him, our hands clasped behind our necks.

"The leader shined his flashlight directly at me. "Lift your face," he ordered, "let me see who it is that's given my men so much trouble."

I lifted my gaze and stared directly at him. Instantly, I recognized who it was: Colonel Felipe Cruz, himself. I pretended not to know, trying to keep a blank expression on my face.

"You look familiar," said the colonel, eyeing me intently. "Have we met before?"

"Perhaps if I knew with whom I'm speaking I could respond to such a question," I said noncommittally.

"I am Colonel Felipe Cruz…in charge of military counterintelligence…but I think you know that already. "Your papers, please."

"I've no papers, Colonel. Search me if you like."

"We'll get to that momentarily…but for now I want to know the whereabouts of the ransom money!"

I shrugged and looked away.

"You will either comply with my demand or Professor Sassari here will be shot."

Carlo looked over at me, horrified.

"I'll get it for you…if you'll allow me to get up," I said, again looking him straight in the eye.

"No, I'd rather you stayed where you are…Professor Sassari will get it…I assume he knows where to look."

I looked over at Carlo and nodded. He rose stiffly and tentatively moved around the wing in the direction of the cargo compartment, clearly nervous about the three men holding assault rifles who seemed to track his movement with the muzzles of their guns. He fumbled with the locking mechanism but eventually lifted the hatch and reached in. It took him some moments to extricate the attaché cases as they were nested among pieces of soft luggage to protect them from being unnecessarily jostled. Finally he had them both in his hands and carried them back to where the colonel and I were positioned, placing them carefully on the surface of the starboard wing.

"Open them!" the colonel commanded.

"I don't know the combinations," said Carlo.

"The combinations, please!" A command directed at me.

"I don't think so Colonel. I'd rather you take the chance of damaging the contents trying to bust them open."

"You're rather cocky given the circumstances," said the colonel as he raised his semiautomatic and pointed it directly at my forehead.

But then he hesitated, scrutinizing my face more closely. "I know you...it was in connection with that stolen..."

But just as he was about to continue the engine of the copter started up, running lights came on and the rotors began to turn.

"What's that man doing!" shouted the colonel, who'd turned in the direction of the chopper. "You two...go see what the pilot's doing!" he added, pointing to two of the men holding assault rifles.

Immediately, the two men began to run towards the chopper, yelling at the pilot as they ran. Both the colonel and the other guard stared after them, trying to make sense out of what was going on. With their attention directed elsewhere, I quickly reached over and recovered my gun from its hiding place. I squeezed off two shots at the guard—dropping him instantly—then turned towards the colonel who had spun around at the sound of the gunfire and was about to shoot. I fired first, placing three rounds in his torso. He fell to the ground. I could sense he was trying to say something despite being mortally wounded. I leaned over, close enough to catch a whisper: "You're that FBI agent."

"No longer, Colonel," I replied softly, "just a man called Church."

"Stow the cases back in the cargo compartment, Carlo," I said, going over and picking up the guards assault rifle, "I'm heading over to the chopper to see what Boris is up to."

By the time I made it over to the chopper Boris, assault rifle in hand, had both guards lying flat on the tarmac, their hands clasped behind their heads. The pilot was still at the controls but nervously eyeing Boris.

"Well, it looks like you've got everything under control," I said.

"Yeah, sometimes it's good to be forgotten…they even ask you about me?"

"The subject never came up," I said with a laugh, "so, what's our plan?"

"I take it you've got a couple of dead bodies over near the plane…my thinking is we detain these three guys and the two corpses until we're ready to leave then let them fly themselves back across the border."

"You okay with that?" I asked the pilot once I'd translated Boris' proposal into Spanish.

He nodded.

"And you guys?"

"Yeah, we're okay with that," said one of the guards.

"Now, here's the deal," I said, continuing in Spanish, "the three of you are going to have to make up a story as to how the colonel and one of your men got killed. Whatever it is can't include your illegal violation of the border or pursuit of Professor Sassari's plane since that'll ring alarm bells diplomatically for your country. You can talk all you want to about two bad *gringos* who speak Spanish who've been causing all sorts of problems in your country this past week. Where you met up with us is up to you to figure out. Also, you can report you think we're badly wounded but were able to get away…probably died somewhere in the woods. You think you can handle that?"

They all nodded.

"Okay, my friend here is going to tie you up and you'll stay that way until 0300 hours. At that time you'll be free to go. We'll allow you to keep possession of your weapons…although they'll be fully dismantled…but we'll discard all ammunition…you clear on that?"

Again they nodded.

I had the pilot shut down the chopper engine and join the two guards on the tarmac. Boris tied the three up while I stood over them, assault rifle at the ready.

"Where are the body bags?" asked Boris once he'd finished.

The pilot told him where to look. Boris climbed into the chopper, retrieved two body bags and headed for the plane. Some minutes later, Boris and Carlo approached dragging one of the body bags. I helped them hoist it into the chopper and slide it into the open space behind the seats.

"We'll get the other then I'll relieve you," said Boris.

"You sure?" I asked.

"Yeah, let me take the first shift…you can relieve me at midnight," said Boris.

"Okay, but grab some food while you're over there."

"Will do," said Boris as he and Carlo headed back to the plane.

* * *

Carlo and I sat cross-legged on the tarmac sharing the meal the village women had prepared. The night was tropically warm, with only modest air currents to break the humidity. I wanted to get his mind off the violence he'd just witnessed and sought to engage him in a running conversation, mostly about his fieldwork but also about Italy. He spoke about the small town north of Milan where he grew up, about the years spent in Rome earning his academic degrees, and of the difficulty finding a suitable university posting. If it weren't for the research support he received from international granting agencies he admitted his efforts in Central America would be impossible. As he spoke, I came to understand more fully why he'd been willing to take the risks associated with helping Boris and myself leave the country. The ten thousand dollars I'd offered would go a long way towards defraying his expenses over the coming months.

We had no bedrolls or anything with which to improvise a cushioned surface, obliging us to simply lie back on the roughened asphalt surface of the tarmac and hope our fatigue would be enough to encourage sleep.

DAY 8

I COULD SEE BORIS was just as much out of breath as I was. We were running towards Carlo's airplane—having positioned flares at intervals along the runway. It was three o'clock in the morning, pitch dark, with only the revved-up sounds of the airplane engine breaking the stillness of the night as Carlo prepared for takeoff at the far end of the tarmac. The flares came from the chopper—liberated, one might say, as a kind of payment for the trouble we'd been put to: having to stand guard over the three surviving members of Colonel Cruz' recon unit. They didn't seem to mind the loss—hell, it wasn't their gear—they were just grateful we were giving them the chance to get back across the border before daylight.

Boris reached the plane first, quickly climbing into one of the rear seats. I followed soon after, taking care to maintain my balance as I climbed onto the wing of the shuddering craft.

"Okay, let's hit it!" I shouted as I secured the door and strapped on the seat harness.

Carlo released the brakes and the craft lurched down the runway, finally becoming airborne a safe distance short of the last set of burning flares. In minutes, the few shoreline lights around the village of Santa Cruz all but disappeared, leaving us with nothing to focus on except the subdued lights of the instrument panel. Boris quickly fell asleep but I struggled to remain alert, hoping to ensure Carlo didn't inadvertently nod off.

* * *

It was well passed daybreak when Carlo pointed to a slender speck on the horizon and announced we were approaching the island. I woke Boris and the three of us poured over the aeronautical chart. Carlo was already in radio contact with the control tower at the airport and soon received landing instructions. The airport lay immediately east of the downtown area of the capital, requiring an approach over the commercial district.

Soon the white smudge of the surf line became visible, along with the faint silhouettes of coastal housing. Minutes later the lush green foliage of the residential neighborhoods came into prominence as Carlo brought the craft lower and lower.

"There's the end of the runway," I shouted, pointing to the white markings at the end of the twin strips of concrete that seemed to go on forever.

"I see it," said Carlo who was busy bringing the craft into alignment with the runway as he made his final approach. The landing itself was unremarkable and we all gave out a sigh of relief as Carlo taxied the plane over to the apron in front of the general aviation terminal.

Once Carlo finished shutting down all systems we climbed out of the airplane and examined our surroundings. A fairly large number of private aircraft were parked nearby and the terminal looked busy—probably crews getting ready for the long flights to Key West or Cancun. The air was clean and crisp and a gentle tropical breeze seemed to keep the humidity at bay. Boris and I removed our luggage and the two aluminum attaché cases from the cargo compartment while Carlo tied off the prop and positioned the wheel blocks.

"Carlo, come over here," I shouted as I placed one of the attaché cases on the starboard wing and undid the latches.

"Were you really going to refuse the colonel when he demanded the combination?" he asked as he came up beside me.

"No," I laughed, "it was just something that came to mind… just a delaying tactic since Boris hadn't yet sprung his diversion."

I opened the lid and removed two packets of crisp one hundred dollar bills—a hundred in each packet.

"These are for you, Carlo," I said, handing him the two packets.

"But we agreed on ten thousand," he said, expressing puzzlement. "You've given me twenty thousand."

"I know…but Boris and I both feel you've had to put up with a hell of a lot of aggravation and sacrifice these past twenty-four hours…a lot more than you bargained for. Regard the extra ten as hardship pay."

Carlo just shook his head in amazement as he continued to examine the two packets. "You sure?" he asked, looking at both Boris and myself.

"Yeah, we're sure," I replied, placing a hand on his shoulder, "now don't worry about customs…there aren't any limits on the amount of U.S. currency you can bring into Grand Cayman."

"Well, okay," he said, slipping the two packets into the canvas document bag he'd removed from the cockpit that held all his airplane papers.

"You going to stay on in George Town?" I asked as the three of us walked towards the terminal.

"For a couple of days at least," I imagine," said Carlo. "The airplane needs to be gone over by a mechanic…and Christ, I can use a little down time to recover from all the excitement."

"What then?" asked Boris.

"Probably start to make my way back to Italy."

"You going to fly there?" asked Boris incredulously.

"Not in that single engine craft," said Carlo with a laugh. "No, I'll hanger that bird somewhere in the States then fly home in a commercial jet."

"I'd ask you to join me on the boat but I suspect I'll be putting out to sea before nightfall," I said.

"It's okay, Church," said Carlo, "anyway three's a crowd…can't imagine your woman friend would take kindly to my presence. No, with the cash I've got I imagine I'll check into a real comfortable inn somewhere along the coast and just ease into the Caribbean lifestyle for a day or two."

"Sounds good," said Boris, "wish I could do the same but the wife's expecting me…and hell, someone has to bring the ransom money back."

"Yeah, you've got a rough life," I said, patting him on the shoulder.

"Go to hell," said Boris

A customs officer met us in the terminal and had us complete declaration documents. The only snag was my possession of a firearm. But once I showed my Interpol and FBI concealed weapon permits and assured the authorities I'd be removing the weapon from the island after a week's stay they granted me a temporary permit and let us clear customs.

* * *

We left the airport and headed for a restaurant known to serve breakfast at this hour. While we waited for our orders I put a call through to the guy who owned the boat.

"This is William Church," I said once a guy with a deep gravelly voice picked up the phone, "your new charter."

"Yeah? Where are you?"

"At the restaurant corner of Dorcy and Roberts…how's the provisioning going?"

"Should be done in about an hour they tell me…you want me to pick you up?"

"That'd be real helpful…there's two of us…with luggage… that be all right?"

"Yeah, look for an open top jeep…that'll be me."

"I didn't catch your name," I said before he could hang up.

"Reilly, Jim Reilly."

"Okay, Jim, we'll be out front…but give us about thirty minutes…we need to eat our breakfast."

"Will do," he said then promptly hung up.

"Everything all right?" asked Boris.

"Yeah, the boat owner…a guy named Reilly…says the outfit Chelsea engaged to provision the boat is almost done. He'll be picking us up out front in about a half hour."

"You know anything about this guy or his boat?" asked Boris.

"Just what Chelsea learned…that he's the owner and the boat's a thirty-six foot sloop with retractable sails. I'll check it out once we get to the marina but chances are it's in decent shape…nobody would want to operate a craft in this area of the Caribbean in any other condition…cruising distances are too long."

"Let's hope you're right," said Boris.

Our food arrived and conversation slackened as we all dug in.

* * *

The three of us were just leaving the restaurant when what looked like a military-issue jeep drove up. A big guy was driving; I'd take him to be in his early fifties. He wore a baseball hat, a loose-fitting non-descript shirt and a pair of khaki shorts. "Which of you is Church?" he shouted.

"That'd be me," I said, coming over and shaking his hand. "Thanks for picking us up…the man on my right is my friend, Boris, and this other distinguished gentleman is Professor Sassari… an archaeologist from Italy."

"Glad to meet you all…just toss your bags in the back and climb in…sorry about the sun beating down…haven't bothered to get a new canvas top for this old girl."

"You go along," said Carlo as he shook my hand, "I've got to see to the refueling and find a mechanic who'll check out the plane."

"Well, it's been a pleasure, Carlo," I said, shaking his hand, "hope everything works out for you."

"Things should work out just fine…and Boris, it was good having you along on this wild journey…only wish we could have had more time together."

"Maybe I'll bring the wife down to visit your dig," said Boris, shaking Carlo's hand, "in any case thanks for everything…Church and I would have had a devil of a time getting out of the country without your help."

"As I recall, even with my help the operation involved a fair amount of excitement," said Carlo, smiling.

Boris and I climbed into the jeep and Reilly put the vehicle in gear. As Reilly pulled away from the curb Carlo gave us a final wave then began walking back towards the terminal.

Reilly circled the airport on Crewe Road, skirting the downtown area near the harbor located further to the west.

"You live on board when not chartering?" I asked as Reilly maneuvered around the circle onto Shamrock Road.

"Yes and no," he said, "don't use the sloop for anything but chartering and blue water sailing…make my residence on an old forty foot cabin cruiser that's tied up along the east side of the quay…not far from where the *Lucky Lady* is docked."

"I take it the *Lucky Lady* is the boat I've chartered."

"Yeah, that's what I call her…she's kept in Bristol condition… unlike the cruiser which hasn't been out to sea in years."

"Been out here long?" I asked.

"Retired to the island about four years ago…had one too many dreary winters in the UK. Between my military pension, what I've saved and what blocs like you are willing to pay for a few days of bareboating I manage all right."

We turned onto Marina Drive and soon began to pass a sprawling community of residential homes to the east. Most faced one or another of the side streets abutting Marina Drive, with names like Orange, Domino and Bamboo. "Much too pricey for my taste," said Reilly as we passed by. "Couldn't make ends meet if I had to lay out the money for one of those."

Soon we arrived at the marina and Reilly took it slow, giving Boris and me the chance to inspect the layout. There seemed to be a preponderance of powerboats tied up along the quay or cradled on land, with fewer large sailing craft than I'd expected.

"It isn't the Virgin Islands," he said, reading my mind. "Most big bareboat outfits prefer to operate where there's a tight cluster of islands…most clients like the prospect of sighting land wherever they sail."

Finally, we pulled up beside a gorgeous French-designed sloop. "There she is…the *Lucky Lady*," said Reilly as he came to a stop and cut the engine.

I climbed out of the jeep and walked over to the vessel. It lay alongside the quay, bobbing gently in response to the languid movement of the surrounding water. Just then a young man emerged from the companionway. He was carrying a large plastic container. He noticed me looking at him and paused.

"You the guy who ordered the provisions?"

"Yes, they all on board?"

"Just finished…I can go over what's included if you want."

"That'd be real helpful," I said, stepping into the cockpit.

The man picked up a clipboard from the cockpit table and turned back towards the companionway. I followed.

As I climbed down the companionway ladder I was struck by how beautifully the interior of the main compartment was decorated—a tasteful blend of tropical hardwoods and soft leather upholstery.

"I'm Stuart White, second in command at Cayman Provisioners," said the young man as he extended his hand, "if you'll bear with me I'll go through the contents of each of the galley compartments."

I nodded.

Once he was through with his inventory review and had handed me a copy of the master list of supplies he started back up the companionway. I stayed below deck, wanting to inspect the diesel engine, electronics, bilge pumps and other systems critical to the worry-free operation of the vessel.

"You ever coming back on deck?" shouted Boris from the top of the companionway.

"Be right there," I shouted.

Finally, I climbed back on deck. Reilly and Boris were sitting lazily on the cushioned benches at the stern.

"You find everything to your liking?" asked Reilly.

"Yeah, but I'll still need to check out the sails and all the running gear...you want to accompany me?"

"No, you go right ahead...if you've a question just give a shout."

I nodded, then began my inspection of the halyards, sheets, winches, and other deck gear.

"You know it's getting late, Church, Elena arrives in less than an hour," said Boris.

"Christ, you're right...Jim, any chance I can persuade you to drive us to the airport?"

"No problem, the jeep comes with the charter...keys are in it."

"You sure?" I asked.

"Well, actually we'll share it...but since I don't budge off the docks that much you'll have it to yourself mostly."

I thanked Reilly, finished signing the charter documents and joined Boris who'd already climbed into the jeep.

* * *

Elena arrived wearing a pair of conservative dark slacks, tailored white blouse and a lightweight cotton blazer.

"Not quite the outfit I'd expected," I said, giving her kiss on the cheek.

"Business before pleasure," she said. "We've got an appointment at the U.S. Consular Agency and we'll have to hurry...they close at two o'clock."

"What've you arranged?" asked Boris as the three of us waited for Elena's luggage.

"Courier status for you, my friend," she said, "so when you arrive in Miami our customs people won't have a fit; they don't usually encounter such large quantities of cash except in connection with drug deals.

We collected Elena's luggage and quickly headed for the jeep parked just outside. Boris, who held on to the attaché cases wherever he went, climbed into the rear seat, while Elena took the passenger seat up front. I started up the old jeep and drove out of the parking lot.

"As I understand it the office isn't far," said Elena, "just at the intersection of Dorcy Drive and Industrial Way."

"Yeah, it's just a couple of blocks," I said, "should make it easy to get there in time."

I pulled up in front of the building and waited in the jeep while Elena and Boris rushed in. About twenty minutes later they emerged from the building, with Boris holding up the attaché cases—now festooned with official-looking seals.

"Any problem?" I asked.

"No," said Elena, "the ambassador had cleared it with his counterpart at the embassy in Jamaica so our local consular officials were primed to move expeditiously. How much time do we have until Boris' flight?"

"It leaves within the hour so we'd better head back," I said as Boris and Elena took their seats.

We returned to the parking lot at the main terminal and the three of us quickly walked to the front entrance. I could see passengers beginning to assemble near the departure gate for Boris' flight so we urged him to make his way through security and not spend time on lengthy good byes. He nodded, gave me a handshake and Elena a hug and a kiss on the cheek then joined the security line. We stood around until he boarded the plane then made our way back out to the jeep and climbed in.

"Let's wait until the plane actually takes off," said Elena, putting a hand on mine just as I was about to turn the key in the ignition.

I nodded. We sat there for what seemed like forever until finally the deep-throated roar of a large commercial jet signaled the time had come.

"Well, we're finally alone," she said, leaning towards me and grasping my hand tightly.

I smiled, then turned and placed a gentle kiss on her lips. "With a week all to ourselves."

"So where is this sailboat we're to spend our time on?" asked Elena, sitting back in her seat as I started up the engine.

"Not far…nothing is really far in George Town…we'll be there shortly."

* * *

"Oh, it's beautiful!" exclaimed Elena after I pointed out the *Lucky Lady*. We had retraced the route Reilly had driven earlier and made it back to the marina quay without getting lost.

"Climb aboard," I said, "The companionway is unlocked…at least it was when we left…I'll grab your luggage."

She was sitting on the deeply cushioned banquette to starboard when I climbed down with the luggage.

"Let me stow these in the forward cabin," I said, "then I'll join you."

"No hurry, William, I'm perfectly content," she replied, kicking off her shoes and propping them up on the soft leather.

"Well, rest easy then…I'll go up topside and get us under way."

"Whoa, where are we going?" asked Elena.

"You've got a choice, we can day sail just off Grand Cayman, spending our nights at a pleasant marina just west of here, or head for the island of Jamaica."

"Which involves what?"

"A blue water cruise lasting about a day and a half to two days, depending on the winds, a couple of days in Kingston then back to Grand Cayman."

"I'd go for the cruise."

I smiled, blew her a kiss then climbed up the companionway. Jim was sitting on the deck of his cabin cruiser drinking a bottle of beer. I waved to him and indicated with a gesture that I'd left the key to the jeep in the ignition. He acknowledged with a nod. I started up the engine, turned on the navigational systems and took a moment to study the electronic display of the North Bay nautical chart. I didn't know how long it would take me to run the channel out to deep water but hoped I'd have enough daylight despite the lateness of the hour. While I was mentally working my way through the alignment of buoy channel markers Elena appeared at the top of the companionway. She'd changed into a pair of white shorts, a pale yellow polo shirt and a pair of deck shoes.

"Don't look so surprised," she said, taking in my glance, "it's not the first time I've been on a boat...so, what can I do?"

"Release the dock lines...but watch your step getting off and on the boat...there's a fair amount of chop just now—a big yacht just came in," I said, pointing to a fifty-foot motor yacht being secured to the quay several boat lengths away.

She dismissed my concerns with a wave and effortlessly jumped onto the quay. I watched as she released the spring lines, then the bow line. As she worked to free the stern line the untethered bow began to swing away from the quay.

"You'll need to hurry," I said

She just smiled, tossed the line onto the boat and reached for the stern rail. With a single smooth motion she swung herself onto the deck and down into the cockpit. With the vessel now unencumbered the bow swung all the way around until it was facing away from land. I put the engine in gear and began motoring towards the channel, taking care to avoid other vessels tied up nearby.

* * *

We cleared the channel with the sun still resting on the western horizon and set about the task of getting under way with sails fully unfurled. The vessel heeled slightly as we came up on an east-by-southeast bearing and caught the wind on a broad reach. I shut off the engine, leaving only the hiss made by the movement of the hull through water and the occasional snap of the mainsail's leach to provide an acoustical background for the forthcoming sunset.

"You go change," said Elena, "I'll handle the helm."

I nodded, stepping away so she could get behind the wheel. She had a look of enormous satisfaction as the vessel responded to her tiny adjustments to the helm. Seeing she was well up to the task I climbed down the companionway ladder and headed for where I'd stowed the luggage. I quickly removed the clothing I'd been wearing and put on a pair of bathing trunks I'd had the foresight to pack. I had no boat shoes so my cross trainers would have to suffice, as would one of my canvas shirts—with sleeves rolled up. Looking a little ragged I reappeared at the top of the companionway.

"I think a little clothes shopping is called for once we reach Kingston," said Elena with a smile.

"Yeah, I should have grabbed some stuff instead of worrying about lunch…speaking of food have you had a chance to check out the provisions?"

"No, so why don't you take the helm and let me put together something to nibble on while we watch the sun go down."

"Open a bottle of wine while you're at it," I called after her as she climbed down the companionway ladder.

I occupied myself during the wait by checking out the boat's radar. There was no way I'd sacrifice our first night together by scheduling watch intervals throughout the hours of darkness. I was pleased to see Reilly had installed a radar guard alarm system—one that would allow me to define a surveillance zone around the boat and rouse me from sleep if a vessel entered the zone. I manually triggered the alarm to assure myself it would be loud enough. It was.

"Okay, get the cockpit table propped up," said Elena as she carefully balanced a tray of food while emerging from the cabin.

"What'd you find?" I asked as I swung the table up from its vertical position and secured the supports.

"Tortilla chips, a container of hummus, a jar of pickled herring, some Jack cheese and a package of crackers…here, take a look."

"Looks good," I said, beginning to apply hummus to one of the chips with a knife Elena had placed on the tray. "How about the wine?"

"A nicely chilled Australian Chardonnay," she said, reaching behind her for the bottle she'd placed just to the side of the companionway before climbing up with the tray.

I put the vessel on autopilot and came around to join her on the well-padded cockpit bench on the port side. She put her arms around me and gave me a lingering kiss—a kiss I took to be a promise of intimacies to come. I gently broke free and reached for the wine bottle. After I pulled the cork and poured each of us a glass she raised hers.

"To a brief interlude in our very busy lives," she said with a smile as we touched glasses.

As we sat there, wine in hand, the sun slowly slipped below the horizon, leaving nothing but a shimmering afterglow.

The End